Hooray for Honno! For a quarter of a century its classic and contemporary titles have been reminding us why Welsh women's voices should be nurtured and celebrated, why Welsh women's writing should be read and re-read. Wales, the UK, and the British literary scene would all be the poorer without Honno. I wish it every possible success as it heads into its next 25 years. **Sarah Waters**

Honno so magnificently lives up to the headline – "great books, great writing, great women!" Welsh women, Welsh women's history, and literature owe a great deal to the groundbreaking work undertaken by the team, past and present, at Honno. I certainly owe a debt of gratitude for the publication of my heroine, Elizabeth Andrews' autobiography *A Woman's Work is Never Done*. **Glenys Kinnock**

I congratulate Honno on their magnificent achievements through 25 years. Supporting, encouraging Welsh women writers to make their creative Celtic voices heard, spiritually, intellectually and emotionally. To flourish and achieve the recognition they undeniably deserve. Continue to blossom, you beautiful, bountiful, utterly brilliant female force!!! **Molly Parkin**

Twenty-five years ago Honno began a revelatory publishing history that has become an essential facet of the whole culture of Wales. From classics, forgotten or neglected, to contemporary work across the creative and critical divides, it is Honno which has placed writing by and about women where it should always have been, at the centre of our past understanding and our future sensibility. **Dai Smith**

Well done to my sisters at Honno Press. The press turns 25 years young today. And during this time it has achieved simply remarkable things – shining a light on treasures from our tradition, providing a platform for exciting contemporary authors and being an all-round fantastic indie. Llongyfarchiadau! **Kathryn Gray**

Honno's story is one of heroic and necessary endurance; for a quarter of a century its workers have committed themselves to discovering new and innovative voices and to resurrecting un̶i̶ ̶ ̶ ones. A wonderful and incredible ̶ ̶ ̶ alue of the written word. ̶h̶e

all shall
be well

25at25

all shall
be well

25at25

Edited by

Stephanie Tillotson and Penny Anne Thomas

First published by Honno

'Ailsa Craig', Heol y Cawl, Dinas Powys,

Wales, CF64 4AH

1 2 3 4 5 6 7 8 9 10

ISBN   978-1-906784-46-1 (hardback)
978-1-906784-33-1 (paperback)

Published with the financial support of the Welsh Books Council.
Cover image: 'Paddlers' by Muriel Delahaye
Printed by Bell and Bain

Every effort has been made to contact the copyright holders for these
stories. In the event of any queries, please contact the publisher.

contents

foreword

As the only two founder members still attending executive committee meetings, and still fascinated with Honno's progress, we were delighted to be asked by our team of young dynamic colleagues to write a brief preface to this collection of stories, marking twenty-five years of commitment not only to the development of new writings by the women of Wales, but also to the reprinting of works by long-forgotten female writers (in English and Welsh), neglected by our male-dominated publishing houses, many of whom were taken by surprise when they heard of our intentions all those years ago. 'Why?' they asked. 'Why women only?'

To answer this question one only needs to refer to the title *Blodeugerdd o Farddoniaeth Gymraeg yr Ugeinfed Ganrif* (An Anthology of Twentieth Century Welsh Poetry) published in 1987, the year of our launch. Of the 170 poets included in this collection only six were women (a situation rectified by Honno in 2003 with the publication of the bilingual anthology, *Welsh Women's Poetry 1460–2001,* containing around 250 poems, with sixty-eight poets writing in English and thirty-three in Welsh).

Honno's first meeting was held in April 1985 in a flat in Newport Road, Cardiff, attended by a group of women from different parts of Wales known to each other merely through a variety of grapevines, but with a mutual interest in the promotion of female writers. Proof of a general and growing awareness of this need for more published works by women in Wales was the positive attitude of the 250 female supporters who responded to the letters we circulated around Wales and beyond early in 1986, by buying shares, at £5 each, which gave us a total of £4000 in a space of twelve months.

Confident that we were embarking upon a much-needed venture, the name Honno was suggested by Rosanne for our Welsh Women's Press, and Penni Bestic was asked to create our logo – the tree of knowledge, with Blodeuwedd the owl surveying the scene from the top branch. On 3 June 1986, following many months of heated but fruitful discussions, the constitution which sealed the deal was finally signed by Kathryn Curtis, Anne Howells, Luned Meredith, Althea Osmond, Sheleagh Llewellyn (secretary), Ceridwen Lloyd-Morgan and Rosanne Reeves. We were now an official, legal, bi-lingual Welsh Women's Community Co-operative. In 1987 our hard work was rewarded with the launch of our first two titles, an event sponsored by HTV. These were *Buwch ar y Lein*, Hafina Clwyd's account of her days as a young teacher in London, and *An Autobiography of Elizabeth Davies, Betsy Cadwaladyr (A Balaclava Nurse)*, our first English language classic, the life story of the indomitable Betsy, from Bala, in North Wales, originally transcribed by the historian Jane Williams (Ysgafell) in 1857.

Those early days were hard; we were on a learning curve. Executive and design decisions, administration, communication, advertising, transporting and storing was done by a few individuals from their own homes in order to keep overheads to a minimum. Looking back, our successes during those first few years were quite remarkable. In 1988 we won the annual Pandora Women in Publishing Award for the most impressive new women's venture, organised by the London-based Women in Publishing (WIP). The following year *On My Life: women's writing from Wales*, ed. Leigh Verrill-Rhys, one of our founder members, won the Raymond Williams Community Publishing Award (an achievement repeated in 1995 with our first collection of short stories *Luminous and Forlorn*, ed. Elin ap Hywel). In 1989 we published our first bestseller, *Morphine and Dolly Mixtures,* by Carol-Ann Courtney; we took a risk, without a publishing grant, to print 6000 copies, with stacks piled high in a member's house in Penarth. This title won the Arts Council of Wales Book of the Year Award in 1990; it was included in the Feminist Book Fortnight's top twenty titles for that year, and was subsequently made into a television film by Karl Francis. When a Penguin imprint bought the paperback rights we thought we had arrived. (A full list of Honno awards can be accessed on our website).

The time was ripe for development and now our hard work was recognised and rewarded when Honno, in 1993, applied for, and received, a grant offered by the then Literature Committee of the Welsh Arts Council, towards employing an editor/manager – a significant milestone which transmuted our amateur status overnight when Elin ap Hywel, well-known published writer and poet, became our first paid professional worker. Since then Honno has gone from strength to strength, a number of talented editors, managers, administrators, accountants and marketing experts having ensured our ongoing development, helped by a team of volunteers. A scan of our website under the title 'Authors' shows a list of over 450 female writers; a majority of whom would not have seen their names in print without the help and encouragement of Honno.

It's a sobering thought that as founder members we are now 'history', but satisfying to realise, looking back to the 1980s, that we played our part in a decade of transformation in the lives and attitudes of the women of Wales – academics, campaigners and activists from all walks of life. We wish Honno a bright and successful future and live in the hope that we'll still be around, along with our constant companion and colleague Eurwen Booth, who joined Honno soon after its launch, for future long-term celebrations!

Rosanne Reeves and Luned Meredith

introduction

It's hard to believe, Honno Welsh Women's Press is twenty-five years old and still going strong. That deserves a celebration don't you think?

Today Honno is one of a very few independent women's presses still in existence; not bad when you consider how little cash is available, how much voluntary commitment it takes to run and, having now published more than a hundred titles, just how far we've come.

Set up in 1986, Honno started out as a small group of women who met once a month in each other's houses and refused to let the lack of an office, equipment, or indeed money, deter them from their commitment to promoting women's writing from Wales. They published one title every year, one in English, the next in Welsh. It was a struggle and, let's not fool ourselves, it still is.

Even so Honno has continued to grow, giving hundreds of Welsh women writers a chance to find their voices and tell their stories, finding ever more readers, and achieving success in terms of prizes, awards and funding.

Twenty-five years of a good thing is worth a party, isn't it?

But hang on a minute, what exactly are we celebrating? The fact that twenty-five years ago Welsh women felt so desperately under-represented that they urgently needed to create a place where their experiences could be put on the page? Or that now, in 2012, there is still such a desire for a dedicated space for writing by women from Wales. Wouldn't Honno's greatest achievement have been to contribute to a culture in which it was no longer needed? Yet Honno's origins and existence attest to a deeply felt and continuing need for such a platform. That in excess of four hundred women came forward to buy shares in the newly formed company is ample evidence of this.

What does this say about Welsh culture? When Honno was founded, a story that concerned Wales tended to be set in a world of coal and rugby, where most women were 'mam' figures, bordered by domestic settings. Rightly or wrongly, the founders of the press thought that male-dominated publishing houses discriminated against women writers and were not interested in what they had to say. One example of this is given by Jane Aaron, in her introduction to the first Honno anthology, *Luminous and Forlorn* (1994), which provides a telling snapshot of the history of women's short-story writing in Wales. It's an account that would be funny if it weren't so infuriating and, artistically, such a disaster for excellent writers struggling for the recognition they deserved, and for the readers deprived of their work.

Jane recalls how the first Welsh short-story collection, published by Faber in 1937, included a phalanx of male names that regularly reappeared in subsequent anthologies, becoming part of a team of 'classics'. By contrast names such as Margiad Evans, Hilda Vaughan or Dorothy Edwards 'bobbed up and down like corks on the contents sheets' making any sustained tradition invisible.

This sort of 'now you see it, now you don't' selection continued until, writes Jane: 'The 1970 anthology, edited by Sam Evans and Roland Mathias, solved the problem by ignoring the women altogether and opting for an all-male line up ...'

It's fair to say that since 1986 Wales has seen massive

social and political changes in the personal and professional roles of women, whose lives and stories have moved from the margins ever closer to a shared centre stage. Despite, or perhaps because of, such change, Honno continues to flourish, through devolution, reorganisations and rounds of funding cuts: still representing Welsh women's views of the world, a landscape that is both specific and subsidiary in terms of English language publishing. Without promotion and generous funding by the Welsh Books Council, much of our culture would remain undiscovered and well-nigh invisible. Instead, Honno has inspired the kind of joy that Janet Thomas expresses in her article 'So Many Stories', after discovering a story written by Siân James and set in Janet's home town of Aberystwyth.

'Short stories happened in London,' she wrote, 'maybe Cardiff, but never here.'

For twenty-five years, in the words of one of Honno's founding members Luned Meredith, the aim has been 'to promote creative writing by women with a connection to Wales, past and present, in Welsh and English'. To make absolutely sure that, whatever else is happening in the world of literature:

Now you see it ...

All Shall Be Well is a celebration of a vision that has thrived for the past twenty-five years.

When the idea for this anthology was first mooted there was a heady rush of excitement. Twenty-five pieces to celebrate our twenty-five years. Then reality set in: how to choose? How could we hope to represent so much, and such a variety of work, from the classics to the contemporary in both languages, from beautiful poetry to passionate prose. How to represent the novels – such as the hugely popular crime stories by Lindsay Ashford – or the long autobiographies such as Ann Pettitt's *Walking to Greenham*.

In the end we decided to concentrate exclusively on the twenty-eight or so anthologies, both fiction and non-fiction, published in the period between 1987 and 2012, which often gave writers the first chance to see their work in print. Many of these volumes were themed, meaning that the editors at Honno were often the gatekeepers for what women wrote about – motherhood, sexuality, infidelity, power, the place of gardens in our hearts or our place in the landscape. Some included authors who never submitted again, others have rich and rewarding volumes to their name. Still faced with a wealth of work to select from, we know this anthology can only ever reflect part of the vast and ever-expanding universe that women are currently writing in Wales, a small contribution to the celebration. In the end *All Shall be Well* is a very subjective selection, purely and simply the editors' choice. Ultimately it is our selection, and one we are extremely proud to put before you.

What it is not is an attempt to create a canon of great women writers, neither does it address the question of whether we want, or need, such a roll of honour. We do feel however that all the pieces here are characterised by skill, be that a skill in storytelling, or dexterity in language, rhetorical or aesthetic, a talent for drawing the reader into an experience, or an ability to create a sense of time or place. Much of the non-fiction represents moments of personal or international history, both dark and bright, with all the punch of first-hand experience. The process of selection also gave us a chance to look back and acknowledge that the past twenty-five years have been an amazing time for women's writing from Wales.

Many of these pieces respond to changes that have taken place over the past century and a half. Honno has mapped an undoubted realignment of emphasis in what we choose to write about. The sense of lives half-lived has receded, powerlessness and poverty has diminished. Our lives have changed beyond the recognition of our grandmothers, but though much has altered, much is still the same. Our experiences advise us to question the conjecture that *All Shall Be Well*, but we appear no longer to be governed by an impression that all social, religious and political odds have been stacked against us. Our experience is ours for good or bad, it is not being stolen from us by a wastage of female potential in a maelstrom of disenfranchisement.

Honno is here and needs to be here. The historical lack of education and neglect of women's writing cannot be unwritten. However confident women authors may have become, there is more yet to say, more to enjoy by readers within and, importantly too, beyond the borders of Wales. Twenty-five years may just be the beginning.

Rosanne Reeves, a founding member, recalls how, 'We decided to call our company, Honno, and many who do not speak Welsh ask what this means. It has no equivalent. There are three ways of referring to 'her' in Welsh: 'hon' means 'this one here'; 'honna', 'that one over there' and '*honno*': *'that one (feminine) who is elsewhere*'. There are many who are elsewhere, authors as yet un-recovered, writers yet to be found, much that remains to be done. For what Honno has achieved, hats off, it has without doubt established a tradition of Welsh women writing in English. Because of this we can look at what still needs doing with some optimism – and who knows, all may yet be well.

Happy Birthday, Honno.

Stephanie Tillotson and Penny Anne Thomas

how to murder your mother

Patricia Duncker

Safe World Gone 2007

theme: the turning point
fiction anthology

Nobody takes any notice of white-haired women in their mid sixties, especially if they are wearing flat shoes and carrying unfashionable handbags. But these two are desperate lovers, hiding out in a chic, slick café, on the watch for *Maman*, who might, at any moment, come rampaging down the boulevards, dark glasses lowered, the prize bull at the corrida, entering the ring, late in the afternoon. One of the women crouches near the window on the first floor level of the café, keeping her glass of unsweetened tea close to her face for protection.

'You must involve the clinic now, *ma chère*,' she hissed. 'If she does commit suicide it will all fall on you.'

Maman had thrown a dramatic fit that morning at breakfast, armed with a large bottle of whisky and sixty paracetamol, spread out on the tablecloth in symmetrical rows. She had even yelled, 'When I'm dead, you'll be sorry!' The elderly lovers remained divided.

'She'd sick the lot up. She can't bear whisky. It's all theatre.'

'Don't be so sure. She's working up to something. I know it.'

The lovers lived two houses and one cul-de-sac away from each other. At first, when *Maman* still possessed most of her marbles, this had been extremely convenient. What could be more natural than close neighbours becoming closer friends? In and out of each other's houses, watering plants and feeding cats, putting out dustbins and sharing builders, even perusing the January sales, first through the catalogues then ransacking the shops. But now the problem was *Maman*. The old lady, eighty-four, sporting a cluster of white hairs on her jutting chin, looked small, thin and frail. Poor dear, sighed the district nurse, not long for this world. But *Maman's* duplicitous physique disguised a lithe and wiry energy; she simmered with bottled-up aggression. The early stages of Alzheimer's glittered in her milky eyes. Her mother and her mother's mother had both been carried off by the disease, at first forgetting to eat and to wash, and eventually forgetting how to breathe. But both these women had first passed through a lengthy stage of murderous venom, when their native selfishness, egotism and savagery knew no limits. At last, the end of respectability and good manners. I can do what I like, say what I like, mangle everything within reach. For who shall fathom the depths of a woman's anger? Who will contain her ingenuity? For every calm old biddy rocking her ancient wisdom to her wizened chest, there are ten, no, dozens of frustrated, ageing witches, who glimpse their diminishing territory and fading powers, and who decide to explode, one last time, in a Catherine wheel of malice and hatred, conducted with volcanic intensity. My daughter is my victim, mine to denigrate and criticise, mine to persecute and destroy. Before I dwindle into darkness I will wreck your life too, and if I can I shall take you with me.

The doctor who suggested that *Maman* should eat more fruit and vegetables and drink two litres of water every day, decided that the old girl was not yet mad enough to be sectioned. He rationalised the situation. The daughter could hold on for a few more years. The old lady was still in good health and nippy on her pins. She might make it to ninety before being banged up in one of the locked wards. But this cruel diagnosis took no account of that successful hell on earth that two women, living in domestic proximity, can create for one another, especially when their family history is one of silent animosity and undercover guerrilla tactics.

The descent presented itself as a gradual, uneven degeneration into muddle and gloom. *Maman* sometimes sat nodding peacefully at the television game shows or crouched over her table concocting crossword puzzles, which never quite worked. She even dabbled in a little embroidery. There were days when the old woman watched her daughter and the beloved neighbour leaving the house armed with shopping bags and umbrellas without uttering a murmur; no snap interdictions or threats, no emotional declarations of menace or blackmail. But as the weather improved *Maman's* internal engines began to ratchet up the scale, increasing from a low growl to a gigantic roar. The beloved neighbour served as the main target.

'Get that woman out of my sight,' she shrieked at her daughter. 'She wants you, to enchant you away from me. She's trying to persuade you to put me in a home and lock me up.'

This was true.

'Do you think she really cares about you? She hasn't got a car and she can't drive. Why do you think she circles round you like a buzzard? She only wants someone to drive her around and take her out shopping.'

Most of this was true too.

'She hopes I'll die. And that you'll get the house. Then you'll both be cosy and rich with all my money. And you can dig a swimming pool in my vegetable patch.'

This idea had indeed been mooted as an eventual possibility. *Maman* had abandoned her vegetables years ago and the browned grass waving in the patch, unsightly and abandoned, figured in vague future plans hatched by the daughter and her beloved neighbour. *Maman's* cunning seemed to respect no earthly boundaries. She overheard secrets even when she was not present; she divined their thoughts like the shrivelled sibyl at Delphi. She lurked behind doorways in kitchens, thwarting their careful arrangements. She went on hunger strike until the holiday bookings for five meagre days in Spain were cancelled. She rang up her grandchildren and wept down the phone, then sat, tranquil and malicious, while her daughter fielded their legitimate anxieties.

Maman no longer allowed her only child to leave the house alone. She settled like a black widow spider on the back seat of the car and complained about the heat, the air conditioning, the journey, the shops, the obligation to walk ten yards to the chiropodist. Her paranoid accusations blossomed into colourful fantasies of conspiracies and plots, hatched by her daughter and the beloved neighbour, to whisk her into the clinic and abandon her there or to eliminate her altogether in a carefully devised accident. Her behaviour became so atrocious that at last they left her screaming on the doorstep and drove off at speed to take tea in town.

They crept home at five only to be confronted by the fire brigade, two police cars and the *SAMU* parked before *Maman's* door, with all the neighbours gathered in the street, whispering.

'*Mon Dieu*,' breathed the daughter. 'She's done it. She's killed herself.'

Their horror and relief bloomed before them, like an emergency air bag. A neighbour rattled the car window.

'It was me,' confessed the excited *voisine*. 'I saw the smoke and called the fire brigade.'

And lo, there was *Maman*, bristling with courage, wrapped in a blanket, supported by two handsome men in uniform, applauded for her daring enterprise and startling strength. Stranded on the terrace stood the daughter's favourite armchair, still smouldering gently, the springs charred and hot.

'She must have fallen asleep with her cigarette still alight,' explained the *capitaine*. 'We found the whole place full of black smoke. It's a wonder that she wasn't asphyxiated. She had the presence of mind to cover her face with a damp towel and pushed the thing out onto the back terrace. The neighbours saw the smoke and called us at once.' He lowered his voice. '*Excusez moi, Madame*, but I don't think that you should leave a fragile old lady of eighty-five completely alone all afternoon.'

'She's eighty-four,' snapped the beloved neighbour, 'and she doesn't smoke.'

But the daughter stood, white-faced, confronting her mother, who took a few faltering steps, tottered unsteadily, then gasped, '*Ma fille, ma fille*! Thank God! My daughter has come back to me.'

The smoke damage was so bad that the entire household, *Maman*, her daughter, two cats and one poodle were all forced to move into the beloved neighbour's house while the painters set to work. *Maman* had the whole thing redecorated in vile greens and pinks; she oversaw the improvements with sinister zeal. The grandchildren drove past on their way to the rented beach villa and made a fuss of her. The old lady basked in their attentive warmth; she had forgotten all their names.

Maman took a taxi to the Inner Peace Emporium and returned armed with josticks and incense, which she lit in every room of the beloved neighbour's house, claiming that it stank. Yet she settled in, grim and intent, despite her discomfort in the slandered slum, and consented to be waited upon, from dawn to dusk. She had her own property re-valued.

'Lovely place,' declared the *notaire*'s agent, looking at the new tiling and polished wooden stairs, all paid for through a lavish insurance claim. 'There's enough space in that vegetable patch for a swimming pool.'

Maman hired a gardener to clear the rampant weeds. Was she enjoying a late burst of rational behaviour? Alas, when the gardener arrived bearing strimmers, forks and shears she accused him of intending to bury her in the wasted patch. Everybody heard her screaming from the terrace steps. 'It's the fire,' they agreed, 'it's affected her brain. Poor thing. She's still in shock.'

Maman commandeered the beloved neighbour's television

set to follow her game shows and soap operas. She reorganised the kitchen and the furniture. She threw out all the potted plants. The daughter found her beloved friend sitting cross-legged on the bedroom floor, staring at a Tarot pack.

'What are you doing?'

'Working out how to murder your mother.'

The date set for their removal back into the redecorated house was September 1st. *Maman* refused to purchase any furniture and the plush, fresh rooms stood empty, reeking of paint. Instead she took to walking the streets of their *quartier* with her arms and legs wrapped in bandages, a hat pulled low over her dark glasses.

'Are you going out disguised? You look like the Invisible Man.' Her daughter refused to let the old lady wander the streets alone and traipsed along just behind her, carrying handbags and parasols.

'It's the radiation,' growled *Maman*. 'The radiation levels -have risen to a dreadful height, well beyond the permitted maximum. I must protect my skin.'

These Chernobyl fantasies persisted for weeks despite the heat. *Maman* even appeared in the post office with her face swathed in white cloths. Shoppers stared. A crowd of Arab children ran after her, begging a peak beneath the mask. The beloved neighbour seethed within her corset of self-control as the chorus of well-aimed casual insults, delivered daily by *Maman*, began to rise towards an evil climax.

The showdown came during the August fiesta. The streets were filled with drunken revellers dancing on the boulevards, brass bands, rock bands, a symphony of accordion players and a twirling gaggle of flamenco gypsies. Juicy smoke rose from a thousand open-air grills and the cicadas roared amidst the magic paper lanterns strung between the trees. Come on, get drunk, enjoy yourselves.

Maman forbade her daughter to go out. She turned on the neighbour.

'Why don't you go by yourself for once?' she snapped at her daughter's elderly lover. 'Then we can have a pleasant evening without you.'

There was a dreadful pause. And then, for the first and only time, the beloved neighbour answered back.

'This is my house. And you are a guest in my house.' The woman's voice gurgled forth in a ghastly whisper. *Maman* glared at her adversary, egging her on.

'It's not a house. It's a tip. It's full of rubbish and it stinks.'

She began chanting abuse, each barbed slur more vicious than the last, and rose up from her post at the table, pointing at the other woman's chest. Everyone began screaming. The neighbour's hand closed over the kitchen knife.

Nobody knows what happened in the kitchen, but hundreds of people saw an elderly lady, swathed in bandages, apparently leaking blood from every crevice, yet surprisingly agile and dynamic, tearing through the fiesta crowds and actually dancing before the Polynesian musicians to the tune of 'Everybody loves Mambo!' The old lady's body could not be found. Her house had been sold weeks before, her accounts drained, her savings spirited away, her passport vanished. The plot was utterly clear. The daughter and her malevolent companion had cashed in and hidden all the old woman's assets, then planned to bump her off. Both protested their innocence, but they would, wouldn't they? *Maman's* signature was there on the *Compromis de Vente*. You forced her, didn't you, argued the inspector. *Maman* herself, covered in bandages, had removed all her savings. But she had given an appalling hint to the now tearful cashier that the bandages masked dreadful incriminating bruises, meted out at home when she had refused to eat up her lettuce. She seemed so vulnerable, pathetic, wailed the cashier, I blame myself. I didn't report those two monsters.

No blood was ever found at home. Not even on the kitchen knife, despite all the latest forensic techniques. The daughter and her companion were remanded in custody as the circumstantial evidence against them mounted beyond reasonable doubt.

But where had they hidden the body?

Every centimetre of the neighbour's flagstone patio and rose garden was ploughed up in the great search for final proof. The abandoned vegetable patch behind the old house became a crevasse beneath the digger's jaws. Nothing, of course, was ever found. But the new owner was delighted and instantly created the blue-tiled swimming pool of his dreams.

Where, oh where is *Maman*?

The clinic overlooks the sea and the old French lady, perched on her sunlit balcony, surrounded by palm trees, can no longer remember her own name. She likes the island's traditional music and whenever the nurse comes to check her blood pressure or to help her eat, she turns up the volume and sings along with her favourite band. '*Maman* loves Mambo!'

all shall be well

Jan Fortune

Strange Days Indeed 2007

theme: motherhood
non-fiction anthology

I settled into the coach, a protective hand over the life within, and closed my eyes. In three hours, Meg, you will be one of the first women priests in the Church of England, I told myself, in three weeks a mother again.

I had woken early, gone straight to the tiny octagonal chapel. The walnut altar was drenched in a kaleidoscope of light filtered through abstract stained glass. After the bishop's address, we remained; thirty-two women waiting to make history.

'The glorious eve of Mothering Sunday,' one ordinand whispered.

Settled in the coach on the way to the Cathedral, I recalled my selection conference ten years before.

'You're how old, dear?' My interviewer, an elderly man with pale eyes, pale skin and a faded paper-grey cardigan, nodded to himself repeatedly.

'Twenty-four.' I leant forward in the threadbare armchair that dwarfed me.

'Right... been married long?' The head continued to nod, mesmerising me so that I had to concentrate not to do the same.

'Six years.' I wound a hand into long dark hair, smiled to cover my unease.

'Ah. Well, I should have thought a nice young lady like you would be more satisfied staying at home to have babies.' It was said with such a tranquil smile, his pale blue eyes turning liquid with the romance of his own notion. My stomach lurched, but I smiled again.

I began theological training a year later, thirty-two weeks pregnant with my first baby.

The ordination was to be a grand public spectacle, every dark shadow of the cathedral illuminated by the world's cameras.

'Praise to the Lord,
the Almighty ...'

We processed in, a chain of hope winding through the aisles. Thirty-two white-robed women each wearing a stole, individually embroidered pieces: rainbow thread crosses, diamanté-encrusted symbols of bread and wine flashing in the camera lights. The aisles were barely wide enough for the procession, so packed were the chairs on either side.

When we finally stood in an arc before the bishop I felt the baby leap inside me. 'Send down the Holy Spirit upon your servant Meg for the office and work of a priest in your Church.' The bishop's hands rested on my head.

Our stoles, previously knotted like Miss World banners across our torsos, were untied to hang like triumphant scarves. The cathedral erupted in Peace. The congregation surged towards us in excited greeting. Amongst them I caught sight of Ben being pulled along by Lauren, fair curls escaping in wisps from her long blue ribbon. She shook hands with everyone in her path.

'That new priest is our mummy,' she repeated over and over. I moved towards my shy seven-year-old son and confident six-year-old daughter; elated like her. I felt the baby squirm inside me again and remembered my first pregnancy, when I was at theological college.

'It's okay, Meg. The Ministry Board just needs certain reassurances.' My Director of Ordinands' voice on the phone had been breathy and defensive.

I'd stood in the cavernous hallway of my new theological college, mind reeling, trying to steady my own voice. 'Reassurances?'

'About the pregnancy. They need to be sure that you can combine studying with being a proper mother.' He'd spoken slowly, as though explaining to an idiot.

'What?' Too loud, I'd told myself. I'd glanced away from the enquiring eyes of passers by, wound my free hand into my hair, and breathed deeply. 'How am I supposed to do that? The baby's not even born yet. Do they ask all the men with pregnant wives to prove they can study and be fit fathers?'

'No, of course not, it's just a matter of thinking through how you'll manage.'

It was an unpromising start to my theological career, but at that point I had still been confident that all would be well.

It had been harder with Lauren.

'Dennis, can I have a word?'

'Of course.'

I'd spoken quietly, craning towards my tutor, aware of the students around me in the crowded narrow common room. 'I'm going to have another baby.'

'What?' Dennis started backwards, attracting interested glances. 'You're not serious, Meg! I don't want to worry you, but you'll never get a post. If I were a bishop I certainly wouldn't take you on.' How nearly right he had been.

'I've had a conversation with a representative from the Ministry Board,' the next phone call began tentatively. 'They're rather concerned that your concentration on babies must be interfering with your full participation in college life.'

'But Rob looks after Ben, and this baby won't be born till the last term, when college life is almost wound up.' I'd laid a protective hand over the secret baby, winced at the note of fear in my voice and wished I wasn't standing in the public hallway of college.

'Be that as it may, they are concerned. These people have your best interests at heart, Meg. They do feel it very important that you get a full picture of community life and they're also concerned for Ben's welfare.' He was brisk and businesslike now.

I'd closed my eyes hard. All would be well I told myself, blinking back a stray tear.

A few weeks later I was 'released' by my sponsoring diocese as though they were freeing me from bondage, rather than washing their hands of me. Five months pregnant, I started the search for a parish. The first rejection was tortuous, the second swift and blunt – the parish was not suitable for a 'working mother', the letter explained, assuring me of their concern for me. By the fourth parish I'd been ready to accept anything, or so I thought until the offer letter arrived with a copy of the parish news sheet.

St Helen's News
I have today offered our title post to Meg. Meg, 27, is married to Rob. They have a little boy of one and Meg is expecting their second child in April. Rob stays at home with the children. The decision to offer Meg the post was a very difficult one; similar to the decision it would have taken to offer the post to a very effeminate gay male candidate, because of the perversity of her lifestyle. However, I am sure that she will make a great contribution to our life at St Helen's.

Two weeks before Lauren was born, I found a parish.

Lauren was born on Tuesday in Easter week. This caesarean section took longer than the first, the thick layer of scar tissue resisting the scalpel, but at last Lauren Elisabeth was born into a life-giving universe. Within two days I had an infection in the wound. In the second week, my breasts became hard and hot and ached with the fever of mastitis. Lauren systematically regurgitated the milk that I poured into her, painfully curling into tight knots of her own private discomfort. The young, newly qualified health visitor breezed in and out of my life, the latest Monsoon clothes draped over her neat, dry breasts and flat stomach.

I'd returned to college when Lauren was four weeks old, dragging myself through morning worship each day, visible and smiling before I collapsed into my college study to wait for the day to end.

'Peace be with you,' Lauren said solemnly, bringing me back to the present. She held out a tiny hand.

'And also with you,' I echoed, beaming.

'And me,' Rosa was at my side; her plump palm grasping my new stole. 'And you!' I agreed, swinging her into my arms. She was more solid than Lauren had ever been, warm and malleable as dough, her dark hair a riot of thick curls. I swung my two year old into Rob's arms as he approached, smiling.

I had been halfway through my curacy when I announced that I was pregnant for a third time. I was six months pregnant before an ad hoc arrangement for leave was reached; a 'maternity policy' it was felt, would be going a little too far.

An eternity passed under the glare of hospital lights while the epidural was inserted, and another eternity before there was a cry and the glimpse of a baby being whisked away. Rosa was a beautiful baby – round-faced, eyes that were the darkest pools of clear, midnight blue, the devastating fragility and enormous strength of new life. I loved her immediately, a comfortable, well-worn love for someone I'd known for a very long time.

But there was an uneasiness in the parish after the maternity leave. Although I had nearly two years to go on my curacy, my archdeacon decided, without explanation, that it might be best if I move on and sent me on a wild goose chase of impossible parishes. The last one had a woman deacon already in post and I was grateful that I decided to defy my archdeacon to talk to her.

'I believe you're leaving,' I began cautiously. Rosa was asleep on the sofa at my side, soft and dark. Outside Ben and Lauren were blowing bubbles in the garden, warmly wrapped against the chill spring air. I stroked Rosa with one finger as I talked, curling into the big red sofa that took up most of our tiny living room.

'Certainly am, the sooner the better.' The voice on the other end was eager to divulge.

'Would you mind telling me a bit?' Rosa stirred slightly and I placed a hand on her arm, nestled closer to her.

'It's been hell from the start. There's this charming non-stipendiary minister – misogyny really doesn't say it. Let's put it this way, my vicar has promised him faithfully that any woman curate here will never be priested no matter what Synod decides.'

I gulped, I had no idea how long it might take for Synod to decide to allow women to be priested, but I wanted to be ready when the call came. 'Sounds appalling.' I twisted a hand into my hair anxiously.

'You've heard nothing yet,' continued Tara, grateful to pour it all out to anyone. 'I had maternity leave last year ...'

'I'm on maternity leave at the moment.'

'I had twins, total shock. Anyway, while I was away, the church council decided that I couldn't possibly work full-time with two babies so I could only come back part-time. No consultation, nothing. They got the bishop's agreement before they even sprang it on me.'

'What?'

'Part-time indeed! Forty hours a week for £5,000 a year! My husband had given in his notice to look after the twins, so you can imagine what it's been like for us.'

'It's unbelievable!' I sat upright, wound my hand tighter into my hair.

'You'd better believe it or they'll have you for breakfast too.'

'So what are you going to do?'

'Give up. Tom's got a job and we're moving out of London.

Don't mind if I never see the inside of a church or vicarage again.'

'Oh, Tara!'

'Just don't come here.'

The archdeacon sounded flustered when he next rang; 'James Lockley says he hasn't heard from you yet,' he began curtly.

'No, I was going to ring you. I really don't think St Mark's is for me.' I wound my hand into my hair, steadied my voice.

'But you haven't looked at it!'

'I spoke to Tara,' I felt determined. I was not going to take my babies to live in a place like that.

'I did warn you that that wouldn't be helpful.'

'She was very helpful, actually. I'm not very happy about working with colleagues opposed to women's ordination.'

'Not James, he'd be very supportive,' the voice was terse.

'Tara says he's agreed with the non-stipendiary that no woman deacon could ever be priested in that parish.'

'Well, yes, but for practical purposes ...' the voice was smoother now, oily, but I was not going to be persuaded.

'I'm sorry, that's not what I call supportive. I also understand that the parish is not happy with working mothers.'

'Oh, but Tara had twins,' the archdeacon lost his calm again. He was defensive now.

'And I've got three children aged four and under!'

'Meg, I must urge you to see this parish and meet James. If you really don't want to, then of course that's your decision, but I must tell you that it may mean there is nothing else for you in this diocese.'

'What?' My moment of triumph evaporated, my hand reached for another twist of hair. I thought I heard Rosa stirring from a nap upstairs.

'We can't just go on making offers for you to turn down, Meg.' I could hear the smug smile in his voice.

'I hardly turned down the last one. I think ...'

'Perhaps you should consider your future, Meg.' The conversation terminated abruptly.

Rosa began to wail.

All shall be well, I told myself over and over. Another parish, another diocese: March 1994 – standing in the cathedral, my children around me, another one due, ordained and offering peace.

The next morning I woke as a priest on Mothering Sunday, eager to celebrate Communion for the first time. When I arrived, the crumbling 1950s concrete church was bursting with daffodils. After two years of serving a disconsolate congregation of twenty, it was a shock to see so many people crowded into the uncomfortable pews.

As I stood to say the Prayer of Consecration over the bread and wine, the baby kicked hard, rippling my new purple chasuble. I spread my arms, a gesture of invitation and blessing. 'On the night that he was betrayed he gave thanks ...'

Thanks and betrayal – odd companions, I mused. The baby kicked again. There would be no six-month maternity leave this time, but it was not a thought to entertain in the midst of my first 'Prayer of Thanksgiving'. I pushed the remembrance of the letter that had arrived a few weeks before ordination to the back of my mind.

Although clergy are not employed and there is therefore no compunction on the diocese to make arrangements for maternity leave or pay, we have none the less decided to adopt a generous policy and to allow ...

I had passed the letter over to Rob, unable to read on.

'You've been a deacon for six years and they hadn't even

mentioned that you are not employed?' Rob held the letter like a viper and looked as white as if he had seen one. 'And they call this generosity?' Rob flung the letter onto the table. 'So now what?'

'Did you know that I can take eight weeks sick leave before I even need a doctor's note?'

'So?'

'So, ten days after a caesarean section, do you think I will be fit to return to work?'

'Ah,' he hesitated, the light coming back into his eyes, 'I see.'

'Maternity leave till ten days after the birth, then sick leave and when that runs out I have all of this year's holiday saved up to take in one block. I'm also going to trade some time from before the birth – holiday cover. That gives me just over eighteen weeks, including their generous ten days, plus a week before the birth.'

'You've been thinking about this?' Rob grinned, reached over to cup his hands over mine.

'Endlessly.'

'This is my body ...' I went on, coming back to the prayer, holding my hands cupped in consecration over the bread. In three weeks I would feed a baby with my own body and all would be well, it always was.

I was alone with the baby when the call came. The week-old caesarean scar ached as I walked round and round the living room in an effort to comfort Silas. I struggled to hold onto the telephone, rocking as I strained to hear the archdeacon, his tone formal, his words tumbling out fast to ensure no interruptions.

'I've had a chance to have a word about your next post, Meg. I think I should warn you that there are going to be no parishes becoming vacant. I really think that you must look to your own future. The bishop will, of course, be willing to release you.'

I put the phone down and buried my face in my quieted baby; released again.

The final release came seven years later.

The first assault became a media circus overnight. How brave I was to go straight back to work only two days after being held at knife point while the church safe was robbed, the image of Silas seared into my inner vision throughout the attack. Surely a three year old wouldn't even remember me if I died now?

The second attack was ignored; I should forget it like everyone else. He was only a harmless schizophrenic, after all, his promises to take us both to God couldn't have been too terrifying and he'd only held me for half an hour while the police were called.

The third attack made me an embarrassment. I was wrong to have informed the police, the hierarchy told me; it would only lead to bad publicity for the church.

Becoming ill after a series of assaults rendered me beyond forgiveness; how would such weakness look to the outside world?

'It is in the crucible of our own fallibility; in the patchwork of love and abuse that we somehow learn again that all will be well ...' I had sermonised on that first Mothering Sunday after being ordained a priest.

Seven years later, I walked out of the service for All Souls knowing that something had changed forever. The vision of motherhood and ministry, one informing and enriching the other, was shattered, but my family were still there and waiting for me in the Vicarage; four children for whom the last few years had been clouded by living with an increasingly sick and broken mother.

I walked into my youngest child's room and held him tightly. I remembered the pristine promise of each baby, the immensity of love and hope that came with each birth. 'This is life in all its fullness,' I said aloud to the half-asleep child, 'You, not them.'

No more chasing parishes in a church that seemed only to be afraid of mothers and resentful of children. The choice was made and I knew that all would be well.

the forest

Christine Harrison

Power 1998

second fiction anthology

The smell of resin in the forest was strong, like the smell of the sea. And, as the salty sea smell clings to the clothes of sailors, so the pungent smell of resin clung to the clothes of the foresters. Their shirts and trousers were stained with it. Their hands were stained with it. And it ran down the bark of the felled trees.

To Barbara the forest was like a home, and its moist smells nourished and comforted her. The trees made a roof over her head, a dark sheltering roof.

Every school day she had to cycle through the forest, keeping to the narrow path thick with several years' fall of pine needles, softly bumping over tree roots and occasional stones. As it happened, in truth, it was the best thing in her life, this ride through the forest to and from school. She came out of her dream. For the rest of her life seemed shadowy, as if lived by someone she hardly knew. It was only in the forest that she felt fully alive, As if it was her real home.

The foresters themselves, Polish nearly all of them, lived in caravans in clearings in the forest, and even in converted horseboxes. Living mostly without women, they worked hard, getting quietly drunk at weekends. On Sundays a lorry-load of them with hangovers went to Mass in Taunton. They worked throughout the daylight hours, sleeping rough, drinking their sweet black tea which they brewed on little fires that glowed in the dark forest. A few of them though did have women, wives or common-law wives, and there were a handful of children – these were the children that Barbara taught. One or two of the women helped with the work in the forest, trimming the smaller branches from the trees and peeling the bark with a sharp tool. One or two women had young babies, and lived isolated and uneventful lives, their men at work all day long.

Every day, on her way to school, Barbara passed one of these women. This was Lily.

Usually Lily was looking out over the half-door of her converted horsebox. She was married to one of the Polish foresters, and had a baby of about six months. Barbara thought she was probably a local woman, her accent seemed local – though it was hard to tell as she spoke very little, and in monosyllables.

Lily was thought to be simple. It was a word that did not quite convey her half-baked complexity. Simple perhaps in her needs – these were scarcely human in their restricted simplicity. There was something amoebic, anchorite, in the way she never left the horsebox and the little patch of cleared forest round it. Lily's complexity lay in the depths of her obscure, unknowable personality, layer on layer, clear on top, murky and unset and raw underneath.

The horsebox was very compact, like a ship's cabin. Everything had a place. During the day the baby's wooden rocker was stowed gipsy-style under the marriage bed with its thin hard mattress. On one wall there was a glass-fronted china cupboard hanging on two huge nails. Lily had beautified the shelves of this cupboard with empty silver foil cases from shop-bought jam tarts and she had spaced out the three chipped and stained tin mugs, nicely laying them on lacy paper doilies. A red enamel kettle for tea and a large kettle for hot water for washing were permanently on the boil on the stove. The stove was the heart and life of this home. Lily had her washing line tied between two trees, but the dripping and moisture from the trees seldom allowed anything to dry properly and she had to string the half-dried things above the hot little stove, where they sometimes scorched. The place smelled of scorched flannel, babies – and resin.

Barbara always waved, and called out something cheerful, 'It's going to clear up later I think,' or 'Lovely morning to put the baby out,' and Lily would sometimes wave – but sometimes look as if she had not heard or did not want to hear. She might be simple, thought Barbara, but she's temperamental. She regarded the woman's life with horror, terror almost. It was not that Barbara did not love the forest. But to be trapped in it?

On her ride back from school Barbara would pass Lily again. The baby would usually be having its afternoon nap. This was the time when Lily got out her book. It was an ancient Girls' Annual. Lily looked at the pictures of gym-slipped girls with lacrosse sticks and she ate jam tarts that she bought from the travelling van.

Once or twice Barbara had got off her bicycle and tried to start a conversation, but was met with suspicion.

Barbara did not realise that Lily suspected every woman her husband might lay eyes on, though these were few enough. She waited all day for him to come home to her, passing her day looking out over the half-door, her baby on her arm, hauling the water from a rain butt to wash the baby's clothes, or getting the stove to burn. All day she kept her hair in rags to curl it, taking them out before she polished the red kettle and set out two enamel plates, two knives and two spoons ready for the evening meal.

When he did come home at dusk, Lily would watch him while he washed, his hands and body still streaked with the strong-smelling resin. As he washed his naked body, the rivulets of resin which ran down his arms would not wash off. At night he would lie beside her in the fug of the horsebox – she, enveloped in the folds of her huge flannel nightdress (for she was prudish in her primitive way) which was rough with fierce washings and warm and scorched with drying over the stove. The baby slept in its rocker beside them.

At night the voices of wood pigeons and owls came from the forest.

Barbara sometimes wondered what it was like at night in the forest. She rented two rooms in the village pub. Cool dark rooms. Her bed by the window allowed her to see the night sky.

On the windowsill Barbara put things she had brought home from the forest – fir cones, a few wood anemones.

In the evening she sat preparing her lessons for the next day.

If they were busy downstairs, she would help out in the bar. Sometimes two or three of the Polish foresters would come in for a drink, but they were always well behaved and quiet and never had more than one drink during the week. She had a peaceful, ordered life, her supper brought up on a tray by the publican's wife. Emotionally it was a solitary existence. The best thing, the thing she looked forward to, was the ride through the forest in the mornings, and then after school, the ride back. Then she felt inside her skin as at no other time or place.

As she cycled steadily on her way back and forth to school she heard, as well as the soft bumping of the wheels of the machine, the whine of the rapacious chainsaws. It was the foresters who worked – felling, stripping and stacking the fir trees – they worked piece work, and so they worked fast and hard, in a regular rhythm, never stopping for long. From time to time Barbara passed one or two at work by the path-side. Sometimes they looked up, sometimes they laughed and said something to each other in their own language. If she said good morning they would smile back with bold shy smiles, their reticence overlaid with a certain male swagger. But they scarcely paused in their work. Occasionally she passed a man who preferred to work alone. Felling a tree alone is very skilled. As it crashes down with an accelerating speed, bringing with it a shipwreck of broken branches and twigs, it could kill a man.

An ex-army hut had been hauled through the main forest road and set up on the edge of the forest to use as a schoolroom. Altogether there were about a dozen children between the ages of four and ten, after that they had to go to school in the town. Half of them spoke no English, and Barbara had only a few words of Polish. She managed with sign language and smiles. If they had not been a quiet docile lot she could not have managed. Only one or two spoke good English.

She taught them to read. She taught them little songs. Sometimes they painted pictures of the forest and their fathers wielding huge chainsaws, their mothers stripping the smaller branches from the fallen trees. The older ones frowned over mathematics books, while the little ones threaded beads and wound them round their brown wrists like bracelets.

At lunchtime they brought out their packed lunches and then they would chat to each other in their native language and eat little shrivelled apples and heavy home-made cake.

At the end of the afternoon school, their mothers came to fetch them, strong women in wellington boots staring in at the window. Barbara locked up the schoolroom and packed her books into the satchel on the back of her bicycle.

She usually took more or less the same way back through the forest, though sometimes she chose a slightly different path which met up later with her usual homeward way. Once or twice she had become briefly lost for a while. She was not really lost this warm May afternoon. Not lost. But she had wandered off her most direct path. She did not want to get to the village too quickly. It was lovely in the forest, quite magical, the sun slipping through the leaves of fir, beech and oak which grew on the periphery of the main fir forest, whose heart was thuya and sitka. Beams of sunlight streamed through the leaves and branches, silky bright as from some angelic source.

Barbara got off her bicycle and pushed it over the knotty tree roots on the little narrowing path.

In the distance she could hear the frantic whine of the chainsaws rising and falling.

She was so sure she was alone in that part of the forest that the sight of a man standing quite still there beside a tree frightened her. She had thought at first he was a tree and then that he was an animal of some kind. She recognised then who it was. It was Lily's husband, a thickset man of about forty, with a dark drooping moustache. Lily's husband.

He just stood there, as the sun flickered leaf patterns over his face and body.

She remounted and rode slowly on, nearer and nearer to him. He stepped towards her and took hold of the handlebars, nearly making her fall. But she was not frightened at all now. It was just Lily's husband. She dismounted.

'You have come the wrong way,' he said, in good English.

'You are Lily's husband,' she said. He did not answer. Then he said, 'I will show you another way.'

'I can find my own way.' Her words rang out between the trees.

'I will show you,' he said, pretending not to understand her rejection. Still holding the bicycle by the handlebars he set off into the wood. He walked quickly, not looking back, and if she had not followed him he would soon have been lost in the trees. She could think of nothing else to do but follow him.

After a while he stopped though, and let her catch up with him.

She stood there beside him waiting for him to relinquish her bicycle. He held on to it, saying nothing, looking at her – with a curious expression, both shy and as if he was nearly laughing at her, looking at her yellow full skirt, her soft white sweater, her bare legs and old brown laced-up shoes. She felt transfixed by his gaze, and at the same time she was experiencing a horrible crawling sensation in her flesh. She was revolted by him in some peculiar way as she might have been if her own father had made some forbidden approach.

She did not understand this. She was aware of his maleness. She could not avoid it, sidestep it. She thought of him in this context in a strange way He is a used-up male, she thought at the back of her mind, dimly, father of a child, another woman's husband; sex to him is an everyday thing, a habit. To her it was not, it was delicate and new, hardly tried. These thoughts of hers did not form words in her mind.

She started to become angry with him, that he would not hand over her bicycle, and immediately he sensed this, and with a small laugh, handed it to her. He pointed out the path she should take, and she felt him watch as she got on the bicycle and unsteadily rode off.

After she had ridden for a while, she came to the clearing which was Lily's forest home.

Lily was putting curling rags into her brown hair, which was all different lengths. She was doing this expertly, with quick fingers, without using a mirror.

She looked at Barbara, who at once thought the woman somehow knew what had happened. But that must be imagination, as it was impossible. And anyway there was nothing to know.

'It's a lovely afternoon. Is the baby asleep?' she said.

'Yes,' said Lily. She twisted another rag into her hair.

Barbara decided she would not think any more about it. She put it right out of her mind.

And she did not see Lily's husband for several weeks. She had forgotten all about him.

Then, one day, there he was in her classroom. He had actually come into her classroom, just walked in. She had been drawing a star shape on the blackboard, she was colouring it in with yellow chalk, writing its name beside it for the children to copy. A star.

Suddenly he was there, standing beside her, and the children had gone very quiet. They weren't used to seeing a man there, except once a week when the vicar came in his robes and smiled strangely at them. This man was out of place in the classroom. He might have sprung from one of the story books, a giant streaked with resin.

'I have come to ask for something,' he said. It was as if the children were invisible to him, he was not aware of them. He spoke only to her.

Barbara did not reply. Her tongue had frozen in her mouth. She was as if stunned, unbelieving, her thoughts stilled inside her head. That he should come into the classroom like this. None of the other men, not one would have done this. The classroom was an alien place to them, territory that would never be broached even if they had a child in the school. Even the mothers did not seem to want to come further than the door. It was the way it was. He began searching for words. He came very close to her.

'Will you teach Lily to read,' he said.

'Lily,' she said faintly whispering.

'Will you say yes,' he asked. He insisted.

She was overwhelmed by him. She agreed without thinking. She wanted him to go.

And so, after that, on her way home from school, all through that summer she stopped at the horsebox that was Lily's home and began to try to teach Lily to read.

She made cards which said 'baby' and 'jam tarts' and 'book' and all the things she thought Lily was interested in. She taught Lily the sounds of the letters and how to write her husband's name – Oscar – she already knew how to write her own name, but that was all. She tried to teach her how to build up words, and also how to recognise word patterns, in case she found that easier.

She would call in and have a cup of tea with sterilised milk and teach Lily how to read 'tree, baby, milk, apple, bird'. Lily copied the words, her tongue between her teeth.

Lily wanted to read her book about the girls who played lacrosse. She was not very interested in the book Barbara tried to teach her from, about two small children called Dick and Dora.

She made very slow progress, if any at all. She wanted to learn, but could not retain anything in her head from one day to the next. Barbara began to feel that her task was impossible. Lily was indeed very simple. And although Barbara had now spent many hours with her, she knew as little about the woman herself as she had at the beginning. It was as if it would have needed something different from words to communicate with her. She began to think she was wasting her time trying to teach her to read, and began to lose heart. She did not know if Lily was losing heart.

One day Lily's husband came home early from work. It had never happened before, wasting daylight when he could be earning money. Lily still had her hair in curlers and was overcome with embarrassment. She went to the darkness at the back of the horsebox, and bending her head away from him started to pull the rags from her hair.

'Can Lily read yet?' he asked Barbara.

Barbara could not bring herself to tell him that his wife probably would not be able to learn to read. That she was too – simple.

'She is not learning very fast,' she said.

'It will take time,' said the Pole.

The baby woke up, hearing its father's deep voice, and began to cry. The man picked the child out of his little wooden bed, and began tenderly speaking in Polish to it. Then, with an encouraging nod of his head, as if to brook no refusal, he gave the baby to Barbara to hold.

As she held Lily's baby, Barbara felt fear and disgust at the smell of its wet nappy and the sight of milky saliva dribbling from its gummy mouth. It stopped crying and gave her a toothless smile, but she was not won over, only now felt guilt at the hardness of her heart.

Nevertheless something had moved within her. It had to do with the feeling she had as she cycled home through the forest. But less pleasant, more disturbing and new and imprisoning. Now she knew why the forest smelled salty and milky. It had to do with this warm baby in her arms.

She felt disgusted by it all. Everything. The cramped little place where they were all squashed in. The warmth of the stove on this fine evening. The Pole's hairy arms, stained with resin, as he washed his hands in the tin basin, the pathetic doilies and jam tart cases on the shelves. Everything.

'I must go,' she said.

'Have some tea,' said the Pole, drying his hands on a nappy he had taken from the line over the stove.

'I must go,' she said, handing the baby to its mother, 'I'm sorry, I must go.'

'Come again. For another lesson.'

She looked at him helplessly, not knowing what to say.

'It will take time,' he said.

the food of love

Elin ap Hywel

Mirror, Mirror 2004

theme: the other woman
fiction anthology

'Vincigrassi alla Romagna on a terrace in Naples,' says Jayne. 'Fresh pasta, white truffles, moonlight on the water – bliss!' She picks up a ripe green olive and pops it, laughing, into her lipsticked mouth.

'Beans on toast,' says Sandy, 'washed down with half a bottle of Newkie Brown, and a fumble on his mum's sofa after.'

Estelle leans over the table to pull the bottle closer. Sauvignon blanc glugs into our outstretched glasses. 'Your turn, Alex.'

'I don't remember eating coming into it much,' says the languid blonde on the sofa. She curls and uncurls one slim brown foot. 'Unless you count licking whipped cream off each other's ...'

'Ugh! Tack-y!' Estelle turns to pour me more pale wine. Smiling, I put my hand over the glass, shake my head, mouth 'thanks'. Her duty done, Estelle leans back against Sandy's hair. 'How about you?'

Four pairs of eyes turn to look at me speculatively. Light from the candles plays on Estelle's shiny dark hair, on Jayne's rouge éclat-lacquered nails, on the thin silver chain girdling Alex's slim ankle. They are young and glossy, these girls. They reflect the light. With them, I feel parched and ancient as papyrus.

'I don't remember.'

'Come off it, Mum,' grins Estelle. 'You remember everything. You've got the nearest thing to a photographic memory this side of MI5.'

I twirl the stem of my empty glass between finger and thumb, balancing the weight of the bowl against the heavy green foot. What am I doing here?

I'd engineered the whole weekend, or so I thought. Chosen a date when I knew David would be away. When I rang Estelle, her voice had been warm with approval. 'Brilliant! D won't be back from Hull until Sunday night, so we'll have a lovely, girlie time – just you and me. Plenty of time for a proper chat.'

It was now nearly midnight on Saturday and, after a breezy 'How's Dad? and a kiss, Estelle and I had only been alone together when we walked from my train to the station car park.

'Sandy's giving us a lift,' said Estelle. 'The bloody Astra's failed its MOT.'

When we arrived home Sandy, of course, had been offered a drink, pressed to stay and share our Chinese takeaway and, long after I'd gone to bed, had crashed out on the sofa.

It was Sandy, too, who drove us to the beauty salon the next morning. ('My treat!' said Estelle.) When we stepped through the swing doors into the gleaming treatment suite I had hopes, at last, of an hour's peace and silence. Surely, somewhere in this hushed temple of pristine towelling and potted palms, there would be a chance to talk to my daughter?

Skincare intervened. Complexion analysis revealed Estelle as a Type A, me as a 'mature Type D'. Obviously remedial, I was escorted to the Deep Treatment Suite, while girls in white coats led my daughter towards the dubious delights of a Bare Earth Facial. Twenty minutes later, beached on a couch, swathed in a deep-pile white robe, I felt my face tighten and set in its mask of green clay, a Greek tragedian's comic rictus of woe.

In the salon, in the supermarket, on the bus home, we have been surrounded all day by other people. And now this.

I had imagined our evening unwinding as lazily as bread rising. The two of us pottering together in the kitchen, making supper. General dogsbody and bottle-washer to her head chef, I would slice carrots and chop parsley while she stirred sauce into pasta, set plates to warm: the evening a fresh tablecloth before us. There would be plenty of time to tell her.

But at seven o'clock, The Girls had giggled into the flat, clutching bottles of wine and bags of designer snacks, draped themselves over various pieces of furniture, and clicked Sinatra into the CD player.

My mouth feels dry. Sinatra's creamy voice curls around the room. 'Remind me again what I've got to remember.'

'It's simple,' says Sandy. 'Just the time, the place and what you had to eat on your first memorable date with the Love of your Life. The point is—'

'It's meant to symbolise,' breaks in Jayne, looking at me sideways, 'how your relationship has turned out since. Sort of encapsulate it – the whole thing.'

'Like – for example – my first meal with Andrew was so-o-o romantic,' says Jayne. 'A cliché really. Almost too good to be true.'

'A bit like Andrew.' Sandy offers me a pesto-flavoured crisp. One of Estelle's linen cushions flies past her head.

'You don't have to tell me,' Jayne snaps. 'I'm married to him, remember?' She takes another sip of wine. 'The real secret of a happy marriage is knowing when to turn a blind eye. And he's always been able to make it up to me.' She grins. 'I just love the making-up.'

'Chocolates, red roses, champagne,' Sandy smiles. 'What's not to love?'

'Puh-lease. I'm not the one living in sin with a Geordie plumber and his mum.'

'Girls, girls!' Estelle flips over on the sofa so that her chin rests on its arm. She looks like the nine year old she was twenty summers ago, lying on her belly on hot summer sand.

'Come on,' she says to me. 'Don't tell me you've forgotten.'

'It was donkey's years ago.' But I remember, of course. I remember exactly. It's a story John and I have quite literally dined out on many times. I haven't told it lately, though. I try to remember how I used to do it. 'It was quite funny, actually. It was the first meal I ever cooked for him.'

I can't imagine, now, how I got mum and dad out of the house: even in 1970, the permissive society was just a flash of fishnets on the horizon of Goodman Street. Gerry, my brother, was away at college, so they might have been visiting him. More likely, though, I'd just commandeered the parlour, banishing them to chilly exile in the back kitchen.

I was in the Upper Sixth then, mad to go to art school, to ride through the streets of Paris on a scooter behind a beatnik poet, paint my eyelids silver, smoke pot, get laid, get out.

'You can do what you like when you're eighteen,' said my mother. 'I just hope to high heaven I'm not around to see you do it.'

In the meantime, straight-laced Goodman Street required that my bohemianism be translated, for the time being, into adventures of the culinary kind. Armed with the complete works of Elizabeth David and the *Good Housekeeping Book of Foreign Cookery*, I stirred, sifted and baked my way through strudel, risotto and bolognaise sauce. I'd even attempted a curry.

For my first real date with Gerry's quiet, good-looking friend, though, I thought I'd try something new: mushroom stroganoff. Ever-attentive to the dictates of the divine Mrs David, I knew that the success of any dish depended on the quality of its ingredients. The fresher the better. Use only local food, in season. Mushrooms would be perfect. It was autumn in Goodman Street, and in the woods above the paper factory I remembered seeing the brown, fleshy caps of fungi nestling in the misty grass.

'Fresh and seasonal,' I muttered as I left the house at first light, armed with mum's wicker shopping basket, lined (an authentic touch, I felt) with a checked red-and-white napkin. The mushrooms would be dewy, delicious, and better still, free, leaving something left over for a bottle of Chianti, if I dared smuggle one into the house. I shivered with anticipation as I stood in the morning chill.

Back in our kitchen, I surveyed the catch. I'd been right. The woods were full of mushrooms, their thick stalks satisfyingly yielding to my eager fingers. Carefully I laid them out on yesterday's *Daily Mirror*. One or two looked different from the rest: rather more yellow, a longer, thinner shape.

'Hey, mum, what d'you reckon to these?' I asked as she moved past me to fill the kettle at the sink.

'I don't know, love.' She peered. 'All this fancy cooking looks the same to me. I'd have done him a nice steak-and-onion pie, myself. Men like meat.'

Sighing, I riffled through my culinary bibles. They weren't forthcoming about the various species of British edible fungi, preferring to dwell on the delights of the tomato. I'd never heard of anyone in our street being poisoned by a mushroom. Hell, I didn't have time to dilly-dally anyway if I wanted to wash my hair before he got here.

Cold anxiety gripped my stomach. I mustn't muck this one up. I really liked this boy, and I thought he liked me. I'd better get my skates on.

The next couple of hours were a whirr of chopping, stirring, tasting, adjusting, adding thick cream, finding clean nylons, rinsing my hair with vinegar to make it shine, and slicing cucumber for the green salad. When the doorbell rang, my hand shook so much I could barely open the door, and by the time I served the stroganoff I was too nervous to do more than toy with some salad. John, eager to please, ate everything, praised everything, said how nice it was to have something different and adventurous to eat instead of his mother's eternal steak-and-kidney pies ...

'So you made him sick?' says Sandy. We all laugh.

'Literally. He was in hospital for a fortnight. A captive

audience. I visited every day, and by the time he was better, we were engaged.'

No beatniks, no pot, no Paris for me. Just a house in the suburbs, a baby daughter and the love of a good man. And for him, over the past few years, more hospitals. Diagnoses, prognoses, radiotherapy.

The room is quiet, and I realise my story has taken much longer than I thought. The Girls sigh, stretch, look at their watches, smile at each other. They gather their jackets and bags and float out, leaving empty wine bottles, olive stones and cigarette smoke unfurling in the candlelight. As she picks up the ashtrays, Estelle's voice is even. 'Dad all right then? Haven't been feeding him any mushrooms lately?'

My heart feels like a huge, overripe fruit, pulpy with grief and the need to tell.

'Estelle—'

Her face crumples. She's known all along. The car ride, the beauty salon, the Girls' Night In – all ways not to arrive at this moment.

'It's come back, hasn't it?'

I nod. I put my arms around her and slowly we rock, a metronome tipped by the relentless ticking of grief.

A long time later, we pull away from each other. Estelle's neat dark features are puffy with tears. We talk about the practicalities, about what I know. How much he knows. Hospital appointments, treatment. Where. How long.

'Leave those,' I say, uncurling her fingers from the dirty glasses she's been clutching all this time. 'We'll do them in the morning. Let's go to bed.'

As I open the door I'm touched, again, by the way she's set out the spare bedroom for me. A small vase of cornflowers on the dressing table, a blue bottle of mineral water and a glass by my bedside lamp. I turn the overhead light off, strip down to my slip and lie on the duvet, my eyes closed but my mind horribly awake. After a while I hear the door open softly. Estelle creeps in.

'Mum? Are you asleep?'

I put out my hand to her and she climbs under the duvet. Hand in hand, we lie there, not talking, watching the occasional headlights stripe light across the ceiling.

'Do you remember the barbecue at Sandhaven?' she asks into the silence.

'Which one?'

I'm surprised she remembers. We rented a beachside cottage the year Estelle was six. It had an almost-private cove in front of it, a jumble of glistening black rocks and a few feet of bare sand when the tide was out. Still, room enough for a barbecue.

'The one with the fish.'

I know at once which one she means. We had fish every day, of course, bought fresh from the quayside, wrapped in foil and baked, along with small, sweet potatoes, in our driftwood fire. Cider for John and me, apple juice for Estelle. We'd drink, tell stories, sing songs, until it was time to poke the parcels from the embers with a long stick and peel them open, laughing, with burning fingers, to show the fragrant, salt-rimed flesh inside.

It was John's job to brave the dead, accusing stares, cut off the heads and tails, deftly fillet the meat from the translucent bones and pass it to us, piece by piece. With the ghoulishness of children, Estelle watched every move. That night a slit from John's knife revealed a cluster of eggs nestling in the fish's belly.

'What's that?'

'Eggs, darling. It's a mother fish. Look, you can see all the spawn inside.'

Estelle peered gravely at the grainy grey dots. 'How do they grow into big fishes?'

'Well ... they won't now.'

'Because we cooked their mummy?'

John looked at me. He could sense the quiver in our daughter's voice. He pulled her gently from the rock on to his knee. 'Yes, because the fisherman caught their mummy and we cooked her.'

Estelle cried, her face scrunched, small fists thumping her father's guernseyed chest. 'I hate you, Daddy. I hate you, I hate you.'

'Steady on!'

John wrapped Estelle more tightly in his arms. He rocked her from side to side as he told her that this little fish was unlucky, but that the world was full of lucky fishes. He whispered into her hair that out there, in the moonlight, under the sea, there were thousands and thousands and millions of fish who would never be caught, never eaten. Who would swim through underground forests of yellow coral, past wrecks spilling Spanish silver, and, with a flick of a fin, scud away from danger.

By the time he'd finished, Estelle was sleeping, her thumb in her mouth, her legs limp. For years afterwards, she wouldn't eat fish.

In the here and now, too, Estelle is breathing gently, making small puffing noises through her nose, falling slowly into exhaustion. Carefully, I pull my hand away from hers, turn over on my side.

I lie awake for a long time, staring into the night. Then I, too, start drifting. As I fall into a net of darkness, I dream of silver fishes. Their eyes are round and bright, the light on their scales a petrolly sheen, their fins flicking their bodies away from danger, out of my reaching hands. Away, away across oceans, across time, past galleons frosted with ancient barnacles, to forests of yellow coral where no net will ever catch them.

walking through

Christine Evans

In Her Element 2008

theme: nature writing
non-fiction anthology

It seems to me I have always loved walking in the dark. More especially, at dusk; walking through from one day's end to the growing stage of the next. Night doesn't 'fall', nothing so abrupt and graceless: as Macbeth observed, *light thickens*, so that for an instant colours flare against the retina, then fade. Shadows clot into a vagueness so that things are seen clearer out of the corner of the eye. At last only pale objects beckon: an outcrop of white limestone snags the glance, a new lamb glimmers, tucked in under an earth bank; petals drift soundlessly from a hedgerow rose. Sometimes – particularly on calm summer evenings when the air is cool silk on bare arms – it seems darkness seeps up through the ground, as if easing an aquifer, an ancient core of black wrapped within the rock since the earth's first cataclysms. It is a transformation we fail to appreciate only because it takes place so predictably, so often in a lifetime. We do not even notice it any more.

In winter it happens early and surprisingly quickly. I take a path my feet know well: up our sheep field behind the house, scramble over a stile and then through gorse and rough pasture past the cottage where the Pritchard family came to live in 1925 after their uncle, King Love, led the Exodus from Enlli. As the twilight deepens, things become first dark shapes, then outlines, and are absorbed, as if in a metaphor of all living matter. And the thickening air accepts the human walker too, takes you into itself so that far from other people's torches and fuss, you move with as well as through the night. There's an occasional rustle in the hawthorn as a bird tucks its head in, a whisper of dry grass that betrays a rabbit or a hedgehog's purposeful tread, but otherwise a settling into quiet. Soon enough though, car headlamps – two, three, as if racing each other – will leap up and over the fields, there'll be a scattering of houselights and far below, the chapel windows glow, like long yellow lozenges, for a meeting of Merched y Wawr or an after-school practice for the Spring Eisteddfod. And then down the road home, the dog and I padding round to the back door, throwing it open to a blare of bright noise and the smell of baking potatoes. They look up – whoever's there – stupid with warmth and television news, and I feel an intruder, too big for the room, more real, charged. Fully alive.

I have done it in reverse, this walking through: slipped out of the marital bed in the greyness before dawn, pulling on tracksuit trousers and fleece in pulses of glare from the lighthouse, for my summers are spent on the island of Bardsey, two miles off the pointing finger that is the Llŷn Peninsula. Each white flash is less sharp on the wall, so when I get out of the gate, the sky is paling over the hunched mountain and the stars are disappearing, swallowed up like shellfish on wet sand as the tide comes in. But morning usually advances too quickly to get the feeling of crossing over: by the time I have followed the crumbling mountain wall up to Pen Cristin I can see my feet and the crouched shapes of gorse bushes, with the furtive shuffles of dangerously belated shearwaters between them. As soon as my shadow starts to throw itself on the ground ahead of me, I feel distinct, conscious of myself as separate, scrambling and puffing. Already, on this sunrise-facing side of the hill, birds are stirring. There's a guillemot churring on the rocky ledges, and gulls are circling and calling high above in the lightening grey, white tips on their wings catching first light like signal flags. When I turn to look the other way, there's warmth on my shoulders and little spiders catch the light and glisten, their webs strung across the bracken turned to fine silver. I stand and watch the island's huge shadow shrinking back into itself so fast you can feel the roll of the planet towards the sun. It is wonderful and exhilarating. I gallop back down, but not as satisfied as when I've been walking through the dusk and felt absorbed.

The habit of walking in the dark started when I was ten

or eleven years old and circumstances forced my family to a farmhouse perched above the Calder valley in the Pennines. The only way of getting to it was a cart track winding steeply up through fields, straggly woods and then moorland, miles of its dark pelt rolling over the rim of the horizon past wild, witchy Whirlaw Rocks and beyond Stoodley Pike to Crow Hill and Top Withens. A huge sky, blowing bogcotton and forgotten Roman roads among the heather, dead farms that stared out over mill towns, sunk under their own smoke. It was a harsh landscape but I knew it, first out of necessity, then with a growing sense of connection. Our home life was fractured, makeshift: my little sister turned to animals for love and companionship while I found satisfaction in landscape and then literature about landscape. I learnt the shapes of the hills against the sky, the slow motion gestures of trees, the clouds and changing colours in the sky that 'would move all together if it move at all' (we 'did' Wordsworth in Form 4) and I longed to be part of that unity. Walking at night, I found, was a good way of losing self-consciousness, or perhaps having the space to be more your self. Because other children, and even adults, were afraid of the dark, it lent a feeling of power, too. We lived remote from other houses: until I lived in cities and travelled through them, I was never afraid of what I might encounter. These were not great expeditions, you understand, just going from place to lighted place – walking home from school in winter, or after babysitting for Dorinda in the council houses. Running down to the farm because the milk in its white enamel billycan had been forgotten on the wall, or slipping out to look for badgers at full moon. The childless couple at Cross Stone had a television and would sometimes invite me: after an evening sitting in a row on their lumpy sofa I'd feel the smell of horses streaming off me in the cool night wind, and my dreams would be wild with cantering and whinnies.

Longer, more purposeful walks followed. As a student I sought out vacation jobs in places where I could indulge my passion for being in the landscape: summers at a farm on the slopes of Dunkery Beacon on Exmoor; nannying for a hunting family near the Long Mynd and a first taste of Clawdd Offa; looking after dogs on Tintagel cliffs; waitressing in the Lake District. Once I came to live and work in Pen Llŷn my life was filled up with astonishing scenery; I could do my walking from home and have hardly needed to travel anywhere else. In my first summer here, a teaching colleague invited me to stay on Enlli, Bardsey Island, and my fate was sealed. Reader, I married the boatman, and my relationship with the natural world moved up quite a few notches. For one thing, living surrounded by the sea and learning to swim was a new exultation: it's as near as most humans can come to another world, another element we can exist in only briefly.

Swimming with Seals

Somewhere far's a memory
of gills, a sense of being somewhere,
something, she has always known:
just as her life is settling into
womanhood, her story seems untwisting
to a dream of a sealself
sleeksided, free, somewhere between
indigo and singing green.

Blue light sinks deeper.

She glides through airless vaulted chambers
over a silver-mottled shadow
that moves as she moves, watching,

until she's not sure which is herself.
Time lengthens ...

Then heart bangs, lungs burn, and she must
spin to the surface
while slower bubbles of her passage
prickle far below, fizz out
in an exultation of silver.

She will climb back on the rock
feeling the lightness drain away,
her body like a coat that does not fit;
hands opening on empty air.

I have only spent half-years on the island, though. There
have always been other commitments in late autumn –
earning a living, schooling, family and friends – and the lure
of mountains, wooded riverbanks, and estuaries to explore
on the mainland. For the most part I am happy within my
own *milltir sgwâr*, the 'square mile' of fields and gorsey
headlands I know well, either on Bardsey or on the tip of the
mainland overlooking it. However busy, my daily practice
would always include a good walk or a wander – an hour or
so, usually in late afternoon after work – until the day before
my sixtieth birthday.

It was the last day of August, perhaps the last of a glorious
hot summer that we'd enjoyed without being disconcerted
by good weather. The baler had broken and everyone on the
island had been out in the hayfield helping to carry a late
crop, having fun forking the sweet-smelling dry grass on to
the trailer, and dancing about on top to trample it down.
Evening brought a sense of satisfied weariness, the body
mildly protesting in all its joints, as I took our grey-muzzled

Labrador for her last-thing walk. Along the cleared field, all gates open now, easy walking, the grass stalks like cut hair, and then up the bank by the old school and back through the bracken. Just ten minutes; I was tired. But what a night! Clear and cold, almost frosty. Too light for shearwaters to come sweeping in, screaming to make contact with their chicks waiting in the burrows, so the island was utterly peaceful under a sky seething with stars above the hill's black shadow.

As I turned briskly for home, invigorated now, there, suddenly, was the moon. It stopped me in my tracks. Full and serene, much more energetic than a mere mirror for the sun, the moon blazed silver across a vast calm expanse of sea. I had heard on Radio 4 that Mars was at perihelion this week, the closest it would be to the earth for another twenty years. I looked for and found its reddish twinkle thirty-five million miles away and just to the right of our moon, and then – a real rarity, this, only seen on the clearest of nights, and never before by me – the rhythmic loom of the lighthouse on Strumble Head, right across Cardigan Bay. It caught my eye like someone waving a torch, signalling from below the southern horizon. There – yes, again – and again – a fan of white light opening against the dark and distance.

I suppose it was a dizzy spell, but I remember what happened next as a moment of rapture. In my happiness at the beauty of the night – of being rapt and wrapped in it – I think I sprang up towards the moon, literally jumping for joy. The world tilted, there was a surge of movement and wind brushed my face. For a fraction of a second I felt weightless, as though I might actually take off, as though the lift-off we all dream of were being offered. Peter Pan has a lot to answer for. Instead of a moment of transcendence, it was a foolish and no doubt comically lumbering expression of exuberance, followed immediately by a lurch, a reel of stars and bracken, a wrenching crack and a thudding into blackness as head hit rock. In memory it's all in slow motion, though of course there's no knowing what actually happened. I fell to earth. It feels exactly as though I had been picked up – and gone willingly, eagerly, into the sky – and been dropped, clumsily. The universe rejected me.

Bracken was scratching my face. It was dark, and the dog was pushing her nose at me in a worried way. I was lying awkwardly in a small hollow in the path, where a scatter of stones points the ruins of an old cottage and gardens. My left ankle was hot, and running fingers gingerly down it, that cliché of bad novels came to mind – twisted at an impossible angle. At least it wasn't my neck. Broken. I'd heard it go, and it was almost midnight and all sensible people had gone to bed. I tried shouting – in case someone from the bird observatory, had gone out to look for owls or shooting stars – calling out in a strained, sorry-to-bother-you tone, Hello? Is anybody there? Hell-Oooo. And then, sounding utterly unconvincing even to myself, Help!

The dog groaned, as if she was embarrassed too, but otherwise the night was silent. The smiling moon sailed on, the lighthouses flashed their indifferent, automated warnings, the light from the stars was ghost-fire, centuries old.

There was no more dizziness, but standing was impossible. I tried leaning on the dog and dragging myself along, but the pain of the limp foot banging on the stony, ground was too intense. I had to get back before the numbness wore off or I'd lose consciousness again. And already I was cold, beginning to shiver, and my teeth aching. (Later, I found out that I'd cracked three on the stone that knocked me out.) So, in a half-crouch, with lots of swearing, I walked. And of course, that is what caused most damage, together with the delay in getting to hospital. I know now that I should have woken people, radioed for the Air Ambulance, disturbed everyone (the noise! the lights! the drama!) and made a fuss – and if anyone could have told me what I'd lose, I would have done. But at the time it was enough to get back down the hill, crawl down the steps and on to the sofa by the Rayburn. Time enough to try to make sense of it, to get mended, tomorrow.

But eight days in hospital and all the skill of the orthopaedic surgeons with titanium pins and screws, followed by physiotherapy, calcium supplements and even acupuncture, can't make it so right again. Four years on, the most I can tackle, with two walking poles, is forty minutes or so of fairly gentle hill. Any more and the ankle protests, and often as not the right hip – the other hip – gangs up on me as well. I put it in these personal terms because – even more than the vertigo and tinnitus I've suffered intermittently ever since – the biggest change is an awareness of and even dialogue with, my own body. Laid up alone with it for whole days back on the island – all the holidaymakers gone by then, husband and son busy with lobstering and ferrying sheep and cattle to mainland markets – I learnt at last to appreciate it. Racked with guilt at my carelessness, as you might be for damaging a car if it were the only one you could ever own, I took an active part in the healing, talking to the leg in plaster and tending it like a hurt friend.

As some children fantasise about being discovered as royal – Laurie Lee in *Cider with Rosie*, for one – when I was young, I harboured a belief that the shape I found myself in was only temporary. I can't remember what I hoped my metamorphosis would bring, if I even got as far as imagining it; but my first feeling on waking was often disappointment that I was still the same. As far as I could see: now I realise that our bodies, especially women's, are constantly changing. They are not our selves, just our miraculously adaptable lodgings, and they deserve looking after.

Steer clear of rough ground, say the specialists, here are

special shock-reducing insoles. Sit down to do the ironing, advises my GP, we can give you a special slanty stool. The physio tells me to keep on with the exercises and get a shopping trolley. My son sets up a system of tanks and pumps behind our island house so I don't have to fetch water from the well, and my husband buys a buggy so I don't have to walk to the jetty or the Abbey tower or the lighthouse. Everyone is kind. I try to take to sedentary activities sitting watching seals or sketching rocks at sunset. Not ironing. Each day I walk for a little longer, a few minutes further. Even on crutches I managed to struggle up the path to the shoulder of the mountain to use my mobile phone, but I haven't made it to the top yet. Perhaps this summer. I said that last year, and the one before that.

But worse than the physical restrictions is having to think for my ankle, not being able to trust it will sense when to avoid tripping or sliding, for it seems to have lost some instinctive connection. Not being able to take energy levels for granted, gauging them like a fuel tank would have come anyway with age, but most irksome is the first taste of being looked after: having to account for where I'm going, how long I might be. How would I know? I want to set off where the fancy takes me, and it has to be on my own. But isn't it a bit late? Look, it's getting dark. Shall we come with you?

So here I am, grounded. But flapping.

fish

Fiona Owen

Catwomen from Hell 2000

theme: the wicked women of Wales
fiction anthology

In the hall stands the goldfish tank, gone all green now. The fish can just be seen, idling among the few strands of slimy reeds. Sometimes they come up to the edge of the glass and peer out, their mouths working, their gills flapping in the thick pea-soup water. Their gold is dissolving into the gluey depths of the tank, settling on the bottom like a discarded robe; in the breathless hush of water, they are preparing to die.

When Huw tells his father about the fish, his father seems not to listen. He seems not to hear. It's that woman, thinks Huw. She's brainwashing him. Each time they go to visit Mrs Jackson and Grettie, Huw sees the fish and the fish see him. Each time, they come right up to the very edge of their world and stare out through the glass at him, with round flat eyes.

'Why don't you clean out the fish?' he asks Grettie, when they're alone.

'She won't let me,' says Grettie, eyes wide towards the door. 'I think she wants them to die.'

'Why did she get them then, in the first place?'

'They were Daddy's,' says Grettie, and then her eyes fill up and overflow.

The hall is the only room in the house that hasn't got carpet. The kitchen has carpet and the toilet has carpet. This makes Huw uncomfortable. What happens if someone pees onto the floor, like his dad does sometimes, in the middle of the night, and like he himself does, often? Boys haven't got such good aim. He remembers his mother always calling him a sprinkler. 'You're as bad as your dad,' she used to say.

Huw thinks there's a smell in the toilet, beneath the floral air-freshener. It's all that sprinkled pee that's soaked into the carpet. You can't vacuum it up. He doesn't fancy the idea of having a bath at Mrs Jackson's house. He doesn't want to walk barefoot in the pee. It's bad enough wearing socks.

Mrs Jackson calls herself *house proud*. She likes Huw to take his trainers off at the front door. He has to leave them alongside his dad's boots and Grettie's shoes, all lined up underneath the fish tank, which sits on a dark old leggy table with twirling edges. Huw tries not to look at the fish tank when he's taking his trainers off, in case he meets eyes with the fish.

'Come on, Huw,' shouts his father, from inside the house.

'Yes, hurry up, Huwie,' comes Mrs Jackson's voice, thick like golden syrup. 'We're all waiting to eat.'

Huw has a knot in one of his laces. The harder he pulls at it, the tighter it gets. He knows without looking up that the fish are lined along the glass, all three of them, mouthing at him in soft liquid voices, whispers that wake Huw from sleep or pierce through his dreams.

'I can't undo my lace, Dad,' he shouts, too loudly. He can hear himself breathing quickly and has a vision of himself in a relay race at school when he was younger, trying to catch up, to catch the boy in front, feeling the blood in his ears pumping, that sense of time overtaking him.

Belinda Jackson appears in the doorway.

'Can't you, love?' she says, cooing like a pigeon. 'Here. Let me help.'

Huw doesn't look up, but struggles harder with the lace. He has a sense of bulk beside him, of soft cushioning breasts and flowery perfume. Just as her hands reach towards his, the knot comes apart between his fingers.

'Done it,' he says, a stark note of triumph in his voice. He jumps up and away from her.

'You're so independent, you are,' says Mrs Jackson. She says it in a voice like honey, but Huw can't meet the hard grey of her eyes.

The table is round, with a peach-coloured table cloth and blue patterned crockery. There is a bottle of wine on the table and wine glasses. Grettie is sitting between Mrs Jackson and Huw, her hair long and straight down her back. She eats without looking up and sometimes she rocks slightly, as she swings her legs under the table. Huw can see his father's face is flushed. That means it's almost time. Huw holds out his leg so that Grettie kicks him accidentally.

'Ow,' he says. 'Why did you do that?'

'I didn't do anything,' says Grettie, her enormous pale eyes gaping in her face.

'Huw,' says his father, warningly. Mrs Jackson is pouring him more gravy, and chuckles.

'It sounds just as it should do,' she says. 'They're starting to relax with each other, that's all.' She beams round the table. 'Pour the wine, Tom. Give the kids just a teensy-weensy bit, eh?'

'I don't want any wine,' says Grettie.

'Oh go on, just a little,' says her stepmother. 'It's a special occasion.'

'I'll have some,' says Huw, anxious not to miss the opportunity and also keen to out-do Grettie. He is thirteen, after all; she is just a kid.

'You can have some orange instead,' Huw's father says to Grettie, as he pours wine into Huw's glass. 'And half a glass will be enough for you,' he says to his son. 'And just this once.'

Mrs Jackson holds her glass up for him to fill and she smiles at him the whole time.

On their way over to see Mrs Jackson and Grettie, Huw's father had said, 'How would you fancy Grettie as a little sister?' Huw had made a noise like being sick, which was only a slight exaggeration of the way he was really feeling. He'd known it was coming; he'd read all the signs. But it still came as a jolt, like an electric shock striking him just under the ribs. 'Because I know she'd love to have you as her older brother.'

Huw could feel himself sealing shut, tight as a clam.

'I mean, poor kid. No dad ...'

And no mum either, thought Huw, feeling an unexpected pang of compassion for her.

'Belinda does her best, of course but it's been hard. She's looked after Grettie like she was her own daughter. I mean, how could a father just up and off and leave his own kid, eh?'

Huw suddenly wanted to ask Grettie questions, things he'd never thought of asking before, about missing fathers and wicked stepmothers. Because Huw was convinced Mrs Jackson was somehow wicked. The fish had told him. Mrs Jackson was really a witch who'd put a spell on his father.

'Dad,' he said, bursting his own silence. 'Do you *love* Mrs Jackson?'

'I wish you'd call her Aunty Belinda. Mrs Jackson is so formal.'

Huw tried it out in his head. *Aunty Belinda*. The sound made him shudder.

'Do you love her?' he repeated.

'Well, yes. Sort of.'

'Like Mummy?'

'No, not like Mummy,' said his father. His father always talked about his dead wife in hushed church tones and his eyes would drift away from Huw to some other time.

'How then?'

'Well, she's good company. She's companionable, a good laugh. She fills a hole in my life.'

'Made by Mummy dying?'

His father said nothing for sometime and Huw thought he'd forgotten the question. Then he said, 'Nothing could fill that,' and Huw sighed deeply. He hadn't realised that he'd been holding his breath.

Huw has a ritual. Every Sunday night, he locks himself in the bathroom and drags the old wicker chair to the sink, so that he can climb up and kneel on it. Then he stares at the mirror non-stop and after about five minutes, his mother comes. His face changes ever so slightly so that it gets more oval. His curling hazel hair grows around his face and falls to his shoulders and his eyelashes grow longer and curl up more. Those are the only necessary adjustments. Then, with his mother's face smiling back at him, he whispers her his secrets, his worries, his latest fears, and she whispers back the answers in her soft wise voice. Her brown eyes brim with love for him, her only son, and her thick hair gleams under the strip-light. Before she goes, she kisses his lips a cool lingering kiss. Then she vanishes back into the mirror, leaving only her breath on the glass.

'We've got a surprise for you two,' says Belinda Jackson. 'Haven't we, Tom?'

'Well, yes we have.'

Huw picks up his wine glass and swills the wine down nervously, all in one go. Then he burps and Grettie shoots him a quick contemptuous look from beneath her eyelashes.

'Can I have some more wine?'

'No, you've already had half a glass. That's quite enough.'

'Tom, let him have a drop more. He needs something in his glass for the toast.'

Huw can feel the wine already working. His lips have turned to rubber and his lower abdomen feels soft and pulpy.

'Yes, the toast,' he says, wanting to giggle out something about marmalade.

'Oh, all right then. Just for this once.' His father pours him half a glass more.

'Your father has something to tell you, Huw,' says Mrs Jackson. 'That's what this meal is all about.'

Huw knows she wants him to look at her, to look up and

smile expectantly as if keen to know the secret. But he has already guessed what's coming, so instead he stares at her breasts. They look even more enormous than usual, as if they're all squashed together and are clamouring for space. They appear over the top of her blouse in mounds and Huw has the insane impulse to lean over and bite into them as if they were ripe juicy fruit.

'Huw and Grettie,' his father says, scraping his chair back awkwardly, so that his napkin slips from his lap. 'Belinda and I have come to a decision that will affect us all.'

Huw sticks his legs out under the table, trying to catch at Grettie's swinging legs.

'What we figure is this: Belinda's on her own with Grettie and I'm on my own with you, Huw, so it makes sense to pool our resources.'

Huw has hold of one of Grettie's feet between his ankles and Grettie is going pink in the face trying to pull free.

'So we've decided to get married and then we can all live together as one family.' Huw lets go of Grettie and stares across at his father. 'Married.' It sounds like an echo. Now that the word is out and hanging suspended over the table, it seems too close, too real. Huw feels as if he's fallen into a nightmare.

'Yes, Huwie,' says Mrs Jackson. 'Isn't that wonderful?'

'No, it's not!' Huw jumps up, knocking his chair over backwards. His head has filled with a giddying red fog. 'You're a witch and you've put a spell on my dad. He doesn't love you. He only loves my mum.'

'Huw! What are you saying?' His father stands up too and comes round to Huw and takes his shoulders. 'Huw, you apologise to Belinda.'

'No, I'll never apologise to her. I'm not going to live here with a witch!' And Huw shakes himself free and runs away, up to the bathroom.

Huw is panting so that his breath mists the mirror. It is cold against his cheek, and through the glass, he can see the whole bathroom in reverse: the pink bath, the pink washbasin set into an ivory cabinet, the rows of creams, shampoos and talcs, the wall-to-wall pink carpet, and the toilet in the corner, from where Huw can already smell the dirty yellow under-smell of urine. Huw knows he must speak to his mother, but it isn't Sunday and this isn't his house, so he's not sure the magic will work and he's not sure he should even try. But his eyes are prickling with hot ready tears and he feels that, if ever there was a time to test the magic, then this is it. He goes to the door and checks the lock just one more time. Then he goes back to the mirror. It is full length, so all he must do is stand in front of it and wait. He knows how to focus his eyes so that everything around him fades into grey background and all he can see is himself. He knows he must stare into his own brown eyes without blinking until he is squeezed to a hot pin-point shape on the glass. Then he feels himself grow loose and limp and it is at that moment that his mother steps forward, out of himself and into the glass.

'*Cariad*,' she whispers to him. Huw feels himself wrapped by cool slim arms. She kisses his forehead, his cheeks, his lips.

'How's my baby boy?'

Huw licks away his salty tears. 'I wasn't sure you'd come to me, here,' he says.

'I'll come whenever you call me,' his mother whispers, with gentle eyes resting on him.

'This is the house of a witch,' he says, wiping his nose with the back of his hand.

'I know. But you have stronger magic.'

'Dad is under her spell.'

'Yes, but you can break it.'

'How?'

His mother smiles at him through the glass, her hair the colour of autumn.

'You must rescue the fish.'

'The fish!' Huw can feel his face flush in excitement. 'They whisper to me. She wants them to die.'

'I know. They are part of the spell. If you rescue the fish and set them free, the spell will be broken and all will be clear to you.'

'Then I'll do it,' says Huw, and he places his palms against his mother's and their lips meet softly.

Just then, Grettie's voice comes through the door. 'Huw, let me in.'

His mother vanishes and Huw is left wiping the smudges hastily from the mirror.

'Who were you talking to just then?' Grettie stands in the bathroom, while Huw locks the door again.

'Nobody,' he says.

'But I heard you.' She is looking at him curiously, more openly than before.

'No you didn't,' says Huw. Then, 'What do you want?'

'They sent me up,' she says, indicating the door with her head. 'First your father was furious and wanted to come after you and make you say sorry. Then he thought he should maybe let you cool down first. Then *she* sent me up to bring you down. Really, I think she just wanted me out of the way.' She looks at Huw through long fair lashes. 'You're right, you know.'

'About what?'

'About her being a witch. I've known for ages. It's because of her that my daddy left home one night and never came back. Now I don't know where he is.' She is looking down again, her pale hair falling across her face like a thin veil.

'I know how to break her spell,' says Huw, lowering his

voice. He moves closer to Grettie, feeling suddenly protective of her, suddenly akin to her in spirit.

Grettie wipes at her face and looks up at Huw through wet eyelashes. 'How?'

'It's to do with the fish. I have to rescue them.'

'They're Daddy's fish.'

'Yes, but they're dying. If I – we – don't get them out of that tank and into fresh water, they've had it.'

'But where could we take them?'

Huw's brow crinkles in thought. 'I don't know yet. A river, maybe.'

'Or a lake,' says Grettie, her eyes widening. 'I know one.'

'Do you?' Huw takes her arm. 'Where?'

'It's in the woods, not far from here.'

'Then you must take us there. Tonight.'

'Tonight?' Grettie sounds suddenly doubtful. 'It'll be dark,' she says.

Huw waves a hand dismissively. 'There's no time to waste. Now, we must go downstairs and pretend. I'll say I'm sorry, but I'll cross my fingers, so it won't really count. Then tonight, late, I'll come for you, and we'll go to the lake.' He peers closely into Grettie's face. 'Okay?'

Grettie nods, but she is chewing at her bottom lip and her pale face looks bleached.

Huw dreams he's in a dark wood, alone. He is searching for something, but he can't quite remember what. He is walking with his arms outstretched, as if he's sleepwalking. Brambles tear at his pyjama bottoms. An owl hoots overhead. There is a rustle among the ferns: something is approaching. Huw turns to see an orange glow, like the prelude to a sunrise, and as he watches, the orange becomes golden. Soon, the light is dazzling, filling the glade where he now stands and out of this sunbeam light rides a beautiful lady with lustrous russet hair astride a gilded stallion that is somehow both a horse and a fish. Suddenly, the beautiful lady holds out her arms and Huw sees with joy that she is his mother and he opens his mouth to call to her, but instead of his own voice, another voice comes. There is a moaning low in his throat, a deep groan that builds and builds. Huw puts his hand to his mouth, forces his fist down his own throat. His mother is calling to him but the moan is louder. It's blocking out all other sound. As Huw struggles, with his hand tearing at the inside of his throat, the moan crescendos, rises in pitch, becomes a high mocking cackle …

Huw wakes with a jolt. He is breathing hard and his nose and mouth feels wet. He reaches to the bedside table and turns on the lamp.

'Damn,' he says. His hand is smeared with the red of blood and the pillow is stained. His nose is still bleeding, so, tipping his head back and cupping his hand underneath his nose, he slips out of bed and goes out onto the landing. The house is in darkness except for the thin light from his bedside lamp. Downstairs, the dining room clock chimes the hour of two. Huw shivers. He tip-toes across the landing, walking carefully to prevent creaks. He'll have to go to the bathroom, until his nose-bleed stops. But he has to pass the room where his father is lying with the witch. The blood is dripping from his nose onto his pyjama top and it's awkward trying to step noiselessly with your head tilted back. He knows this is the dangerous part of the landing and their door is slightly ajar, too, so he must take extra care. Then, from within the witch's room, come noises: grunts and growls and breathy groans. A moaning like pain. And Huw knows it's time and, true enough, the fish begin calling to hurry, hurry, and he abandons his search for toilet tissue. As if carried along by air, he finds himself in Grettie's room and by her bed.

'Grettie,' he hisses, shaking her roughly. 'Wake up.'

Huw has prepared. He stole a plastic food bag from one of the kitchen drawers. Now it is filled with water and Grettie is standing holding it, while Huw is up on a chair, netting the fish. The hall is filled with an eerie green light, emanating from the fish tank.

'Here they are,' Huw whispers triumphantly, as he lifts the net from the tank. He climbs down from the chair and they both gaze into the net at the fish, who lie placidly among the sludge scraped up with them. Even in the dim green light, the fish look tarnished and ill.

'It's almost as if they know we're helping them,' whispers Grettie.

'Of course they know,' says Huw, carefully releasing the fish into the plastic bag. 'Not long now,' he tells them. 'Soon you'll be free.'

The night is black and still, and Huw is wishing he'd brought a torch. He has his anorak on over his pyjamas and although it's mild, he feels on the brink of shivering.

'How much longer?' he says.

'Just up here,' says Grettie. She is walking ahead slightly, with quick small steps, and Huw is suddenly struck by her whiteness, by the way she seems to glow in the dark. Her cream-coloured hair spreads around her shoulders, and her face, pasty at all other times, now gleams as if lit from within. Even the length of white nightie that hangs beneath her jumper seems to be giving out light. Now she stops by a wooden stile set into the fence.

'This is it,' she says, and her eyes fill her face like moons.

Huw has tied the plastic bag at the top and carries it in front of him in case the brambles tear it.

'Where's the lake?' he says.

'It's in the middle of the wood. It's quite easy to find once we get onto the main track.'

The path they are following is narrow and uneven and the

trees seem to close in behind them. Grettie glides ahead, lighting the way for Huw, who stumbles along, catching his feet in tufts and trailing vegetation. The trees clutch at him as he walks, stroking his hair and patting his shoulders. And all the time, he carries the fish ahead of him, as if presenting them as a gift.

Suddenly the path opens out into a clearing. Either Huw's eyes have adjusted to the dark or it has got lighter, for he can see more easily around him. They are standing in a glade which is encircled by trees and undergrowth.

'Where are we?' he says.

Grettie is walking the circle, lighting the air as she goes. Then she stops and cocks her head to one side, like a dog listening.

'Grettie,' says Huw, uncertainly. 'What are you doing?'

'We're near,' says Grettie. 'I'm just finding the direction.'

Huw looks about him. This clearing is like a cul-de-sac. He can't see another way out. He turns back up the path they came down. There might be a path leading off it that they missed. It's dark, without Grettie, and the brambles seem worse. He holds the plastic bag higher. But his foot hits against something and he goes sprawling down among the vegetation. He can think of nothing other than the pain, as the nettles and brambles close around him, stinging and striking at his hands and face like a hundred vipers. There is a moment of blackness, of silence. Then he remembers.

'Oh God,' he whimpers, and struggles upright. 'The fish.'

The thorns tear at his clothes as he feels his way forward. It's so dark. It's as if the trees have grown in minutes to shut out the night sky.

'Grettie,' he moans. Then louder, 'Grettie. I've lost the fish.'

She appears at his side like a candle.

'I fell and I've lost the fish,' says Huw, crawling up the path on his hands and knees. 'They could be anywhere.'

Grettie is behind him, rummaging. He can hear her rustling in the bushes. Then she says, 'Here they are!' and Huw clambers unsteadily to his feet. Holding the bag up, they can both make out that it's spurting water like a watering can. Huw tries to cover the holes with his hands, but it is useless. He gives out a howl of frustration that stirs the trees like a breeze. Then Grettie says, 'Follow me.'

They head back down the path into the clearing. Huw cups the bag in his hands, feeling the water leak out like blood. Grettie floats across the clearing and slips behind a tree and Huw follows, close behind. A narrow rabbit track leads them round a thicket and down an avenue of closely growing evergreens. Then, without warning, the trees seem to side step, and there in front of them is the lake.

They both kneel down at the water's edge. The lake is like a black mirror, stretching out into the darkness. Huw struggles with the knotted bag. The water's all run out and the plastic has closed around the fish like cling-film. He rips the bag open and they peer in.

'Are they alive?' whispers Grettie. As if in reply, they see the faintest of wriggles: the flutter of a tail, the flap of a gill.

'Good luck,' Huw says to them, and then tips the bag inside out, so they fall with a plop into the lake. For a minute, they float on the surface and Huw thinks he's killed them. Then there is the kick of a tail, the flash of old-gold and, one by one, the fish swim away, down into the depths of the lake.

Huw leans over as far as he can and stares into the water after them. As the ripples subside and the surface of the lake smoothes over to its mirror finish, a face seems to compose itself upon the water. The detail is missing, but Huw recognises the smile. He lowers his face closer to the surface of the water, and whispers, 'Have we done it? Have we broken the spell?'

The face smiles back at him tenderly, then seems to dissolve, leaving him staring into his own reflection.

'Huw,' says Grettie, and her face glides into view like a swan. 'Will everything be all right, now?'

Huw pushes himself to his feet and wipes under his nose with his forefinger. He feels like crying. But also, he feels grown up: wise and responsible.

'Maybe. Yes.'

Grettie is gazing up at him and shifting from one foot to another, pointing her toes like a ballet dancer.

'You should see yourself,' she says. 'All blood-stained.'

'I had a nose bleed,' says Huw. 'I forgot.'

His eyes wander across the lake's smooth surface. Detail is appearing out of the grey dawn light. All around them, the birds have started up a rowdy chorus.

'Might as well go home, then,' says Grettie, attempting a pirouette.

'Okay,' Huw says, turning for the trees. 'Might as well.'

rash

Janet Thomas

Safe World Gone 2007

theme: the turning point
fiction anthology

Karen was one of the first to get a sun-lounger and she lay by the pool in jeans, a long-sleeved white shirt, wide straw hat, trainers and sunglasses. Every so often, she moved the blue umbrella so her hands and ankles were in shadow. Around the kidney-shaped pool, at least fifty other people, also tourists, almost all also British, lay around her, in swimsuits and bikinis. The Greek sun softened the tarmac on the road. People whispered, stared openly, nudged each other, but not as much as they had yesterday. Karen lifted her book and pretended nobody was looking at her. For all they knew she always sunbathed fully dressed. I don't care, she told herself, this is my holiday, my one holiday, and I'm not sitting in that little room any longer. Her skin, under her jeans, shirt and trainers, itched and raged.

The rep had said it was a photosensitive rash. 'We see them quite a lot, especially on British skins. An allergy to the sun, basically.'

'But I've sunbathed all my life.' Karen turned so the rep could see it was all over her back as well as her arms, legs and chest. Her skin was like pink sandpaper. 'I put on tons of cream.'

'Just keep covered,' the rep suggested. 'It'll go.'

Jim came walking up the beach with the group from Newport he'd palled up with while she'd been hiding in their room taking cold baths. She watched him from behind her sunglasses, as he chatted to the two girls, both wearing strappy tops and tiny shorts, their exposed skins honey and caramel. Her stomach clenched so hard she dropped her book. He'll sleep with one of them, if he hasn't already, a voice in her head whispered, sounding like her mother, as she struggled to find her page and look relaxed. You look repellent, he thinks you're infectious and you wince when he touches you, so what do you expect? He's on holiday. And how can you be allergic to the sun? It's like being allergic to life.

She smiled as he came closer. He was going pink along his freckly cheekbones. 'You might burn a little, love.'

He waved his hand, dismissing this. What idiots can't handle the sun? The Newport lot looked at her, the freak, one tilting her head to get a better look. Karen pulled her sleeves over her hands. The movement stung. 'I was thinking of going shopping in Corfu Town. I'm fed up of wearing these, thought I'd treat myself.'

Jim pointed to the others. 'We're going paragliding. We've booked.'

'That's fine, love.' Karen smiled brightly. 'There's a bus trip. I'll get that.'

'Oh,' one of the girls said, 'that's going in a minute.'

Karen hugged her bag. She didn't want to leave him with them, didn't want to walk away alone. But what was the option? Stay in her room in the bath? Watch them paraglide, dressed, scratching? She had four days and eight hours of this holiday left. 'Right. Well, I'd better move then.'

She stood and Jim leaned an inch away from her. She hurried off, holding her hat, smiling away as if a bus trip alone in the heat was the only reason she'd come to the island.

The stuffy coach swung back and forth along the twisting roads. The hill dropped down at the side, small stones skittering into nothing as they passed. Six boys from Birmingham drank beer in the back seats and sang obscene songs, mostly insulting Greek men's balls. Karen picked at her nail varnish and wondered what everyone at home was doing, how work was managing without her. She imagined facing them all, with no Jim, no tan, and felt sick. She closed her eyes, blaming the swaying bus. She itched.

About half an hour later the bus stopped, and she looked around for Corfu Town, but it was just scrubby hillside. The Greek bus driver stomped to the back and shouted at the boys from Birmingham in Greek. Karen sank down in her seat. The bus started again and so did the singing. Everyone else pretended to be deaf. Another ten minutes and the bus shuddered to a halt. The bus driver shouted, got off the bus and walked down the road. The boys cheered.

Karen was sweating, sticking to her seat, itching and itching. The boys kept singing. Soon they started to sound bored, looking for the driver, egging each other on for Round Two. Ten minutes. Fifteen minutes. Okay, he'd made his point now.

All the British tourists sat in the bus for half an hour. The singing had finally mumbled into silence. Karen knew she'd scream if she had to sit there itching against the plastic seat any longer, so she got up and everyone looked at her. Desperate to move, she climbed off the bus down on to the dust road. The olive trees twisted their branches around themselves in grey-green rows. The sun stared down at her, burning her centre parting. There was no sign of the bus driver, or anyone else, or any houses. Her phone played 'I Predict a Riot' when she turned it on, making her homesick. No signal. What the hell did she do now? Her skin seethed, nagging her on. She was wearing her trainers, so, unfolding her sunhat, she started to walk. There would have to be a village with a phone eventually. Behind her, she was aware of people spilling off the bus.

'Hey, you gonna walk all the way?' A Birmingham accent. Noisy scuffing footsteps followed her down the hill.

'On your own, darling?'

'I saw your man with those Welsh girls, didn't I? That why he's not with you?'

'Aw, I'll keep you company.' Sniggering.

She carried on walking, eyes ahead, as if nobody was saying anything.

'Hey, don't be unfriendly.'

'Why'd you come, if you just want to be so fucking miserable?'

They caught up with her, moved around her, their shirts off, showing their soft flesh. They had bottles in their hands, their eyes covered by big ugly sunglasses, like flies' eyes. The lager smelt like sweat. Why didn't the sun turn their skins pink and spiteful? Her body remembered a party when she'd suddenly been circled by gatecrashers, when she'd had to be rescued, and trembled. She stared desperately at the horizon, trying to show nothing on her face at all.

'Bitch.' One grabbed her left arm. They all stopped. She realised they had walked out of sight of the bus. Why had she thought they were boys? Her tongue was too big in her throat. 'That's more like it,' he sneered, pushing her back against the wall of his friends. 'I've seen you, stuck up, avoiding everyone, thinking you're so fucking great.' His grip bit into her rash, stinging. The rash that was why Jim wasn't here.

'Careful,' she said, her voice shaking. She pulled back her sleeve and the spots glowed in the sun. 'It's catching.'

He let her arm go. She pulled back her collar, showing her shoulder round. They all stepped back, one scuffling on the edge.

'That's why my boyfriend couldn't come. Nothing yesterday. Today he's covered. *Everywhere*. And he'll be scarred.' The thought of Jim burning added bite to her voice.

'Fuck.' The man wiped his hand on his shorts.

She took a tiny step up the hill and they backed off. She wanted to laugh. Move, her brain screamed, and she slipped through them and ran for the top, her breath rough. Her legs were so tense it was hard not to trip over herself, waiting for a hand on her shoulder, in her hair. The bus was at the top – and the bus driver, beckoning her. She grabbed the bar and swung herself on after him. He was talking away in Greek. 'Those men,' she panted.

He waved dismissively and drove off, his smile stretching his moustache wide. None of the others said anything about the group left behind. She sat on the seat behind the driver, clinging to the rail. I'm all right, she told herself, shaking.

After the hotel complex full of British people, Corfu Town felt Greek. She bought a glass of white wine in the first bar she saw and a pudding she couldn't pronounce, all layers of pastry and nuts and honey, sweet enough to make her fillings ache and yet dry on her tongue. It was the first thing she had eaten on this holiday that she couldn't eat at home and she felt a little heartache of joy, as if it was a mini adventure just eating it, but it didn't still the shakes. She drank her wine and licked honey from her fingers, and all she could think of was the way she'd stared at the horizon as if nothing was happening. Why do that? That was always how she handled the bullies at school, that was how she'd handled those men at that party, before she'd been rescued. Pretend it isn't happening – why was that her defence mechanism? When had that ever worked?

But I did something this time, she thought. I'm here. She stretched out her hand and smiled at her raw angry skin.

And she thought of Jim – pretend everything is fine. Pretend you aren't bothered. Ignore it and it isn't happening. Why did she do that? When had it ever worked?

The waiter offered her another glass, smiling, and she felt an urge to flash her rash at him, just to see the start in his eyes. Surprised at herself she almost giggled. She nodded to the wine, and pointed at random to something on the menu. It came back deep-fried with tentacles. She laughed openly then. Was she really going to eat that? She looked around for someone to notice that she was about to eat tentacles, but everyone else was caught up in their own business. She stared. What did these people do on holiday, away from the beach, seemingly sexless and so dressed? She bit into her seafood, which was crunchy and chewy and didn't particularly taste of anything, and waited to feel sick. She thought, I am alone, foreign, repulsively pink and crusted, and waited to feel afraid.

And instead, like a loosening, she had this sense of Corfu Town spreading out around her, and beyond that other towns, other countries, on and on, like a map unfolding. It was a weird feeling and she didn't know quite what to do with it. But she knew what she wouldn't do.

She sat in the bar, swaying in her chair, eating tentacles, until she knew the bus would have gone. She rang Jim, left a message at reception for him as he was out. She rang her mother at home, shouting to her over the music. And as she told her mother about her allergy, stretching out her arm, she realised she wasn't itching any more. As she listened to her mother panic, the phone clamped between her cheek and her shoulder, she scratched her arm and waited to feel the pain. She picked at her spots, dug her nails in, attacked them. She wasn't ready yet to lose her rash.

e d

Eloise Williams

Cut on the Bias 2010

theme: clothes
fiction anthology

This is my green cardy. I call it Ed. People tell me it is strange to call your cardigan something. I don't care and that's a fact.

My mother says I am twenty-five now. She tells me all the time.

– Don't do that, you are twenty-five now.
– Don't say that, you are twenty-five now.
– Don't look like that, you are twenty-five now.

I just stay quiet, but I think I don't know how to look any different. I can't really change my face.

My green cardy is my favourite thing in the world because it is mine and I chose it and I didn't choose any of my other clothes. Usually my mum, or my nana, bring me clothes that they have bought for me, and they are all like, pink, with pictures of puppies or cats, and I think I am not twelve anymore.

My green cardy is nine years old and smells of grass when it has soaked up the sun; it reminds me of being in a tent when the rain starts falling lightly in the spring. I sleep with it under my pillow now, in case they throw it out 'cos it is missing a button, has a hole in the arm and is

– way too tight
or, as I like to call it, cwtchy.

My name is Eleri, which either means unknown, or people don't know what it means when you look it up in a dictionary. It is sad that Eleri rhymes with scary. This gives all the people who

– don't know better
a really easy way to make me angry.

I had a banana sandwich before we set off, and I had toast with eggs this morning. Sometimes I have toast with jam, but that is usually on a Thursday when I get up later to rest after my Wednesday outing. Today is Wednesday. Today my friend takes me out. His name is Mikey, and he is cool, and lets me do pretty much anything I want

– within reason.

He is the only man I have seen who wears a scarf on his head, and has ribbons on his bag which are sun yellow and sky blue, which makes it easy to spot him in a crowd.

The walk is four miles, he tells me, so I wear my walking shoes.

Mum makes a fuss before we leave about it being

– too far
– too dangerous
– too everything,

this just means I want to go more.

Mikey ties Ed around my waist and we set off into the forest of trees. The ground beneath my feet is crunchy and stumbly, and my balance isn't good like other people's. I've got a scab on my knee from where I fell over the other day, so I have a big plaster which makes my friends ooh and aah, and that is good. We see a butterfly flutter by, and Mikey whistles a song which sounds like something from a telly commercial, and I sing along like lalalalala. Even though I never heard it before I sound pretty brilliant.

We are walking to the waterfall today. Mikey showed me

pictures of it in a photograph book and I wanted to go there right away, but that was not our going out day so I couldn't. We've been planning it for three days. I looked at a map and copied it onto paper for us. He got us two walking sticks off a tree out the back garden and put bells on them. They jingle, jangle, tinkle as we walk, though I've given mine to Mikey 'cos it is too much like hard work and that's for sure.

The waterfall we are walking to is called 'Sgwyd yr Eira', which means 'Falls of Snow', which doesn't make hardly any sense at all until you see a picture. You can walk behind it. I never heard of any waterfall you can walk behind in real life before, and so that's why we are on our way.

I've got water in a bottle round my neck and I keep sipping some even though it tastes of plastic. The sun is big. Like a giant gold coin and I can't look at it for squinting, and Mikey says I'll get crow's feet, which makes no sense at all 'cos why would my feet change into a bird's because I look at the sun? He puts my glasses on and the world becomes pink and shiny, and we walk some more.

And then we walk some more again.

I'm following the map with my finger, and on the red dotty line there is a river which I have put as three blue wavy lines, and we haven't even reached the river, and I think we are lost, and to be honest I'm a little bit fed up because this was meant to be an adventure not an endless trudgety trudgety trudge. Mikey is in front of me and his footsteps kick up dust in clouds and puffs. I scuff my own shoes for a bit, listening to their sound as it matches my heartbeat, and then I cough a lot to make a point about his walking habits and to get a break. We sit and I cough some more, like a lady that I saw on *Casualty*, and I try to get some blood up but there is none to come. When that doesn't get me much attention I start to cry. This is a certain sure way to get a hug, and to go back to the car and go to get some chips.

'What's up, kiddo?' Mikey sits down next to me which I usually like but he smells of hot and his skin is wet.

'I am not a kiddo.' This is a sure for certain sign to him that I am in a strop.

'You're not giving up on me already are you, my intrepid explorer?' He smiles his big white teeth smile and I catch a spark of gold in his mouth, like buried treasure and it makes me think of pirates and how they were brave, and I don't know what intrepid means but I think he is calling me a scaredy cat.

'My knee hurts.' It doesn't but I need a reason to be cross.

'Let me see.' Mikey takes off the plaster and it leaves a black square where the dirt has stuck around the edges, and my skin is very bluey where the plaster was. He tuts a bit and shakes his head. 'Do you want to go on? Or shall we take you to the hospital?'

A bee buzzes past, and he is lucky I don't bat it into his eye.

'I never said I wanted to go back.' I am stubborn

– at the best of times.

We have been walking for a hundred and fifty years now. Mikey has pointed to lots of mountains that all look the same. He keeps showing me flowers though which are nice colours like lemon and lilac and candyfloss pink, and for a while we play 'he loves me, he loves me not' which is strange for both of us 'cos Mikey is a boy and I don't have a boyfriend.

I had a boyfriend once at music club but that was
     – not allowed,

so now I just have boys who are friends and the difference is we don't hold hands, unless it is for a game like drama.

'Listen.' Mikey puts his hand on my shoulder and I let him put it there 'cos he is safe. The wind makes a sound like a moan, then a whine, then a rush and I turn around quickly as I'm sure that a tidal wave is on its way to smash me into smithereens.

Smithereens is a good word. I've smashed lots of things into smithereens. Mirrors, plates, cups, mum's photo frame, mum's glasses, the shower door, part of the car, the shed window, that kind of thing. I listen with my ear to the sound and my hair splashing across the front of my face in waves. Mikey's face has lit up like an electric bulb, and he is saying excited things like 'wicked' and 'awesome', and I copy him because it makes him happy, and he is good to me and he has the money for chips.

The wind blasts past us with a smash and a crack and is gone.

It excited Mikey so much he wants to walk a bit more quickly, and I try my best even though I am not

– nimble
or
– dainty
and I'm
– certainly not going to be a ballerina.

I drink my last bit of plasticy water down and am just beginning to get really super mad when we come to the edge of the world, and Mikey points down and through the trees you can see it.

Now when I said you could understand the name 'Falls of Snow' from the picture, I believed it and that's for certain sure, but looking at it now I know that you could never understand it till you seen it with your own

– baby blues.

Me and Mikey and Ed hug and jump up and down a bit, only I jump a bit less 'cos my feet are sore.

'And now for the ultimate challenge.' Mikey points at a million steps down and I think that he is wrong cos the ultimate challenge will be climbing back up, but the water is so beautiful and looks frothy, diamondy, and glittery like Christmas and magicy like fairies, and I haven't got any plasticy water left so we go.

'Mum was right.' We are halfway down and I am crying, not to get a cuddle but just 'cos I can't stop.

Mikey sits down next to me and smiles. He is always bloody smiling.

'Your mum is right about a lot of things, Eleri, but not this. This is your time to prove to her that you are a grown-up. Show her that you can do things for yourself. I promise you it'll be worth the struggle if you make it.'

And his voice is so soft it is like a pillow on my head, and I look up at the steps behind us and see how very far I have come already and I know that he is right, it is kind of now or never, I can't be like this for always.

'You aren't Barack Obama you know,' I say, because I am always sarcastic when he makes a speech even when he is saying the right things, and I am very well up on current affairs. Ed squeezes me extra hard around my waist, and I use him to wipe the tears from my eyes, and the snot from my nose, which he is used to 'cos he is my oldest friend apart from Mum.

I could tell you about the rest of the steps, and how I banged my knee and gashed my legs till blood ran red into my sock, and how we had to walk sideways on the rocks holding hands 'cos it was high up and slippery, soaking and silly dangerous, but you would be scared and I want to tell you about the waterfall.

*

Shut your eyes and think of white. And then think of that white falling in front of you, like a curtain of heavy thick snowflakes, and then specks of that white landing on your face like tiny giggles or kisses. Imagine a noise in your ears, like a train rattling through a tunnel, or a million people playing drums, or everyone in the world jumping up and down all at once. Think what you imagine heaven to look like, and then make it better and louder by a hundred, and take out the harps.

I look at Mikey, and his face is shining like a lamp, and his eyes are on fire they are so bright, and his mouth is in the shape that a mouth makes when there is a whooooooo hooooo coming out, but I can't hear it because the water is filling my ears with its own happy shouts.

I take a step back as some big splashes hit my face with an ice cold slap that would wake up a hibernating hedgehog, and step on something soft.

And there he is. Ed. My oldest friend. He has loosened himself from around my middle where he usually cuddles, and is lying in a pool as clear as the shiniest, cleanest mirror.

People think I'm strange. Most people don't understand their clothes like I do, but then most people really don't listen.

We come to an understanding without speaking, Ed and I. This is our time. This is our moment to be free. This is the time we will grow up, and we will take on the world on our own, and not cow down to the bullies, and not let Mum tell us what we have to do, or where we have to go, or that we

— aren't strong enough
or
— clever enough
or
— brave enough

and sometimes we'll have eggs on a Thursday too, if we want them.

I pick Ed up and I am shaking. Partly with the cold and partly because I am excited and afraid, but in a good way. Ed drips tears down my arm, but they are happy tears. Mikey gives me a little nod, though he looks serious as hell. I hold Ed to my face, but just for a second 'cos he already smells different, and soon we will be strangers. We don't need to speak our goodbyes 'cos we know.

Ed flies when I throw him, through the fall of snow to the wide open world. I see him in jigsaw bits and pieces through the always-changing white. He swims hard in bubbles and gurgles, the sun catching him as he bounces off rocks in bright meadow green. And then he is gone, all the way to the sea.

I salute. I don't know why I salute, it just feels right. I suppose I feel like the captain for a change, and even though there are a hundred and fifty million steps to go straight up, and about a hundred and twenty miles to get to the car, I can't wipe the grin off my face, and I'm sure that Ed can't either.

s w i m m i n g

Sarah Jackman

Safe World Gone 2007

theme: the turning point
fiction anthology

'Ready?' Lisa asked.

'Yes,' Mattie said slowly, but she didn't move. She was thinking that even though Lisa was dressed in a brand-new tracksuit and was carrying a brand-new sports bag, she didn't look like she was about to go swimming.

In fact, if Mattie had opened the door and found Lisa's disembodied head bobbing in the air in front of her, it wouldn't have been at all surprising to hear it start grumbling about how, once again, Mattie had misunderstood the arrangements and impatiently telling her to go and get changed for the disco.

Lisa's hair was secured in place at the back with a clasp and held neatly off each side of her face with heart-shaped diamanté clips so that Mattie had an unimpeded view of Lisa's blue eyes nestled in thick mascara.

'Have you got your cossie on underneath?' Lisa's tongue flicked across her bottom lip, then the top, making the lip-gloss gleam.

'No.'

Lisa frowned. 'It saves time when we get there.'

Mattie seriously doubted this was true, but she recognised the casual certainty of Lisa's declaration and knew it would be best to keep quiet. It had been the same yesterday when Lisa sprung the idea of swimming on her as they were walking home from school.

Lisa had said, 'We need to get fit.' She'd said, 'Swimming's good exercise and there's nothing else to do on Wednesday evenings anyway.'

Mattie fished her costume out of her bag and shut herself in the downstairs loo. She sat on the toilet seat to remove her trainers. Outside Lisa had started singing and Mattie knew that she'd be practising the dance that went with the song; Lisa only needed to see the video once to be able to copy the moves. Mattie struggled to pull her sweatshirt over her head.

She tugged it to and fro but it was stuck on her scrunchie, and the more she tried, the worse it seemed to get. She was panting with the effort, her arms felt weak held above her head, her ears hot from friction.

Outside Lisa stopped singing. Mattie froze.

'Matt? Have you died in there or what?'

Mattie's muffled laughter filled her top with warm, minty air. She pictured it frosting the inside like a coating of icing sugar. She yanked herself free and stood up giddily to take off her tracksuit bottoms and knickers.

Mattie eyed the photo on the wall in front of her, picked herself out in the middle row without intention or hesitation. For the millionth time, the desire accidentally to knock the photo to the floor swelled inside her, but she knew it was futile; it would only be promptly replaced by one of those plastered all over the living room. She noticed the costume that she was wearing back then was the same one she was now about to step into; she seriously doubted it was going to fit.

Swimming had taken up too much time.

There had been practice at least four times a week and then competitions most Saturdays, which meant that she could never go shopping in town with Lisa and the others. It meant going to school on Monday and having to ask Lisa to fill her in on what everyone was talking about until Lisa started snapping at her and saying, 'You had to be there, Matt.'

She glared at Tony's face on the photograph, her face reddening with the thought that she had once nearly fancied him and at the memory of that evening when he'd turned up at the house.

She'd heard the doorbell and people talking hush-hush in the hall, so when her mum had called her downstairs with a strange urgency in her voice, Mattie had burst into the living room full of anticipation and excitement. Three serious faces had turned towards her and stared, until her dad said, 'Where are your manners? Say hello to Mr Mills, Mathilda.'

It had taken a moment to register that he meant Tony.

The moment she sat down Mum started throwing accusations and questions at her: *She'd lied to them. Where had she been going on Saturdays all this time? What had she been doing? Who was she with?*

Then Tony had his go, telling her that she'd need to be dedicated and how there were plenty of others to take her place if she wasn't. Perhaps not as good, he'd added, but reliable members of the team. As he spoke he kept looking at Dad, who had jumped in as soon as Tony had finished speaking. 'What do you have to say for yourself, young lady?'

When Mattie said that she didn't want to swim anymore, she was sick of it, she hated it, Dad leapt up.

'You're an idiot for wasting a gift,' he shouted, grabbing one of her cups off the shelf and holding it aloft as if he'd just won a race himself. 'Look at what you're giving up, look at what you're giving up,' he kept repeating. When Mum started crying, Mattie had closed her eyes. Anyone would have thought she'd been doing something terrible instead of just shopping and hanging out. She couldn't understand how swimming had ever got that important.

With a final wriggle, the costume was on. It was way too small and cut across her cheeks so that they bulged out like the lumps of raw dough they'd made pizza bases with at school. Mattie tilted backwards, which loosened the material on her bum but tightened it across her stomach and tits which, with nowhere else to go, started to ooze into her armpits. Mattie squished them back in as best she could.

Outside Lisa was singing, 'Why are we waiting?'

On closer inspection, Mattie saw with alarm that sprigs of pubic hair were also escaping down below. She poked those back in too.

'What *are* you doing in there, Matt?' Lisa rapped crossly on the door.

Mattie went straight to locker number 193 without thinking and the same queasy feeling came over her as it had in the ticket queue when she inhaled the familiar smell of rubber and sweat and cleaning fluid. Her heart was beating fast, like it used to before a race. She stuffed her belongings inside and stood for a moment trying to breathe deeply, but her lungs felt like soggy sponges soaking up the warm, damp air.

She wrapped her towel around her; tying it at her waist; she stared at the bump her stomach made which seemed to be growing bigger every second. She clenched her muscles and sucked it in when Lisa emerged from the cubicle.

'Do I look okay?' Lisa turned this way and that in front of the full-length mirror.

Slice Mattie in half and there would still be more of her than Lisa. She reminded Mattie of one of those brittle shavings Dad planed from hunks of wood in his workshop and which Mattie liked to pick up off the floor just to feel their fragility.

'You look great.' She tweaked the elastic that had cut grooves into the top of her thighs and rubbed at the red marks. 'Mine's too small.'

Lisa made Mattie undo her towel. Under her scrutiny, Mattie clenched and sucked so hard her muscles trembled and her jaw began to ache from holding her breath.

'It's not too bad,' Lisa announced after a long pause.

The air was bitter with chlorine and tainted sea-green, so that Mattie felt as if her eyes were open under water. Ahead, Lisa handed her ticket to the lifeguard attendant. He peered at Mattie as she approached. 'Haven't seen you for a long time.'

Mattie felt caught. 'I've been busy,' she finally said, hanging her head.

She walked past the baby pool filled with tiny children splashing along in their armbands like wind-up toys let loose; past the cordoned-off inky-blue diving pool where she'd always imagined if you dove down like an arrow, you could break through into a magical world. When she came to the main pool she was shocked by how busy it was; there was barely a centimetre which didn't contain a body part; the water was so thrashed up that the black lines on the bottom looked as if they'd been painted by someone who couldn't keep their hand steady. Everyone was shouting and somewhere a child was crying, jagged shrieks which reverberated around the hall.

Mattie had always tried to be the first to get to training. She liked nothing better than treading through the echoing quiet early in the morning to stand at the deep end and look across the motionless blue of the pool. She would dive into the exact middle and once she'd reached the other end, look back at the perfect 'v' trail she'd created unfurling across the water until it bumped into nothingness at the sides and stillness was restored.

'Come on, Matt,' Lisa shouted. She was sitting on the edge with her legs dangling in the water and her arms hugged around her.

Mattie threw down her towel and angled her body sideways down the steps so that neither her bum nor her stomach faced the pool. She plunged into the water and spotting Lisa's feet, came up with her mouth gaping, pretending to chomp at her toes. Lisa squealed and Mattie splashed her – only once, but it was a big mistake. Lisa hissed a single word, '*Don't,*' before retreating to a bench at the side of the pool where she sat shivering until Mattie promised not to do it again.

'Are you really wearing those?' Lisa asked, looking down at Mattie as she adjusted the goggles to sit tightly over her eyes.

'How else will I see under water?'

'Why do you need to?' Before Mattie had a chance to reply, Lisa spoke again. 'You go away,' she instructed, 'until I'm in.'

Mattie held her nose as she sank down, feeling the water close over her head. She began a slow glide along the bottom, her tummy grazing the floor. She swam through a forest of pasty legs to the other side and then back again before surfacing.

Lisa was a couple of metres away swimming with jerky strokes, her neck stiffly arched, her chin pushed forward, her nose held high. In the swimming club they'd called the people who refused to get their heads wet 'snouts'.

Mattie dove down and surfaced just behind Lisa, touching her leg to let her know she was there. Lisa yelped, began flailing around, gulping for air and kicking out plumes of spray as she headed into the side.

'If I'd known you were going to muck around so much, I wouldn't have asked you to come.' Lisa's face was screwed up and pink with anger. 'I could have drowned,' she said, clutching the rail of the steps, her voice shrill and her eyes wide.

'Sorry,' Mattie said. 'I was only ...'

'Has my mascara run?' Lisa cut in. 'It had better not have.'

Lisa's hairline at the back of her neck was damp and Mattie watched as a single drop of water slid slowly down her forehead; but the mascara and lip-gloss were untouched.

'No, it's fine.'

Mattie turned back to face the pool. Without thinking, she pushed off and began to swim, keeping alert to the gaps between people. Her body stretched and curved as she dipped and rose. Then she altered her stroke and began to cut through the pool, narrow and fast. She'd forgotten how strong her body was, how her skin felt coated in silk as it slipped easily through the water. People cleared a pathway for her as she tumble-turned and began another length.

Mattie counted twenty more before easing to a gentle halt in the shallow end. She looked around for Lisa, felt a bump of guilt when she saw Lisa hadn't moved but as Mattie started towards her, she noticed Lisa wasn't alone. She was talking to Robin and Sammy from their school.

Mattie quickly submerged herself but as soon as she came up for air, Lisa started waving to her. She swam reluctantly forward.

'Robin and Sammy come swimming every Wednesday,' Lisa told Mattie and giggled. Mattie remembered Lisa fancied Robin. 'Mattie used to be in the swimming team. But I'm useless, half a length and I'm exhausted.'

'You need to build up some muscles,' Robin told her and Mattie watched him gently squeeze one of her thin arms; they both laughed as if it was the funniest thing in the world.

Mattie quickly lowered her arms out of sight. She had bigger muscles than either of the boys and now that she was stationary her whole body seemed to be expanding; her tummy was ballooning, the fat on her thighs was rippling with the flow of the water. She sank deeper and half-listened to the others chat.

Mattie didn't know what to say to boys anymore. In the swimming club it had been easy, she just talked to them about techniques and times and normal things too, like what they'd watched on television the night before. There wasn't a big deal made about girls and boys like there was at school where you weren't supposed to forget about it for a single moment.

Whenever a group got together, Mattie felt sick with nerves, much worse than she ever felt before competing. At least then she'd known what the rules were and that her team was always there cheering her on, calling out her name, wanting her to do well. Now, Mattie was constantly confused and was always in danger of getting it wrong. Girls who were friends one minute were no longer talking to her and Lisa the next; and one time Mattie had made the big mistake of just chatting with a boy only to have Lisa drag her away, whispering how she was causing loads of trouble because he was 'somebody else's'.

It was safer, Mattie had decided, to look stupid and stay silent.

Lisa giggled again and suddenly Mattie saw how it was.

She left the side without saying a word. She would not, she promised herself, stop swimming until Lisa had stopped talking to the boys.

At each turn when Mattie checked whether they were still in the same spot, the words 'she knew, she knew' bubbled through her. She had to force herself to forget, to concentrate on placing her body within the water, getting the stroke exactly right. She was too out of practice to achieve this all the time, but whenever she did, it felt good and purposeful.

She stopped to catch her breath and couldn't resist glancing over. When she saw them huddled together, the words swept through her: 'She knew they'd be here.'

She swam over.

'I'm getting out now,' she told Lisa.

'Me too. See you later, you guys.'

Mattie was up and out in a flash. She retrieved her towel from the bench and set off for the changing rooms. The lifeguard called out to her as she passed, 'You've not lost the knack, I see.'

She slowed her pace, smiled over her shoulder. 'Thanks.'

'Don't leave it so long next time,' he said and winked.

In the shower, Mattie closed her eyes as the water cascaded onto her head, over her face and shoulders. She could stay like this for hours.

'Was that lifeguard chatting you up?' Lisa stood shivering

at the entrance to the shower room, her towel wrapped tightly around her shoulders.

'No.'

'What did he say then?'

'Nothing. He remembered me from before that's all.'

'I think he fancies you.'

'He was just being friendly.'

'He's old anyhow,' Lisa said. 'He'd be a perv.'

'Aren't you having a shower?'

'I haven't got any stuff with me.'

'You can borrow mine.'

'It's okay. I don't want to get my hair wet.'

Mattie began shampooing her hair.

'I told them we'd meet up after, in the café,' Lisa said.

Mattie said nothing.

'Sammy says you're a great swimmer. I think he likes you. Do you like him?'

Mattie began rinsing her hair. She couldn't think there was anything to like about Sammy. He was shorter and skinnier than her, and spotty. He told jokes that weren't funny. She peered through the streaming water at Lisa. 'You knew they'd be here.'

'I thought they might, but I didn't know for definite.'

'I think it's out of order, that's all. Not telling me.'

'Don't get stressed, Matt, okay. You wouldn't have come if I'd said.'

'I might.' Mattie paused. 'It's out of order, that's all,' she repeated but less firmly. Lisa's attention was drifting; she was looking towards the changing cubicles.

'Sammy's a wet,' Mattie said, turning the shower off. 'But Robin's all right. He fancies you.'

Lisa waited for her. 'He doesn't.'

'He's mad about you. It's obvious.'

Lisa touched Mattie's hand and they stopped, centimetres apart; face to face. 'Do you think so, Matt, really?'

Mattie hesitated but only for a second; it was her chance to make Lisa smile. 'Yeah, I really, really do.'

In the cubicle, Mattie peeled her costume from her body, kicked it off her feet onto the floor.

'I do feel,' Lisa shouted over a long hiss of aerosol spraying, 'kind of good, you know, having made the effort. Do you know what I mean? We'd only have been stuck indoors otherwise, watching television or something.'

Mattie felt suddenly tired; her stomach growled. 'I'm hungry.'

'You can get something upstairs in the café.'

'I fancy a tomato. A lovely, red, juicy, fresh tomato.'

Lisa laughed. 'You're mad, Matt.'

Mattie imagined the tomato, perfectly round, with a perfect green flower stalk on top. She pictured biting into it, the juice and pips squirting onto her tongue, the sweet, meaty flavour.

'They might sell spicy tomato flavour crisps in the café,' Lisa called out.

Lisa had changed into jeans and her best black top. Mattie had on the tracksuit that she came in. 'Okay, ready?' Lisa asked.

'I've got to dry my hair a bit. You go ahead.'

'I'll wait for you.'

'Don't bother,' Mattie told her. 'I won't be long.'

'Okay.' Lisa paused by the door. 'I'll get you a coke, and some chilli crisps or something.'

'Great,' Mattie said. 'Thanks.'

She inserted twenty pence in the slot for the hair dryer which roared into life, then settled into a low drone. She aimed the lukewarm air at the top of her head. She wished she'd asked Lisa to wait after all. She saw she'd been mistaken to think that it was better to go up alone than to stand side by side with Lisa. Now she'd have to break into their group, interrupt their laughter, their chat. They'd all three turn and look at her and there would be no one to hide behind.

'You are a great swimmer,' she said out loud. 'You are a better swimmer than all of them, put together.'

The dryer came to an abrupt halt.

What worth did swimming have, anyway? It would be more useful to be good at practically anything else. She looked in the mirror. Her hair was frizzy and the goggles had left a red impression round her eyes. She placed the tip of her index finger on the glass, traced the outline of her face, then along the bridge of her nose. Or – best of all – why couldn't she be pretty?

She returned to the cubicle and looked at her swimming costume which was still lying on the floor. Water had seeped out and formed a puddle around it like a shadow. Mattie pushed the toe of her trainer into the costume and watched it squirm before walking away.

# of sons and stars

Catherine Merriman

Of Sons and Stars 1997

fiction anthology

'This can't take long,' said Susan, pulling the heavy latched door of the cottage to behind her. 'I've got to ring your father before ten.'

'Just along here,' said Jamie's voice, disembodied in the darkness, somewhere the other side of the garden lawn. 'It has to be away from the lights.'

Susan sighed, and with an edge of humour she didn't actually feel, said, 'This had better be worth it.' She stepped, reluctantly, onto the dewy grass. Her canvas shoes were going to get soaked. Where was her son taking her? Ugh, she could feel a chilly dampness already. At the bottom of the lawn she heard a familiar rattle and creak. Oh God, he was through into the field. Groping for the swinging garden gate she called irritably, 'Where are we going, Jamie?' Then made an effort – this was meant to be a surprise for her, a treat, even – and called again, more lightly, 'Jamie?'

'Here.' There was still eagerness in her son's voice. She felt a pang of shame, and then gratitude, for the uncrushable optimism and tolerance of her child. She sighed again. Why were his surprises so wearisome? Why did they oppress her so? And what would it be, this time? Probably an animal. That's why he wouldn't use the handlamp. A hedgehog? Toad? Glow-worm? Something of wonder to a thirteen year old. She could hear herself saying, fervently, 'Oh, marvellous, Jamie.' Feeling dutiful, for expressing wonder, and inadequate, for having to pretend it.

In the darkness she stumbled over a tussock of long scratchy grass. 'Oh hell,' she said, forgetting good intentions and thinking of her tights, 'Jamie! Put the bloody torch on.'

'You don't need it,' said Jamie's voice, close beside her. 'This'll do. Stand still.'

Susan stood still. The lights of the house had disappeared behind the garden hedge. She could only just make out Jamie, a darker, denser shape in the blackness.

'Well?' she said.

'Look up.'

She looked up vaguely. 'What?'

'Oh, Mummy.' Jamie sounded exasperated. 'Look.'

She stared up and felt, as a telescopic process, her vision stretch outwards into the night. Her eyes refocused. Millions of stars, from brilliant cats' eyes to diamond dust, arched in a frozen swirl across the night sky.

'It's the Milky Way,' she said. Of course, she had seen it before, often. But still. Sincerely she said, 'Beautiful, isn't it.' Her son had brought her out to see the stars. How touching. She wondered how long she should stay, marvelling at them, to show her appreciation.

'Now,' Jamie said, sounding not awestruck, but business-like. 'Come closer.'

Oh dear, there was more. Susan twisted her wrist, before realising she wouldn't be able to read her watch. Suppressing a tick of impatience – it must be nearly ten – she moved closer.

'Right,' Jamie said. He was so near she could hear the catarrhal rasp of his breathing. He's as tall as I am, she thought. He seems even taller in the dark. But he still breathes like a child. His elbow brushed against her arm, as he did something with the torch.

'Okay,' he said. 'Now, get really close, and follow the line of the beam. Keep behind it, or you'll be dazzled.'

She heard a click. From his chest a powerful beam shot upwards to the sky.

'Gracious!' she said. For a second the beam looked like a heart-light, emerging from her son, leading straight up to the stars. She recollected herself, and gave a short laugh. 'You must have bought a new battery.'

'Yup,' said Jamie, sounding smug. 'You need a powerful torch for this.'

He swung the beam from horizon to horizon like a searchlight, then steadied it.

'Put your head close to mine.' He waited for Susan to obey him. 'Right, now, that group of stars there. Can you see them?'

Susan followed the line of the beam upwards. How impressive. She could see exactly the stars he meant, just outside the dense swirl of the Milky Way. The beam appeared to bathe them in pale light. She nodded and said, 'Yes, I see them.'

'That's Orion.'

'Is it?' she said. 'How clever of you. And what a good way of pointing them out. It's like using a ruler on a blackboard.' She pulled back. 'Where on earth did you learn to do this?'

'On the geography field trip,' Jamie said. 'Mr Haines is mad about stars.' He moved the beam a fraction away. 'There, that's the Pleiades ... see? And that bright star there ... Aldebaran. In Taurus.'

'Where's ... um ...' It took Susan a second to think of a heavenly body, '...the Plough?'

'Ah,' said Jamie. 'That's the other side of the Milky Way.' He swung the beam across the sky and resettled it. 'There ... see?'

'Goodness,' breathed Susan. 'This really is clever.'

'It is, isn't it?' Jamie sounded pleased. 'And look, there's the Bear. There ... there ... and there.'

Susan looked at the stars that made up the Bear. He'd learnt this on his geography field trip. She frowned. 'But the school trip ...' she said. 'It was ages ago.' Her son must have known how to do this for months.

'Yeah, well, it's a good night, tonight,' said Jamie. 'You can't always see so much, can you?'

It occurred to her, shockingly, that her son must know other things he hadn't told her about. That he was no longer totally known to her. And he must have been out here, surely, practising this ...

'I'll show you something else, too, if you like,' said Jamie. 'Nothing to do with astronomy ... about your eyes.'

'What?' She glanced back from the sky to the faint outline of his upturned face. For a moment it looked unfamiliar. Stronger-featured, solider. Almost adult.

'Well,' he said, adjusting the direction of the torch beam. 'Look at that empty space ... there ... a sort of triangle ... look straight at it.'

Susan lifted her eyes back up to the sky. 'I'm looking.'

Jamie clicked the torch off. 'Now move your eyes somewhere else, but remember where the space is.'

'What d'you mean?'

'Just do it. Don't move your eyes too far. Remember where the space is, relative to where you're looking.'

'Okay,' said Susan slowly. 'I've done it.'

'Now,' said Jamie. 'Don't look back, but what's in the space now?'

Susan concentrated on seeing the space, without actually looking at it. The sky, on that side of the vision, now appeared crowded with stars. 'I can't find it,' she said. 'It's gone. Sorry.'

'Look back to where it was,' said Jamie.

Susan looked back. The black triangle was instantly visible. How could she have missed it?

'I've got it,' she said. 'I don't know why I couldn't see it before.'

'Because it wasn't there,' said Jamie triumphantly.

'What are you talking about?' Susan smiled. 'Obviously it was there.'

'It wasn't,' said Jamie. 'Try moving your eyes away again.'

Susan stared at the space, fixing it, and then gradually moved her eyes away. As she did, the space appeared to fill with tiny dimlit stars. She looked back, and it was a space again.

'My God,' she said. 'Stars appeared in the hole.'

Jamie chuckled. 'Brilliant, isn't it?'

'But how can stars suddenly appear like that? Are they real? Why can't I see them when I look at them?'

'Oh, they're real all right,' said Jamie. 'It's because of the angle light hits the back of our eyes.' He switched the hand-lamp on and pointed it down at the grass by their feet. 'See the bright inner circle ... how small it is, straight down? Now ...' He raised the lamp slightly, so the beam hit the grass obliquely, about six feet away. 'See how much bigger it is now ... how much more grass it's covering? That's why our peripheral vision is so good. Light coming in at an angle hits more cones in our eyes. So we can see things that are too faint to see straight on.'

Susan stared at the oblong of light on the field, then raised her eyes to the sky. She found the empty black triangle. Very slowly she shifted her eyes away. Once more the dimlit stars appeared. Extraordinary.

She thought a moment and then said, 'Is this always true? When we look at things straight on, we never see them as clearly as when we don't?'

She sensed Jamie shrug. 'I suppose so. As long as they're in our field of vision. It's just how the eye works.'

'Did Mr Haines teach you this, too?'

'Mmm ... sometimes we couldn't see all the right stars in a constellation. You move your eyes away, and then you can.'

'It's amazing,' said Susan. She felt truly amazed, at learning something so fundamental, for the first time. And amazed too, in some all-encompassing, revelatory way, at her son.

Jamie turned the beam of the torch upwards, under-lighting his face. He said, 'Hoo hoo,' and grinned at her ghoulishly.

She grinned back at him. Immediately he was just Jamie again, her son, ordinary, unamazing Jamie.

She looked away, back up to the stars, and reassuringly, out of the corner of her eye, saw her son grow amazing again. She felt suddenly light, almost giddy. As if a burden – a burden she had scarcely realised she was carrying – had lifted from her. It was floating upwards: the weight of a child – her child – drifting up to the stars. She watched it rise, dwindling to nothingness in the vast night sky. There, it was gone.

She turned back to Jamie with a smile. Her tall, nearly adult, unwearisome son. And recalled, seeing him, that she had a phone call to make.

'I've got to go in,' she said. She touched his sleeve. 'I must ring your father.'

Jamie said, 'Oh yeah,' with sudden enthusiasm, and bounded towards the garden gate. He swung the beam of the torch behind him, lighting her path. 'I'll tell him about showing you the stars, shall I?'

'Definitely,' she said, and followed him towards the house.

a 'natural' birth

Paula Brackston

Strange Days Indeed 2007

theme: motherhood
non-fiction anthology

The new midwife looked at me with fresh-faced enthusiasm. 'So,' she smiled up from my unread notes, 'are you planning to have the baby at home? A natural birth, perhaps?'

I suppose it was a fair assumption to make. This was my second baby. My first was toddling around the clinic as she spoke. My rural address and slightly hippy appearance may well have given her ideas about birthing pools and aromatherapy pain relief. I might once even have harboured such notions myself. Now all I could manage was a somewhat weary laugh. She looked taken aback, so I did my best to explain.

A few years earlier my partner and I had begun to discuss starting a family. Actually, it wasn't so much a discussion as a game of ping-pong, neither of us ready to be the one to make the Big Decision. 'Kids, then. What d'you reckon?' 'Mmm. Yes, soon.' 'No rush.' 'No. But we're neither of us getting any younger.' 'Hmm, better get on with it then.' 'Best get into shape first. Give up smoking. Drink more water.' 'Okay.' 'Fine.' 'Good.' 'Pass the Shiraz.' The truth was, we were both hurtling towards forty. The prospect of children was both wonderful and terrifying. Making the Big Decision seemed beyond us. So we dithered and we went out lots and had long lie-ins and drank more than was good for us and even began to think this wasn't a bad way of life, when events, as they say, overtook us.

It started as a twinge in my leg, then it became a soreness, then complete agony. After a trip to casualty suggested I had pulled a muscle I munched painkillers, borrowed a pair of crutches, and waited for things to get better. They didn't. A week later a scan finally revealed thrombosis the length of my leg. Or should that be thromboses? Whichever, I was hospitalised and pumped full of rat poison and other such delights. Ten days later, when at last I was about to be sent home, I mentioned I was thinking of starting a family. There were dark looks between the youthful doctors at the foot of my bed. Tests would have to be done. Enough blood was extracted from me to make several black puddings before the reason for my thrombosis became clear. I have a blood condition called Leiden Factor Five. This sounded to me like some sort of sun protection. The haematologist elaborated – I was a thrombophiliac. Still this wasn't getting through. He put it in simple terms – blood like tomato soup. If I continued to smoke my chances of another thrombosis (and therefore possible pulmonary embolism/stroke/death) would increase ten per cent. If I didn't stop taking the contraceptive pill they would increase twenty per cent. If I was pregnant, the likelihood went up to seventy per cent. *Seventy per cent!* These were surely impossible odds. But no, wait, the haematologist assured me, pregnancy was possible with careful monitoring and medication. The monitoring meant half a day a week in the hospital for the duration of my pregnancy. The medication was to be an injection of blood thinners administered daily into my stomach. I could come in to the clinic to have them done, I was told, or I could inject myself. A daily forty-mile round trip was out of the question. In fact, the injections were not as bad as I had anticipated, especially once I had learnt how to do them with my eyes still open.

It is strange how quickly the bizarre becomes the normal. I soon fell pregnant (I love that expression, as if I tripped over a pair of discarded socks on the landing, thudded to the ground and – oops! Pregnant!) and got used to starting my day by 'shooting up' as my partner, Simon, so quaintly put it. There was some local bruising, so that as the weeks went on my tummy began to resemble some sort of psychedelic melon, but it was a small price to pay.

The morning sickness was unpleasant but manageable, though I may never be able to face a ginger biscuit again. With the days and weeks being crossed off at an alarming rate we decided on one last quick holiday as a couple before the little tadpole grew big enough to hop out and join us. We spent a lovely few days in London visiting friends, going out, and generally doing stuff people without babies or small children do. Quick. While there was still time. On the night before we were due to go home I began to feel unwell. At first I put it down to morning sickness, although it was past eight in the evening. But things got worse. Sickness, sweating, severe abdominal pains. None of it good when you are seven weeks pregnant. We rang the nearest hospital. There was a twelve-hour wait in casualty, could we go somewhere else? We tried again. Only four hours at Ealing, good enough for us. Simon drove through unfamiliar streets at speed with me groaning on the back seat, lifting my head every so often to give directions. I have one piece of advice for anyone who might find themselves in a similar situation. Don't try it at the weekend. The world, his wife and his seven children will all be in A & E with splinters in their thumbs or suspicious-looking rashes. I spent four hours on a plastic chair vomiting into a paper cup wondering if I was about to lose my baby while seemingly healthy people breezed past me to be treated. I'm sure they were in extremis, but, for heaven's sake, at least they could still walk! At last I was admitted. I was hugely relieved to be in a proper bed surrounded by people dressed as doctors and nurses. It felt like the right place to be. However, as it was Saturday night the people who could do the necessary scan to determine whether I had appendicitis or an ectopic pregnancy would not be in until the following afternoon. I was taken to a small room with peeling paint and a commode and told not to eat anything. This was no hardship. However, they decided it would be best not to give me any pain relief, in case it masked symptoms. Best for whom?!

Eventually, at six o'clock the next evening, the scan showed I did have a poisonous appendix and it would have to come out. The anaesthetist came to see me to say, very gently, that I had a fifty-fifty chance of losing my baby. Here were those nasty odds again. I should have taken up gambling. The nurses at the hospital were lovely, and I'm sure the doctors and surgeons knew their stuff, but it does not help one's confidence levels to have the wheel fall off the wheelchair you are being trundled about in. The last thing I remember before the anaesthetic claimed me was talking to my unborn child, saying, 'Hold on tight, little tad. Hold on tight.'

When I came round my arms were being pinned to my sides by a particularly large male nurse, two others were standing flat against the wall, and a third was clutching a bloody nose. They kept calling my name until I calmed down. Apparently, some people react violently when surfacing from being anaesthetised. I did manage to apologise, but really all I wanted to know was if my baby was okay. Back in my room a beaming doctor told me yes, everything was fine, and I could go home in a few days. I am, of course, boundlessly grateful to the people who saved my own life and that of my baby. However, the surgery was the least part. How I survived the hospital I'll never know. I was horribly sick and in pain for the next thirty-six hours. During this time an endless stream of uniforms trotted in and out. One screamed at me for eating toast.

'What do you think you're doing?' she bellowed. 'They're waiting for you down in surgery!'

I was stunned.

'To take out what, exactly?' I wanted to know. It seemed they had got me confused with the six-foot, ginger-haired, bearded, Scotsman in the next room. By the following day serious boredom had set in to the point where I picked up my notes for something to read. I was a little surprised to find they weren't mine. I tried to explain this to the next efficient-looking young woman who came into my room.

'My name,' I told her, 'is not, and has never been, Abdul Aziz. I am not a man, nor am I fifty-seven, and as you can see,' I pulled back my sheets with a flourish, 'I am not wearing a scrotum support. These are not my notes!'

She gave me a pitying look, said it was all very interesting, but I'd be better off telling a nurse. Turned out she was one of the cleaners. I still worry that poor Mr Aziz had his appendix whipped out unnecessarily.

Early in my stay a nurse had forced me into a pair of full-length white stockings. This was to help avoid clotting, so I was happy to wear them, even if they did look utterly ludicrous. As I hobbled down the corridor to the toilets I passed similarly attired patients. It seemed they were standard issue. I glimpsed myself in the mirror. I don't know about motherhood aging you, but my first pregnancy seemed to have rendered me one of the living dead within a matter of weeks. The eczema on my face had gone mad. My eyes were bloodshot. And some sneaky four year old had apparently been backcombing my hair while I slept. It was a depressing sight. As I hobbled back to my room I exchanged nods with an equally dishevelled woman. I smiled at her weakly.

'Hospital hair!' I said, a comment meant to indicate patient solidarity.

It was only once I'd passed her I realised she was in fact a visitor.

You can imagine how pleased I was to eventually make it back home. I should explain here that home is a thirteenth-century Welsh longhouse in the Brecon Beacons. It is in the most beautiful spot, completely isolated, peaceful, and magical. At the time, though, it had no telephone, and there was no mobile signal unless you climbed up the mountain to the third rowan tree from the fence. And the house had no electricity. Now, none of this particularly bothered us, but it was not popular with my mother. Here was her only daughter, recently rescued from a life-threatening thrombosis, fresh out of hospital and surgery, increasingly pregnant, and often alone on top of a mountain with no way of contacting anyone should another emergency occur. She came to stay a lot. Little did we realise just how more precarious things were about to get.

I have to say, despite it all, I loved being pregnant. I was the happiest I had ever been, and the near-death experiences soon seemed distant memories and as nothing compared to the wonder of growing a baby and preparing to become a mum.

Autumn turned to a particularly wet winter. We live in Wales, so we're used to rain, but this was something different. One day our neighbour (who lives over a mile away) alerted us to a sinister-looking crack in our lane. This is a proper tarmac, council-maintained road, albeit a very narrow, twisty one. It also happens to climb up the side of the hill with a giddying hundred-foot drop on one side. The crack quickly got bigger. I swear you could see it growing. The man from the highways department came out that very day and declared the route unsafe. This we already knew. We had to move quickly. If the road went and we did not have a vehicle the other side of the landslide we would be seriously cut off. Ordinarily we might not have minded, but it was winter, we needed coal, and gas, and my mother kept on about ambulance access. And there was the teensy matter of my getting to the hospital for all that monitoring. Simon took our battered little car and drove it down the hill. The crack was now a step. The car bumped over it. Still the rain fell. We went about our business, parking the hatchback on the 'civilisation' side of the fissure, clambering above the road for a couple of hundred yards, then climbing into our road-unworthy jeep for the rest of the mile or so journey to our house. As I got bigger this whole exercise got slower. The hillside above the ruined road was slippery and uneven and steep. The jeep lacked anything resembling suspension giving a ride so bumpy even I began to fear it could bring on labour. The road, in a matter of weeks, disappeared into the valley below. It was terrifying to see, and we realised how lucky we had been to have noticed the crack before it became so dangerous. We soon adapted to our new access. The hatchback/jeep combination worked. The tricky part was carting supplies between the vehicles. We ignored the expense and bought a new wheelbarrow. Visitors became fewer, but the die-hards still made it up to see us. We borrowed a friendly farmer's quad bike to cart up coal and gas (though my mother made me promise not to get on it, much as I longed to).

That Christmas it snowed. Beautiful, crisp, deep, alpine snow under turquoise skies by day and spangled ones by night. On New Year's Eve I climbed slowly up the hill behind the house to the third rowan tree from the fence and used a borrowed mobile phone to call people and wish them Happy 2001. As I sat there on a snowy tussock in my wellies, Si's coat (by now the only one that would fit me) and a ski hat, my phone resting on my sizeable bump, I thought the world had never looked more beautiful. The moon was so bright there were perfect moon shadows, and I could see for twenty miles in any direction. I stroked my bump and whispered to my little tadpole that there was a fabulous, magical world waiting for him.

The highways department had promised us a new road, but weeks turned into months and still I was waddling around the crevasse and rattling up the hill in the jeep. It wasn't so much getting to the hospital for the birth that bothered me; it was managing without the road with a tiny baby in car seat/pram/buggy/whatever. Repeated calls to the council yielded nothing but more promises. Something had to be done. I went to county hall and asked to speak to the person in charge of highways. As luck would have it, he was available, and I was shown in. I lowered my largeness onto a plastic chair and explained who I was and why we needed our road back. Soon. In fact, sooner than soon. The Man In Charge was all smiles and placating hand gestures, but the gist of what he was saying was, we'll get round to it eventually. I told him as sweetly as I could that this was not good enough. We were not going to move out (they would surely never have repaired the road), and the baby's due date was looming. I painted him a graphic picture of what might happen if a woman with my blood condition went into labour and there were complications and the ambulance could not reach me. The Man In Charge paled. I settled deeper into my chair and said that, while I hated to be a nuisance, I was not leaving his office until I had his word the road would be fixed as a priority. Within the week, preferably. We stared at each other in silence for one very long minute and then he picked up the phone. Two days later the diggers arrived and within a fortnight we had a beautiful new road. My mother cancelled the air ambulance.

With the coming of spring our thoughts not unnaturally turned to spring-cleaning. I'd heard that pregnant women take up bleaching things and scrubbing floors in preparation for the new arrival, and I have to say I never thought it would happen to me. I'm of the opinion that housework is mostly unnecessary and often downright dangerous. However, our house was an unusual case, and not in a baby-friendly state by anyone's reckoning. Did I mention we had no electricity? We had managed happily with candles, pot-holer's headlamps, and a couple of gaslights, but of course we couldn't use a vacuum cleaner. And the house is very old. And the dust had lain thick for many years before I had moved in. With a burst of energy never before expended on cleaning by either of us, we hired a generator for the weekend and borrowed an industrial-strength Hoover. Not that I could use the thing, as it was too heavy for me to lift, and my enormous bump prevented me bending in the middle. Anyway, several family members and a few friends arrived for the weekend with rubber gloves and crates of beer and we set to. The first shock when we switched on the generator and attached some lights was the extent of the cobwebs. I loathe spiders, and the realisation that the Hanging Gardens of Babylon that dangled from our ceiling were constructed entirely of arachnid nests was horrifying. It took two days of vacuuming, sweeping, shrieking (by me, at spiders), tearing up of rotting carpet, assembling of baby furniture, and general wiping down with damp cloth (sometimes each other) to transform our grubby home into a gleaming, baby-ready dwelling. We were so impressed with all this technology that we went out and bought a little generator all of our own. We were promptly given a washing machine, and with hindsight can see that life would have been horrendous without one once the baby arrived and set about creating Andean ranges of washing all by itself. Now we had lights and a food processor. The twenty-first century had finally arrived at our home. At least by day. At night, when the generator was switched off, I would of course end up changing nappies by candlelight, as women had done up here on this mountain in this very house for nearly seven hundred years. No doubt filled with the same awe and love for their babies, but each fervently wishing the little critter would let them get some sleep.

With the Big Day only a few weeks away I trotted off (no, make that waddled off) to see my obstetrician. Why do so many of them wear bow ties? He briefly explained my options. I could go for a vaginal delivery but should anything go wrong and a caesarean be needed we would be in trouble, because I was on high doses of blood thinners and surgery would most likely cause me to bleed to death. Not a tempting thought. Or I could choose an elective (rather than emergency) caesarean, they would have me in the night before, take me off the blood thinners, watch me closely to make sure I wasn't going to clot and pop my clogs before the main event, then carry out the procedure under a general anaesthetic. So much for breathing techniques and playing your favourite tunes. An epidural was possible, but in my case could lead to permanent damage of the spine. It all sounded a bit bleak. Still, the little chap was well beyond a tadpole now and had to get out somehow. I opted for the planned caesarean and came away thinking my obstetrician was a genius for making me feel I had any choice in the matter at all.

In fact, the whole procedure was very much like having my appendix taken out, though without the feeling poisoned bit. I was given lots of morphine and spent my first twenty-four hours as a mother more stoned than I have ever been in my life. When I was finally able to focus I saw in my arms this gorgeous, bright, strong little boy, and I knew I'd do it all again in an instant. It wasn't the pregnancy I'd imagined, and it wasn't the birth I had hoped for, but here was my wonderful son and nothing else mattered. Perhaps, for me, as this was the only way I could survive a pregnancy and have a child, this was, after all, a natural birth. My son now has a sister to play with, and we have a telephone at the house and the internet. And next summer the landlord is having electricity installed. But it is still the same magical place, and I am thrilled to be raising my babies here. We named our boy Thaddeus, which sounded like a fine and fitting name. But to us he has always been, and will always be, our little Tad.

colliers' row – 1939

Irene Thomas

On My Life 1989

theme: autobiographical essays
non-fiction anthology

When I sit jackknifed on the windowsill of the big bedroom in Colliers' Row, I draw the curtains over the wires behind me and I am in my own house with silky walls and a window big enough to see across the valley to the Morning Star.

Like Alice, I have grown too big, and my head is rammed into the ceiling. Bits of dry cement run down the loose wallpaper behind my back, but I can read in peace without Gran interfering.

'Books will addle your brain,' she says, 'and give you brainstorms.'

Sometimes I look in the hand mirror Mam puts face down on the ecru crochet doiley she made for her dressing table. The mirror is framed with gold-wire lace and around the edges of the glass there are rainbows. I look at my face, peppered with freckles, eyes green as the grapes Gran buys when somebody is bad in bed, with two candles, and I try to remember where I was before I got to Colliers' Row. Mam reckons the stork brought me, but when I asked Gran if she'd ever seen one, she answered, 'Little girls should be seen and not heard.'

I hate that answer.

I can't stand up straight in the bedroom, the roof is too low. Mam says not to grow any more, but I'm shooting up so fast Grancher maintains I've been putting manure in my shoes.

I won't sit upstairs in the night. Gran lets me have a candle to light the way up the stairs at bedtime. Then shadows jump over the walls and into the old pictures. Lions creep closer to Daniel in the den and he looks really scared. Waves smash the lady clinging to the cross in the boiling sea and she prays harder to the Angel.

When I get into bed I have to blow out the candle.

'Waste not, want not,' is Gran's favourite motto.

Now I'm nearly ten, I don't believe in bogey men, but I'm

still afraid of the dark. Gran used to frighten me when I was little, with one of her rhymes. She'd light the candle and say,

'Here is a candle to light you to bed,
here is a chopper to chop orf your head.
Chipper chopper, chipper chopper,
last man's head ORFF.'

It is freezing in our bedroom and I'm glad when Mam comes to bed and I can cwtch up to her, now that Dad is away in Birmingham looking for work.

It is cold in the front room as well. The fire is only lit for funerals and Christmas. We don't have colliers' coal because Gran and Grancher are pensioners and Grancher has finished working up the tip, so we have to be careful with the coal.

Gran stands in front of the kitchen fire when she wants a warm, pulls at the skirts and fills the kitchen with camphorated oil and winter-green, which makes me kek. If I stand there she says, 'Get out from underfoot, you are shielding the fire orf everybody else.'

Gran and Grancher sleep downstairs next to the front room and they have a stove to undress by. We get oil from Mr Davies the oilman, who comes round with his van, and he lets Gran fill up the can from his tap until the little arrow goes from 'Empty' to 'Full'. Mr Davies sells wicks as well, wide white cotton belts with blue threads. You dip them in the oil and then wind them up through the burner.

I love Gran's stove. Wish we could have one upstairs. It is black and has holes in a lacy pattern around it, and a red celluloid window in the front. In the top of the stove are holes which make a flower pattern of lights on the ceiling as the wick burns up. You can slide a shutter and they open and close to let out the heat. It alters the pattern on the ceiling and Mam says I mustn't play about with it, but I go in there when she is in work and watch the patterns and warm my hands.

Wednesday is the best day of the week. It is Mam's half

day off from the shoe shop, and after she has done the washing, and scrubbed the steps up to the front room with left over water, she makes something special for tea. Toast, cut in triangles, treacle pudding or spotted dick. On ordinary days it is a piece of bread and jam in your hand, or one of Gran's welshcakes. She makes the best welshcakes in the Row, and swears by a pinch of spice and Borwicks baking powder. I like butter on them, but Gran isn't willing. She says it's a luxury and I'm not to act like Lady Muck.

On Wednesday nights we sit near the fire, as close as we can get. The kitchen is only four chairs wide. Gran sits by the gas stove, but she won't cook anything in it.

'Not while we have a nice fire oven,' she says.

Once a week Mam lights the two back burners for the wash boiler. The front ring is to boil water for Gran's first cup of tea in bed in the morning. Sometimes, when Gran is in bed on a Sunday afternoon, Mam puts a penny in the red, iron meter by the front door and cooks a sponge in the gas oven unbeknownst to Gran.

Mam sits on the kitchen chair, which has a wonky leg. It's all right as long as you don't lean back.

Mrs Bailey from Number 5 perches on the one with the stuffed leather seat. She comes in for a gossip, cup of tea and a grumble about her husband. She can't sit still when she talks and Gran calls her 'Fidgety Bum'. Mrs Bailey makes her mob-caps from Mr Bailey's old cotton shirts. She pulls the elastic down her forehead, nearly over her eyes. I have the giggles when I look at her, but Mam glares at me with her 'Don't you shame me, my girl', look, and I have to hold the laughs in. Mam never says much – a look is enough.

Mrs Bailey is as dark as the gipsies from Nant-y-glo who make paper flowers to sell over the half-door. You have to buy, or else they'll put a curse on you. She likes embroidering lazy daisies in Anchor thread on white cloths, with home-made crochet lace round the edges. Gran can't abide it when Mrs Bailey sits all morning crocheting away, with dirty dishes in the bosh and ashes piling up in the grate.

Grancher's armchair is on the other corner, but he clears off to the Con Club on Wednesdays.

'Good riddance,' Gran says. 'We can talk better without him.'

They could talk better if I wasn't there, but I want to listen, so I pretend to read my encyclopaedia, or do a jigsaw. They whisper and say things behind their hands, when they don't want me to hear. Gran looks hard at me, and says, 'Little pigs have big ears.'

One day I will get to know all their secrets. I pretend I don't care and scribble on the table.

If Gran sees it she says, 'Don't make marks on that oilcloth, or you'll be getting a fourpenny, my girl.'

She hasn't hit me yet.

When we have used up all the daylight and it gets too dark to see, Gran lights the gas. She is only a twt, so she climbs up on the armchair and kneels on the table to reach the tap.

She turns the gas on, it hisses out of the mantle and smells of dirty socks. To get down quick, she puts her leg out backwards off the table and tries to find the mat with her toe. Sometimes her slipper falls off or catches in her long black skirts and then her tongue clicks.

When she gets to the fire, she climbs up on to the steel fender to reach for a spill from the blue jug, decorated with a picture of a windmill. It would be easier if she kept the jug on the windowsill, but Gran won't have anything moved if it has been there a long time. Every Sunday she and Grancher make spills from the *News of the World*. They cut long strips, wet their thumbs and roll the paper into tight stalks. It saves using matches. Gran says that it is wasteful to use matches when we have a fire.

She rams the spill into a burning coal and then holding

the paper down to catch, carries it back to the mantle. She climbs on to the chair and the table again and bits of burned paper fall on to the oilcloth. I blow them away and they fly like jackdaws.

Sometimes the flame is douted down to sparks.

'Drat the thing,' says Gran and starts all over again.

When she puts the flame to the mantle, I screw up my eyes and there is a loud bang. The mantle spits to green and Gran's white eyebrows go a bit brown and curl.

She won't have electric light, like Mrs Harry down the Row.

Gran says, 'Electricity is dangerous.'

I go to church and to chapel. Gran is church and Mam is chapel. Dad isn't anything and he never gets a say anyhow. Mostly I go to church, St John's, down Libanus Road, but in the summer, I attend the Wesleyans, in James Street. Then I can go to Barry Island with the Sunday school.

Gran knows the Creed and she can say the Lord's Prayer right through, although she can't read or write. She is proud of being confirmed and sometimes shows me a picture of herself in her confirmation dress. She wore a white blouse and a lace cap, with a veil hanging down the back.

Gran is a cockney and comes from Epping Forest. She had three stepmothers and went out to service, cleaning brass and polishing tables. She met Grancher when he visited a cousin in London and he fancied her, wrote to her twice and asked her to come to Wales to get married. She came because she had nothing else to do.

She can't talk Welshy like us and still says some funny cockney words like 'orf' for 'of'. Her first baby, Auntie Millie, died when she was only four. There is a picture of her in the front room, dressed in a white pinny with a lace collar, button up boots and a cap with fur. Sometimes Gran stands in front of it for a while and then her lips flatten into a line and she goes into her room to lie on the bed. I heard Mrs Bailey say that when they buried Auntie Millie up the cemetery, it rained cats and dogs in the night, and they had to stop Gran going out to get Millie back. She didn't want her to drown.

I've never missed school because I've slept late. Mam sees to that, and calls me when she gets up for work.

Pontygof Girls' turns your stomach in the mornings. The cleaners scrub out with carbolic, and the smell of wet wooden floors is horrible. Mansion Polish pongs go down your throat when you open the desks, but that's not so bad. Some girls look for pepsin they stuck under the lids at home-time the day before. Put it back in their mouths and chew it all day, they do. Don't mind if they find somebody else's gum either. It makes me feel sick. You can't eat anything in peace, it's 'give us your stump, or a bite' or 'a suck' or 'a dip', I can't stand anybody licking my toffee apple.

Miss Stevens is our teacher, and calls out the register first thing in the morning.

'Eva Parry,' and we answer, 'Present, Miss.'
    'Olive Adams.' 'Absent, Miss.'
    'Enid Morris.' 'No shoes, Miss.'
    'Betty Solway.' 'Slept late, Miss.'
    'Hilda Morgan.' 'Clinic, Miss.'
    'Violet Griffiths.'
    'Miss, her brother's turn for the coat, Miss.'

Miss Doughton teaches us singing. She says it has got to come from our chests. She's got a huge one, and a voice to match. When she sings she's like a kettle boiling over on the hob. It's always, 'Rise, Rise Thou Merry Lark' or 'Hen Wlad Fy Nhadau'. We have to learn sol-fa from the charts she slings over the board. They are old, cracked and scabby as the whitewash on next door's front wall.

Bronwen Griffiths is my friend from Number 4, and we sit together. She is podgier than me with nearly white hair and blue eyes with bits like gravy browning in them. When she sees Miss Doughton's tongue wobbling on top notes, she dives under the desk not to burst out laughing and then comes up, red in the face. The trouble with Bronwen is that she gets the sulks. She'll walk away for no reason at all, with her bottom lip stuck out a mile.

Gran says we must make allowances, because her mother is dead. On the day of the funeral they couldn't get Mrs Griffiths' coffin out of the downstairs bedroom because it was too big. You could hear them knocking the front window frame out all down the Row.

Bronwen's house is full up. She has a father, a baby brother, three sisters and two uncles. One is a dago and sleeps on the tip. Bronwen is a queer kid Gran reckons, and not because her mother is dead.

They like cooking onions in Bronwen's.

'You've been in there again,' Gran complains, when I come home reeking. 'And look at the tar on your clothes. Stay out or get Bronwen to come and play with you in here.'

Butter gets tar off your hands, but even Persil and bar soap won't get it off clothes.

Bronwen's father paints tar halfway up the kitchen.

'Stops the buggers going up the wall,' he says.

He means the black pats.

We have anaglypta round our walls and our black pats slide. You can hear their legs scratching like mad as they slip back down. If you don't shake your coat when you take it from the back of the door a black pat will run up your arm and round your neck, quick as a winkie.

Every night Gran cooks something from nothing, but when Gran makes brawn the house stinks all day.

She buys her pigs' heads from Tommy Lloyd, the butcher.

He lines them in his window and stuffs oranges in their mouths. Gran gets the orange free.

She forks out the pig's eyes, then cuts off its ears, and splits the head in half with the chopper and a coal hammer. It is horrible to watch. Into the big saucepan go the two halves of the head and it boils for hours and hours on the hob.

When everything has gone to pulp, including brains, Gran tips out the mess on to the big blue meat dish and takes out all the little bones and gristle. The kitchen is full of pig's head steam, so I go outside and bang my clothes to get rid of the smell. Gran chops up everything very small and puts it into a mixing bowl to set in its own jelly, with a board and a flat iron on top to press it down.

Gran's brawn is famous. My aunties even come up from Cwm to taste the stuff, but I can't stand it. I don't even fancy the orange.

Gran leaves most of the shopping until Saturday nights, when the shops keep open late, and only close when there are no more people on the street. We go out at ten o'clock, because Gran says she can get the best bargains when the shopkeepers want to get rid of their goods for the weekend.

I don't have much patience to wait, and I plague Gran to go out at a quarter to ten. 'Get my hat then,' she says.

I get her dark shiny brown straw shopping hat from the top of the chest of drawers in the bedroom, where it sits all week, looking as important as her Very Best. That one is inside the wardrobe in a box, to keep the decorations from fading. It is brown, well, most of Gran's things are brown or black, but there is velvet around it, orange and brown and leaves, and an amber head on the hat-pin.

I scoop out tissue paper from the crown of the shopping hat, and the two mothballs. We have loads of moths and they eat holes in everything but they don't like mothballs because they are camphorated, smell rotten and taste bitter. I know because I thought a mothball was a sweet, once, and licked it.

Gran puts the hat on very carefully and sticks her second best plain black hat-pin through into her white hair.

'Must be careful not to spear me brains,' she says, 'I want to be able to think straight.'

Grancher helps her put on the long black coat and I hand her the fox fur. At the end of the fur is a fox's head. It has glass eyes and a mouth which opens, so that it can grab its tail, and pinch your hand if you're not careful. I think it is sly, keeping its mouth a secret in the fur. Sometimes Gran makes it talk and moves its jaws and then it looks really alive. I used to be afraid of it when I was little, but I don't give it a second look now.

Grancher unhooks the shopping baskets from the beams, where they hang all the week. Gran keeps fruit up there to ripen in the warmth from the gaslight.

Sometimes she buys green pears, wraps them in tissue paper and puts them away in the chest of drawers until they are soft. Then she can eat them by scooping out the middles with a spoon.

'Where are your teeth, Gran?' I asked her one day.

'I gave them to a dentist in Clapham Common,' she answered, grinning with her gums.

She thinks that it is better not to have teeth.

'You can't get toothache then,' she says.

I am always having toothache, so I will be glad when mine are all gone.

Gran's gums are as hard as nails.

I know they are, because I let her bite my finger once to see, and was sorry afterwards.

Grancher has false teeth. I don't think they are in very tight, because they click up and down when he talks, and fall out a bit when he gets excited. When he puts them in the glass in the pantry for the night, his chin goes up to meet his nose.

He puts on his best white muffler and his trilby hat when we go shopping, and walks in front of us, stopping now and then so that we can catch him up. Gran wouldn't hurry if you paid her and Grancher gets mad.

He stops in the pools of yellow light from the street lamps at each corner, and then paces up and down, whistling through his teeth.

'Come on, Em,' he shouts. Grancher was a sergeant in the army and he can shout really loud. You can hear him calling from three blocks away.

'I wish he would stay home,' Gran grumbles.

When he's not in work, he follows her everywhere and never lets her go out of his sight.

'Thinks I will run orf and find a fancy man,' she says. 'As if I'd fancy anyone after him.'

When we get to the butcher's, I stay outside. I don't want to look at the animals hanging upside down, the smell of the blood and sawdust makes me feel sick.

Gran bought a pig's head, so that she can make more brawn; a large piece of furry tripe, some chitterlings, a piece of stewing beef and kidneys.

At the greengrocer's a few rabbits were left. Gran bought one for half price, because there were a few pieces of shot still in it.

The fish was cheap as well, so we bought smoked haddock and a large bag of sprats.

When we came home, we had fried sprats for supper. I like them crisp and brown and so hot that the vinegar sizzles, and the smell jumps up your nose.

Every week I get a telling off from Mam, for getting my best shoes and socks covered with muck.

'It's not my fault, Mam.'

She wags her finger and says, 'You are always running and not looking where you put your feet.' Mam can't be mad for long because she hasn't got time.

When you run through the back bailey, it is hard not to step on a flat loose stone. They are sort of stepping stones put down on top of slops and washing-up water. Some people just throw out over the half-doors, without looking, because they are too lazy to carry out to the drain by the back garden wall. You can get a dirty bath if you are not quick.

Next door, they empty chamber pots on to the front road or down the wall from the bedroom. They never use their front room so it doesn't worry them, but their whitewash is turning green and it makes a nasty smell outside our front room when we open the door.

Mr Griffiths puts ashes into the holes in the road outside his house and if you fall down, cokes graze your legs and hands. Then Gran gets out the iodine. It is a little brown bottle and stings worse than a wasp.

Gran says I have to learn to be brave, because if I had to go to the fever hospital the nurses there pull plasters right off you in one go. They have big wide ones, not narrow bits like we have, from round Oxo boxes.

There are big holes full of rainwater outside Mrs Bailey's front door, because Mr Bailey revs up his bike in the same place. Sometimes he wakes Gran and Grancher from their afternoon nap and then they are cracksy with me. Mr Bailey wears plus fours, which look funny on his short legs. Dad says they are 'plus twos'.

We are clean in our house and once a week, mostly on Sunday nights, I bath. Mam dusts out the tin bath, because it hangs up outside, on a six-inch nail on the garden wall opposite, and crawlies get in it.

Sometimes we run up the bailey and bang the baths with sticks. It makes the neighbours poke their heads out over half-doors and shout. Mr Griffiths swears blue blazes, but Gran says he doesn't mean anything by it.

Mr Hodges, next door up, in Number 1, has never washed his back. He believes it will take his strength away.

'Rubbish,' says Mam, but Grancher says, 'Ahhhh well, the old miners always went by it.'

Mam has a friend in a posh house by the post office. There are pebbles on the front, not whitewash, and a china bath upstairs with hot water from a tap. Her husband won't use the bath. He says it is wrong to take dirt upstairs.

The tip comes down to our front garden. When we walk it in, Gran says it has put its dirty boots under our table.

Where the grass has grown on top of the tip, it is like being out in the country. Bees land on the purple thistles and we catch them in jam jars. When the jars are full, we give them a good shake to rile the bees, knock off the lids and run.

I play 'cowboys and indians', like the ones in the pictures in the Plaza, with Johnny Harry, Number 6. When we quarrel we make faces and I pull down my eyes and push my nose up at the same time. Not when Gran can see me though because she won't let me do it.

'Tain't ladylike,' she says. 'It'll stay that way if you're not careful.'

My face has always gone back all right, but I don't pull too hard just in case. I don't quarrel with Johnny for long because his mother pays for me to go with him to the pictures. He is afraid to come home by himself in the dark, and he's got the cheek to call me a 'Siss'.

Bronwen doesn't like cowboys so if she's in a good mood we find a nice piece of grass which the sheep have cropped, brush away droppings, and mark out a house with stones. We have a picnic in the rooms, with sauce sandwiches and tap water in a pop bottle.

When the summer comes I sledge down the sides of the tip on a shovel or on a tray. The shale shines black as the glass in stout bottles. Some of the boys have real sledges, with steel runners from bedsteads, fastened underneath and they shoot over bumps, and blue sparks flash. It is a bit like the dodgems in Danter's Fair, when it comes to the Drillground, only there's no smell of grease, or a man to tell you to get off.

There is a nasty smell around when a sheep dies, or when somebody throws down an old mattress, but I never go near in case of catching the fever.

If you catch fever, you have to go to the sick bay in the town, for weeks and weeks and never see out because the glass in the windows is painted dark brown.

Drams run down the other side of the tip, which is all shale. Huge pieces of stone thin as wafers are packed together. You can pick them out with your fingers and they make plates, slates or knives. We stand right on the edge of the tip, and when it gives way it takes us down with it. The one to get to the bottom still standing up is the winner.

I like collecting pieces of broken china in a brown paper bag. Then I take them home and wash them in the second best enamel bowl Grancher has mended with washers. Sometimes there is a lovely pink piece or willow pattern or a piece of saucer with 'Present from Barry Island' in gold on it.

Once a week I take up a bucket and look for coal to help out our small.

Mr Griffiths has cemented his back garden path up as far as the lav, and stuck in pieces of china collected from the tip. It looks really pretty. I wanted Grancher to do ours the same, but he said that he wasn't a handy person. He is good at getting coal in and killing chickens.

Grancher used to work on the drams. His job was to throw in a sprag between the wheels to slow them down, but one day a stone fell from the top of Bufton's and broke his wrist. He had the Comp. for it, but I never knew how much. I saw him give Gran a bundle of pound notes on the quiet and we had chunks every Sunday after that. The drams are pulled on greasy wires over rollers and when they are working we stand on the rollers and ride them with our feet until they go too fast and we fall off.

Most of the men in Ebbw Vale have no work and are on the dole. They hang about the streets or go up the tip to play cards in tin shanties, which they built from tin sheetings to keep the cold out. Gran says they are playing with Devil's cards and doing wrong to gamble. They only play for matches, so I can't see it matters much, but I never back-answer Gran.

We dig secret holes in the grass, to make safes, then put in tins, and cover them with clods. We thread long tins with string and use them for stilts. They make a clatter along the Row and we get told off for waking working men on nights. There are hundreds of tins on the tip, corned beef, tinned fish and sardine ones with keys. We collect the ones with labels and play shop with them. If there's any juice left in the fruit ones, Johnny Harry drinks it – dirty devil!

Mountain ponies are pests. They eat peelings and cabbage stalks people throw out. I stood behind one once and it kicked me over and hurt my hand.

'Serve you right,' Gran said. 'Never worry an animal when it's eating. I never talk to your Grancher until he's had his dinner.'

The nit nurse is called Nurse Jones, and we all hate her. She has a face like a funeral and never smiles. Her hair is straight and dyed black and she has hard mean hands. When she grips hold of your arm, you can't wriggle away and then she finds lousy hair.

In school, she can't have a room of her own, so she hides behind the blackboard muttering and getting angry with the dirty children. The whole class can hear her telling them off, and it's not their fault. If you are clean she grunts and pushes you away. Every Monday I have a clean vest and spencer, so I wasn't worried. If you have sores, you are sent to the clinic and the nurses there cover your legs with violet paint. You come back to school, marked for a week. Mam said she would be ashamed if I was marked out. So would I.

My friend Megan, from up Newtown, went to the clinic for bad eyes and when she climbed up the stairs the nit nurse grabbed her and said, 'Take off your clothes. Into the bath with you.' Megan tried to tell her she had only come for her eye ointment, but Jonesey wouldn't listen. Megan said it was a lovely white bath to lie in and she made waves from top to bottom. She didn't mind the disinfectant and she liked having the ointment rubbed on her legs and arms.

'You are a lot better,' the nurse said.

Megan would like to go again, because they haven't got a proper bath in Newtown, and she has never been in a bath with a plug before.

Gran's hair is long and white and pulled back over her head into a bun. She has twenty hairpins. Mam only has one clip to hold in her finger wave, because her hair is short, and cut in a bob. Mam is very tall and tries to look smart, and wears everything navy. I would like her to have curls, but she says she can't afford a perm like Evelyn next door.

Evelyn is an usherette in the Plaza and earns a pound a week before stoppages. She told me she had a Eugene perm and that it will stay in even after she washes her hair. It cost thirty shillings for twenty curlers. Fancy spending all that on your hair!

'She must be desperate and looking for a man,' Gran said.

I didn't tell her that she has already found one. They spend ages every night on the corner kissing and cuddling in the dark. I know because I hang out of the bedroom window and watch them sparking.

Caswell's bring our coal and when the lorry stops outside our door, the house shakes and the front room goes dark. We stay inside until they have tipped the load, because the coal sends up clouds of black dust. When the sun shines through, it glitters and falls very slowly. I think coal is pretty. Gran says the lumps are black diamonds, hard to get and expensive to buy.

As soon as the dust settles we roll up the runner of coconut matting in the front room, and put down newspapers over the oilcloth. Our coal cellar is underneath the front room and the door to it is by the side of the fireplace. We are the only ones with a cellar in the Row, because our house used to be the police station. It is horrible down the cellar, black as pitch, cold and damp and it smells the same as the shaft of the Bakehouse Pit. There was a grating under the front-room window so that prisoners could breathe, but there are slabs over it now. Hundreds of huge spiders hang in the thick webs strung over the walls. They look like black dirt in grey dishcloths.

Grancher keeps most of the coal down in the cellar. He carries the rest of it through the front room and the kitchen into the coal cwtch outside. The trouble is, Dayton's next door, Number 3, sneak over in the night and pinch it, so it is safer down the cellar.

Where my friend Megan and her gran live in Newtown, the coal cots are back to back, Their neighbour took out some bricks from the middle wall and pinched the coal through the hole. They had a roaring fire every day, although they were out of work, until Megan's Gran twigged. Megan is sorry because she could go next door for a warm, as her gran is a meany with coal.

Grancher is not very tall and when he carries the big lumps he gets shorter as his legs bend out and go bandy.

'Out of the road,' he gasps, staggers through the front room and dumps the coal on the top of the cellar steps. He says more than that when he struggles down the steps, but not if Gran is about. They are so steep, he climbs down first and then lifts the coal from the top step. His moustache is filthy afterwards, and so is our front-room floor.

Gran is happy when the coal comes on Wednesdays, because Mam can scrub out with the hot, dirty clothes water and it isn't wasted.

I could hardly wait when Mam told me we were going to have a wireless. It will cost a pound deposit and fourteen shillings a month. Mam says that I can't have it on all the time and will have to turn it off when Gran goes for her afternoon nap, or when Grancher wants to sleep in the armchair.

'He's always doing that, so I won't be able to listen very often,' I said, going miserable.

'Well,' said Mam, 'you can have it on quietly.'

When I came home from school, the wireless was playing. As soon as I opened the front door, I could hear music. It was coming from a large wooden box on the windowsill in the kitchen. The front was pretty. It had three leaf shapes carved out of it, covered with a silk material, and the sound came out through the shapes. Underneath there were two knobs. It is called 'Treve Radio'.

When the men came to put the wires round the window, they had to move Gran's sewing tin. She didn't like that.

'Won't be able to find nothing now,' she grumbled, 'all me bits and pieces are in there, and me thimble.'

Gran won't sew anything without her thimble, but I think they are awkward old things.

The wireless is a bit big for the windowsill, and it makes the kitchen dark, but we don't mind.

We had it on all night, and listened to military bands. Grancher liked those, because he could march up and down the kitchen and pretend he was back in the army, until Gran got fed up and made him sit down.

There was a variety show called *Ronald Frankau Cabaret Kittens*, and they sang some of the old songs which Gran knew when she was a girl, so she looked a bit more pleased and forgot about the sewing tin.

Best of all, there was a play from a book I had read, *Alice Through The Looking Glass*. It was the best thing I had ever heard. The people in it spoke in special voices and it seemed as if they were really next to me in the kitchen.

Then there was the news.

'Fancy being able to know what is going on in London,' Gran said, 'and hearing that man's voice here the minute he opens his mouth. He must be shouting very loud.'

'No, Gran,' I explained, 'they have microphones, which send his voice out.'

'We could do with a couple of them here, when we are calling you to come in to bed then,' she answered, sharp as a needle.

Johnny Harry's mother buys her bread with checks from the Co-op, and we have to go to the bakery to get her bread.

'Don't pick the crust on the way back, either!' she says. 'It looks well if we have visitors, and we haven't got a decent edge to a sandwich.'

Fresh crust is lovely and we can't stop picking bits off once we start.

The bakehouse is up Norton's Hill and along the alley by

Pit Row. The smell is beautiful. Sometimes we go there and stand outside just to breathe it in. The trouble is, it makes us feel hungrier.

You can go in and watch the men pulling and rolling the dough, and then throwing little white dough balls into black oblong tins which they never miss. I'm dying to have a go. I like watching them make the cottage loaves best. One blob goes on top of another like little white bellies, and then they stick their fingers in the middle to make a button. They make Cobs and Batches, Swanseas, Baps and Crowns, but Mrs Harry likes a tin-burnt.

After we get Johnny's bread, we go round the back to see the horses in the stables. They don't half smell, especially when they drop a load of manure. The best one is called Major. He is an enormous, grey cart horse, who wears brasses and leather blinkers. He stamps and flares out his nostrils and snorts and the whole of the stables fills with his steam. He has a mark, 'USA' burned into his back, because he once belonged to the American army.

When he's out on a round with Bryn the Breadman, they go down Station Hill. Major hears the train whistle, and then runs like mad, because he thinks it's a bugle, and he's back in the army. Fred can't stop him until he's run through Pontygof, right to the bottom of Newtown Hill.

Next to the bakehouse is the shed where they make coffins. The black tar wooden doors are closed, but you can hear sawing and smell the wood. Curled shavings, like pencil sharpenings, creep out from under the doors, and when you look through the crack at the side, you can just make out the coffins. It is very dark inside and Johnny says it's because they've got bodies in there, fitting them into the coffins. He reckons that in the night their ghosts wail something cruel. When Bronwen comes with us, she won't go near the door. She is afraid of ghosts.

Johnny is cheeky, because he hollers through the crack of the door, 'Got any empty boxes?' and then we run.

When it is cold Mam makes me wear the combs. I hate them, because they are scratchy and itchy, and I don't like the draughty hole underneath you have to undo every time you go to the lav. She makes me wear them because she says she's not paying a shilling for nothing. I even hate the name – 'com-bin-ations'. I would rather have fleecy knickers, and anyway they are only sixpence in the sales. Besides, there's a pocket for my sweets.

You can change your mind about things. I hate Wednesdays now, even if we have jam roly poly and that is my favourite.

It is all spoiled because of last week.

We screamed out of school, tagging and running up the stone steps between the yard and the 'Prims' Sunday-school wall. The wind uses the steps as a dustbin and dumps P.K. packets, Five Boys wrappers and sherbet bags, and then keeps whirling them around.

'Oh Fish!' Bronwen said, 'I've forgotten my coat. Wait for me.'

'I'll go on,' I shouted.

'Wait for me,' she said and stamped her foot. I could see one of her paddies coming on, so I hung about. The sun never warms down the steps, so the walls are wet and smelly. I was cold, so I ran up the steps into the light and over the road. I waited on the other side. She came to the top of the steps, her blue coat with the black armbands, dragging dirty on the ground. Her eyes were nearly shut with the sulks, and she scraped her feet, hanging about. I saw a bus coming, but it was a long way down the road. I called, 'Come on! Or I won't wait.'

I made her run. I never noticed the other bus.

It hit her in the back and she curved up into the air and fell underneath. I ran across. The driver jumped out of the cab and pulled her from under the wheel. He cwtched her, and her arms hung down, like the rag doll Gran made me for Christmas. Bronwen's eyes were shut, but she only had scratches on her arms and legs.

'Oh my God!' the driver kept saying. 'Oh my God!'

'She's my best friend,' I said.

'Go and fetch her mother.'

'I can't. She's dead.'

'Oh God, has she got a father?'

I nodded, and ran through the Row until my legs wobbled and my chest hurt. Nobody looked at me twice or knew it was a different kind of day.

Mr Griffiths' big door was open and I hung over the half-door. Onions again!

'Come quick, Mr Griffiths,' I shouted.

What's the bloody matter now?' he said in a sleepy voice from under the newspaper he always spreads over his face when he has a nap.

'It's Bronwen, she's been run over.'

He went red and dropped the paper.

'Is she hurt bad?'

'She's got scratches on her legs,' I said. 'Come quick!'

He ran out of the front door, left it wide open. I could see through the dark front room and out again, like looking through a tunnel with a light at the end.

I went home to tell Gran.

'Bronwen's been run over.'

She ran out straight away and I heard doors banging and other people running up and down the bailey. The kettle boiled over on the fire and I pulled it to the hob, so that it wouldn't dout the fire.

After a long time Gran came back.

'She's dead,' she said. Her voice was quivery but her face didn't alter much. Gran always looks serious, even when she's pleased. She didn't say any more, and left me with nothing to do, so I went out and walked slowly down the bailey. When I started to cry, Mrs Harry, Number 6, took me back to Gran.

She put me in the cold front room.

'Sit there quiet,' she said, 'and I'll give you a nice Jaffa.'

Gran drew the curtains to show respect for the dead and I sat by the grate in the darkened room. The Jaffa was a treat I didn't want to waste, but when I peeled it with my thumb, a piece stabbed under my nail and juice spurted into my eye and made it sting.

After that, it was all secrets. I crept to the middle door and listened.

'Her chest was knocked in. He wouldn't let anyone touch her, carried her home under a blanket, right through the Row, tears pouring down his face.'

I didn't tell them it was my fault. I had killed her and would have to go to Cardiff jail. Gran told me about it once. Prisoners sat in cells with only bread and water to eat, not even toast.

I thought I was found out, in school the next day.

'You are wanted in the headmistress' room,' teacher said.

I went through the Infants' class to get to Miss Peck, the headmistress' room. They were playing with red and yellow blocks. The grey rocking horse looked at me with his glass eye as if he knew something was up.

The policemen asked me questions. I gave wrong answers, so they wouldn't know I had done it. Then cried my eyes out because Gran doesn't hold with liars, and I was one.

'This child is confused,' I heard the sergeant say, and they let me go.

Curtains were drawn over every window in the Row. I didn't look at Bronwen's window and my feet made too much noise on the ashes outside, when I had to pass.

The morning of the funeral, old Mrs Hodges next door grabbed my hand and pulled me towards the house. She pushed violets at me.

'Put them in the coffin,' she said. 'Go on, she looks lovely.'

'No,' I shouted and screamed. I did not want to see Bronwen's chest smashed in. I never kicked anybody, not even a boy, but I kicked her.

'Well I'm blowed,' she said, 'I'll tell your Mam on you.'

They wouldn't let me see the funeral or go to the church service that other children went to. Made me sit in the front room again.

After it was over, Gran opened the curtains.

'Thank God we can have some light now,' she said.

I asked her when I would be going to Cardiff.

'Whatever for? Don't ask daft questions,' she said.

In the night I heard her say to Mam, 'Least said, soonest mended.'

The bobbies have never come. When somebody knocks on the door to borrow sugar, I am afraid to open it, in case they have come for me. I have seen them marching through the Row and my heart jumps into my mouth, but then they stop and knock on somebody else's door.

Now, I go to Sunday school every Sunday to pay for my sin. I asked the teacher if God forgave people anything.

'Yes,' she said. 'Well I suppose so, but you don't have to worry. You haven't done one, have you?'

She laughed as if it was funny.

The dark nights go slowly when Mam is late coming home, nine or ten o'clock on Saturdays. Gran plays 'Snakes and Ladders' and 'Happy Families' with me to pass the time. Then I watch while she plays dominoes with Grancher. They peg matches into a board, but won't let me play. They say I can't understand the scoring. They don't know how I think in my head and that is my secret.

Then there are the Wednesdays and the whisperings. I can tell they are about me, as well as babies and other secrets.

I heard Mrs Bailey say that her husband has written to the council to get a barrier put up across the steps, to stop the children running over the road. She looked at Gran and then at me and they both nodded. I wondered if somebody had clecked, and my face went red. I wondered if they had Co-op marge on their dry bread in Cardiff, and if they would put me down the cellar first before they take me away on the train.

Every Wednesday, I wish that Dad would send for us so that I can go away and live in Birmingham.

I wish for the light nights, so I can get out and run on the tip, catch bees on thistles and ride the drams.

towards new horizons

Elizabeth Andrews

A Woman's Work is Never Done (2006)

political autobiography: stories of everyday heroism
between the wars
non-fiction anthology

In the early days, women were very new in politics, and were afraid of being called Suffragettes. Much educational work had to be done in simple language, and made interesting.

Realising this, I decided to interest them by charts, and the first one I drafted was 'Mother in the Home' surrounded by all the laws that affected her in every aspect of daily life.

This chart became very popular and I realised that visual aid was to play an important part in my propaganda work. Our socialist propaganda had to have a sense of reality. We were not only a political party, but a great Movement, concerned about human personalities and their well-being.

Effective propaganda work on Labour's policy was done by means of attractive tableaux and pageantry at out special rallies and 'Women's Months'. One outstanding procession was in Swansea. Sir Alfred Mond, its MP, was minister of health and his plea for economy by cutting down on milk for babies and housing had aroused the women of the country. Our West Wales advisory committee organised a procession through the town with meetings in the park. The band we had engaged failed us, so we had a silent procession carrying banners with slogans like these ...

'LABOUR WOMEN SAY MOND MUST GO'

'STINT THE MILK AND STARVE THE CHILD'

It was interesting to see the public reading these banners as we passed by. *At the next Election Mond did go and we won this seat for Labour for the first time!*

The first Women's Section was formed at Ton Pentre, Rhondda in 1918 with the help of the local Trades Council. I was appointed secretary. There were twelve women present. At that time the South Wales Miners' Federation were agitating for shorter hours and higher wages. When discussing this matter, the women felt that the time was long overdue to get something done to lighten the burden of the miner's wife.

I wrote a letter to the miners' conference saying we whole-heartedly supported their demands and while doing so, thought the time had come when shorter hours for miners' wives should have some consideration. We also made the request that the question of pit baths should be a part of their campaign. This letter was read to the conference and interest was aroused as well as some opposition. The press gave this matter much publicity and I had many lively discussions with some of the miners' leaders.

On pit baths, Katherine Bruce Glasier had already done much propaganda work with the Women's Labour League. A pamphlet was written jointly by Katherine, Robert Smillie (President of the Miners' Federation of Great Britain) and G.R. Carter, MA, which had photographs of pit baths that had been built at a British colliery and in France and Belgium. Katherine had made arrangements to meet the miners' leaders at the 1913 Trade Union Congress to discuss this question. She was aroused to immense indignation when one of them from Wales tore up the pamphlet, threw it away and called her a 'dreamer'. *This pamphlet eventually ran into six editions and was endorsed by the Miners' Federation of Great Britain itself!*

She was delighted when I took up this campaign and gave evidence before the Sankey Commission in 1919 on pit baths and housing, on behalf of the South Wales Miners' Federation. A great bond of friendship arose between us that lasted until the end of her days in 1950.

In South Wales, the Ocean Colliery Company, with the personal interest of the two Misses Davies of Llandinam, gave the movement an impetus, and the first pit baths were built at Treharris. In 1919 I arranged for the Ton Pentre

Section and the Co-operative Guild to visit these baths. Many other parties from the coalfield sponsored by the miners' lodges followed, and thus the campaign went on.

In addition, I had the load of lantern slides on pit baths from the Welsh Housing Association whose secretary, Mr Edgar Chappell, was keenly interested in the campaign. I was able to get the use of Workmen's Halls to show these slides, and with the help of the miners' political organisers carried this campaign to all the mining areas of South Wales.

In many a cottage there were three or four miners having to bath in a tub in front of the fire. The small kitchen was often the only available living room in the house and had to serve as bathroom, laundry, bakery, dining room and nursery. The heat from the large open fire, and the stench from the wet pit clothes made the atmosphere unbearable. The mother and wife had to tolerate all this.

But still amongst the miners and their families, prejudices had to be overcome, old ideas destroyed and convincing facts marshalled to prove the benefit of pit baths.

The Royal Commission on the Mining Industry – generally known from its chairman as the Sankey Commission – was set up in 1918. Dr Marion Phillips suggested that women from the mining areas should give evidence on housing and pit baths. I was asked by the South Wales Miners' Federation to represent South Wales. Mrs Hart came from Wigan, and Mrs Brown from Scotland. We three gave evidence.

When we arrived in London we were besieged by the Press at the hotel, and during the time we were giving evidence we were photographed and a minute description given of our dresses.

Many of the personal remarks amused us greatly. They expected us to be overawed at being in the King's Robing Room in the House of Lords where the Commission was held. They also expressed surprise at our calmness when giving evidence.

I dealt with the overcrowding in the mining areas of South Wales and the strain on the miner's wife, from lifting of tubs and heavy boilers. This accounted for the high maternal mortality. The drying of pit clothes in an overcrowded kitchen played havoc with the health of young children. The infant mortality rate in the Rhondda was 105 per 1,000.

The proposals put forward in the Sankey Commission Report included better housing, pit-head baths and holidays with pay. All these were shelved for many years and the position in the coalfield grew steadily worse. From 1921 to 1932, 250,000 people left South Wales to look for work elsewhere. The aftermath of the 1914–18 war had a disastrous effect on the coal industry in this country. Mass unemployment and the family Means Test drove many young members of the families away from home. Those that remained, unable to find jobs, expressed themselves by mass demonstrations, protest meetings and deputations.

Then came the General Strike and Lock-out from May to December 1926. It was during this period of poverty and distress that Communist propaganda had a good following in the Rhondda, and the township of Mardy became named 'Little Moscow'. The Communists captured the Executive of the Rhondda Borough Party which had to be disaffiliated and reorganised. We Labour people suffered much from their attacks, which were often very personal.

Today their strength has faded. A better standard of life, and better conditions for the workers are the only answer to Communist propaganda. Our experience in the Rhondda is a miniature lesson for the undeveloped countries. Poverty and injustice must be removed.

guilty

Siân James

Catwomen from Hell 2000

theme: the wicked women of Wales
fiction anthology

My mother had a great-aunt Hester. Hetty. She was born back in the nineteenth century, had died before I was born, but of all my relatives, she's the one I'd liked to have known. Hetty.

Her mother had died in childbirth and she was brought up, rather grudgingly it seemed, by her grandmother. Life was hard for elderly widows in those days, and Hetty was allowed a small share in her grandmother's poverty. The cottage was small and sparsely furnished. Food, mostly bread and potatoes, was always in short supply, and to make matters worse, she had no other children to play with, the nearest house being two miles away. She went to school in the nearest village, three miles away, until she was eleven, though her grandmother would keep her home whenever it suited her. In spite of her erratic attendance, she learnt to read and write; indeed when my mother was clearing out her house, forty years later, she came across three or four books she'd had as school prizes.

The headmaster's wife, a Mrs Matthews, had a large family and would often call her in to give her parcels of out-grown clothes and a slice of bread to eat on the long walk home, but, as she told my mother on one occasion, had never invited her in to play with her own children. I suppose no one took much notice of her.

It was her love of wild animals and her ability to rescue and tame them which gave her life a purpose. It was considered a fairly easy task to rescue a fledgling magpie and keep it as a pet until the following spring when it flew away to find a mate, but even her headmaster was impressed when a blackbird accompanied her to school one year, waiting in a tree outside until the end of the day. 'Sir, Hetty's taught the blackbird to whistle "Bobby Shaftoe",' one of the big boys announced. And Mr Matthews listened to their duet, Hetty inside the classroom, the blackbird outside, and afterwards patted her on the head. One spring, she rescued and reared a baby squirrel, a red squirrel, far more wild and shy than the grey, and even after she'd released it back into the woods, it would appear on a branch from time to time when she walked to school, as though still acknowledging a distant kinship. 'I've got a dratted flea in my bed,' her grandmother complained around this time. 'Oh, but I mustn't tell you or you'll be wanting it for a pet.'

In spite of her limited diet, Hetty grew very tall, so that when she had to leave school to nurse her grandmother who had developed sciatica and could do nothing for herself, she was able to get a morning job at Bryn Teg, the nearest farm, with a Mrs Delia Evans who'd been given to understand that she was thirteen, and who was to prove a good friend.

Hetty's grandmother died when Hetty was fifteen and at that point Mrs Evans suggested that she should take a full time, living-in job at the farm. She was about to move in when her father turned up. He'd disappeared when his wife died, probably unwilling to contribute anything to his child's upkeep, escaping to South Wales where he'd got a job in the mines and re-married. His second wife had eventually thrown him out because of his habitual heavy drinking and occasional violence, so that he'd returned to his native village and hearing of his mother-in-law's death, had gone along to her cottage, hoping for temporary accommodation.

He was astonished to discover his daughter there; he'd hardly given her a thought for fifteen years. (By this time he'd had two daughters by his second wife, but was equally indifferent to them.)

Hetty listened to all his troubles, accepted his presence as she'd accepted every other of life's burdens, made up her grandmother's bed and prepared to look after him. He was by this time a sick man.

She cared for him for twenty years. He had a miner's

disease, dust on the lungs, which prevented him from working, but not from drinking; he could manage to cajole money from her even when she had barely enough for food. My mother once asked her whether she'd been able to feel any affection for her father. 'No, only sorrow,' she'd answered tearfully. He died in 1914, just before the beginning of the first world war.

The war caused few changes in Hetty's life; she didn't miss any luxury food items because she'd never had any and having no sweetheart or brother, wasn't as heartbroken about the young men who were being sent to France; she cared and worried about them, hated the idea of war, but wasn't personally involved.

She wasn't again invited to live-in at the farm; by this time Mrs Evans had five children so there wasn't even an attic available, so that she lived alone in her isolated cottage, becoming more and more of a recluse. She worked at the farm as the indoor maid-of-all-work, lighting the range at seven every morning and scrubbing out the dairy and the flagstone floors of the kitchen and back-kitchen and the long passages, washing and mangling all the 'rough', the bed linen, the towels, the overalls and aprons, cleaning vegetables, making bread, churning butter. Mrs Evans didn't ask her to work outside because she knew how upset she got at the way the farm animals were treated; she'd always send her home early when Emlyn Gelly, arrived to kill the pig; she didn't even ask her to pluck a chicken or skin a rabbit. What she was able to do, she did with all her strength, but there were things she wasn't able to do and Mrs Evans accepted that. 'She's not like other people,' she'd say, 'and perhaps that's not such a bad thing.' She was aware that Hetty went round the rabbit snares that her husband laid out around his hedges, but never let on; she herself had often been sickened to see the poor mutilated creatures. 'Shoot them, by all means,' she used to tell her husband, 'I know what damage they do, but it can't be right to torture them.'

'I saw you out in Top Meadow earlier on,' she once said when Hetty had arrived a few minutes' late for work. 'Was it mushrooms you were after?'

Hetty had blushed to the roots of her reddish hair, but had scorned to tell a lie. 'No, not mushrooms. Too early for mushrooms, Mrs Ifans. But when I find some I'll bring them up for your breakfast, be sure of that.'

'I know what you're doing, Hetty,' Delia Evans said after a moment or two, 'and I don't blame you. You've got a soft heart, that's your trouble, but I won't say a word.'

What else did she find to do with her time after her long day at the farm? She occasionally went to evening service at Bethesda chapel on a Sunday when the weather was fine, but Mrs Evans told my mother that she wasn't a great one for God. 'I don't understand what He's doing, Mrs Ifans, letting all our young men face such danger. Ifor Stanley has been killed, they say, and his mother a widow with only him to help her with her bit of a smallholding. And even if those Germans lads are wicked as Mr Isaacs, Bethesda, seems to think, they've still got mothers haven't they?'

'It's not for us to reckon it out, Hetty. But thank goodness my boys are too young to go to the Front. They took Mat Brynhir, as it is, and two of our horses.'

It was in the spring of 1918, the morning of Palm Sunday, when Hetty found the injured man in the woods. She was picking primroses and violets to put on her grandmother's grave and they were so scarce that year that she'd had to go deep into Arwel woods before she'd got enough for a decent bunch. The man pulled himself up to a sitting position and stared at her. 'Don't split on me,' he said. Hetty didn't understand much English, but she understood the pleading in his eyes. She put down her flowers and took off her shawl and put it round his shoulders because he'd begun to shiver and sweat. 'I'm on the run,' he said. 'On the run from the army. They'll shoot me if they find me. Don't let them know.'

'No,' Hetty said. 'No, no, no. I get you food.'

She looked hard at him. She had sometimes seen animals being driven to the slaughter house in town. It was Palm Sunday. She gathered up her flowers and walked quickly back to the cottage.

There was some soup on the hob. She heated it up, put some into a covered pot, placed it, with a piece of bread and a spoon, into a basket, put a blanket on top and walked back into the wood, walked hurriedly, fearing that the man might already be dead: she knew starvation when she saw it, knew the smell of death, too.

He hadn't moved; had either been too weak, or had perhaps trusted her. 'I'm a deserter,' he said – she didn't know that word – 'and they'll shoot me if they find me.'

'No,' she said. 'I say no.'

Then she started giving him spoonfuls of soup, very small amounts at first.

'Good,' he said.

'Cawl,' she said.

'Cawl,' he said.

She went on feeding him until his eyes closed. Then she took the shawl she'd lain on him earlier and folded it for a pillow, laid the blanket over him, and told him, as well as she could, that she'd be back when it was dark. She wondered whether he'd be still alive and wondered what she'd do with him if he was. How ever would she get him back to the cottage? He was certainly too weak to walk. Perhaps she'd have to leave him in the woods until he got stronger.

She still had some of her father's clothes which she'd washed and ironed but hadn't managed to give away because no tramps, these days, seemed to come so far out of their way as her cottage. She'd burn his army uniform and give him clean clothes and he could hide away in her grandmother's bedroom until the war was over.

After her dinner, the remains of the soup, she walked the three miles to Bethesda chapel to put the bunch of flowers on her grandmother's grave. She didn't intend to stay for evening service, but went into the chapel and for once managed to pray, tears falling down her cheeks as she did so. 'Let him live. Let him live.'

The Reverend Isaacs came in as she was coming out. 'Are you all right?' he asked.

'I'm all right. But what about the soldiers at the Front?'

'God cares for them, Hetty, every one.'

'No, He doesn't,' Hetty snapped back at him. The Reverend Isaacs was to report that at her trial.

As soon as it was dark, Hetty set off to the woods with a basin of bread and milk in her basket. She shivered a little, remembering the story of little Red Riding Hood which Miss Jenkins had read to them in the Infants', but then smiled at her fear; she wasn't a pretty little child but a grown woman, nearly forty years old, her hair already grey and her back already stooped. And the poor soldier she was hurrying to see was weak as a sickly lamb.

He was still alive. She got him up to a sitting position and fed him the bread and milk.

'Good,' he said.

'Bara llath,' she said.

He looked worse than any tramp, he hadn't shaved for weeks, he stank of urine and faeces, but Hetty was ready to risk everything for him. He was a frightened man on the run and she had to hide him. She had no option.

He wasn't ready to try to walk, whimpering when she tried to get him to his feet, so, reluctantly, she had to leave him where he was for another night.

The next morning she was up before dawn to take him some gruel before going to work. She found him a little stronger, got him on his feet, said he had to walk a short distance to a place where he'd be more adequately hidden. After walking a few steps, he collapsed onto the ground and wept. 'My feet are on fire,' he said. 'No more walking.' She undid the laces on his boots and as she tried to ease them off, was almost overpowered by the stench of his feet. He smiled at her for the first time. 'Thank you,' he said. She began to feed him the gruel, but he was able to take the spoon from her and feed himself.

She left him a bottle of tea and a piece of bread for his dinner and hurried to the farm.

'Hetty, you're not yourself this morning,' Mrs Evans said. 'Aren't you well?'

'Thinking about this war, that's all. When will it end, say? What does it say this week in Mr Ifans' paper?'

'Always telling us it's going to end, but nobody knows is my guess. And all our boys getting killed. Katie Williams, Hendre Fach, has lost three of her four sons and she won't last long, doesn't leave her bed, they say. Joe Morris' boy has been sent home but he'll never be right, his feet are like webbed feet, Joe says, something to do with being in those wet trenches for months at a time, and he may have to have one leg off because of the gangrene ... Great Heavens, girl, sit down for a minute. Put your head between your legs, you've gone as white as milk. You'd never do as a nurse, would you? Too soft-hearted, by far.'

Hetty sat for a whole five minutes before she felt up to getting on with the butter making. And the whole time she was churning the word gangrene, gangrene, gangrene went round and round in her head.

That night she went off again with her pot of soup. 'Cawl,' he said, as she lifted the lid. 'Good cawl.' He ate heartily.

'Walk now,' she said when he had finished. She helped him to stand, hoisted his arms over one of her shoulders and half-carried, half dragged him along the dark path. Four times, when his groaning became too much for her, she had to let him rest for five or ten minutes. The journey, less than two miles by her reckoning, took almost four hours.

She let him lie on the doorstep while she went in to light a candle and re-kindle the fire. The kitchen had an earth floor with a rag rug in front of the hearth. She dragged the rug a yard or two into the room and brought down the quilt from her bed; she knew he'd never manage the stairs that night. When she went out to help him in, he was already asleep. She had to wake him and force him, quite roughly, to take the last few steps. He lay down with a groan and was asleep again in less than a minute. Then she banked the fire, put a china chamber pot at his side and set out again for the wood to retrieve the blanket and the shawl.

It was after midnight when she got to bed though she had, as usual, to be up at six. Her body ached with tiredness, but she couldn't sleep. She knew she could find him food, knew she could hide him away since no one ever called on her, but what would happen if he had gangrene? At last she slept but dreamed about the war, about soldiers, Joe Morris' son amongst them, turning into large green frogs croaking in the slime of the trenches. The plague of Egypt, she was saying as she woke.

'You're looking ill again today,' Mrs Evans said. 'Sit down and have a basin of porridge before you start on the dairy. Can't have you fainting away again.'

'You're very kind to me, Mrs Ifans,' Hetty said. And burst into tears.

'Are you in trouble?' Mrs Evans asked her. But then realised that she couldn't be, she was surely too old, had never even had a sweetheart as far as she knew, she was tall as a man, her chest was flat, her hair scraped back in a bun. 'Are you unwell? Are you having heavy bleeding, something like that? It's quite usual, you know, at your age.'

'No, it's nothing like that.'

Hetty sat over her porridge, still weeping, and Mrs Evans suddenly decided that what she needed was a bottle of tonic. 'I'll send you home early this afternoon, Hetty, so that you can go up to see Sal, Penpwll. She's got all the old herbal powders and mixtures that are better than anything Dr Forest prescribes and you save a guinea as well. Sixpence is all she charges. Spring is a hard time for man and beast and as you know I've got my sister and her family coming for Easter so I'll be depending on you at the weekend.'

Hetty was pleased to have an excuse to visit old Sal, though she lived on the far side of the moor. She told her how she'd lost her appetite, how tired she was all day and how she wasn't able to sleep at night. 'Please give me the strongest tonic you've got. It was Mrs Ifans, Bryn Teg, sent me. She says you're better by far than the doctor and cheaper, too.'

'She's right, gel fach. This is my special mixture, this green one. It's bitter, mind, but it purifies the blood like nothing else. You'll be strong as a stallion when you've got this down you. A teaspoonful twice a day in half a cup of water and that will be sixpence halfpenny.'

Hetty felt buoyant as she walked home, confident that the bitter green medicine would be just the thing for her soldier.

That evening she managed to get his boots and socks off, and though his feet were sore and bleeding they didn't seem disfigured. He whimpered like a puppy as she put his feet into a bowl of warm, salt water, but seemed ready to do whatever he was asked. The next morning before she went to the farm she managed to get him upstairs and felt he was now safe. She washed him and gave him one of her father's old shirts to wear and helped him get into bed in the best room which had once been her grandmother's. The English she'd learnt at school was coming back to her and she was beginning to understand most of what he said, though she found it more difficult to talk to him.

'I'm Hetty,' she said when she came home that evening. 'You?'

' Billy. Billy Mason.'

'Mam? Dad?'

He nodded his head. 'Live in Gloucester. You have parents? Mam and Dad?'

'Dead.'

'I'm sorry.'

'You write to Mam and Dad?'

'No,' he replied in an anguished voice. 'No. They mustn't know I'm alive. No one must know.'

She picked up his uniform which was caked with mud and sweat. 'Burn,' she said. She took every piece of his clothing out into the garden, built a bonfire and stood over it until nothing remained but clean ash. She went upstairs again to try to tell him that he was no longer a soldier, but he was fast asleep. She breathed more easily.

'The tonic is doing you a lot of good, Hetty,' Mrs Evans said at the end of the week.

'Oh, it is.'

The next three weeks passed with relatively few problems. Billy, though unable to eat much, seemed a little stronger each day. He walked to the window of the bedroom and sat there for much of the time she was at work. It was a warm spring. Hetty was pleased that he didn't mention coming downstairs.

Occasionally he'd talk about the war. When he did, he'd forget that she was there, talking fast and wildly so that she wasn't able to follow much of what he said. 'Jack. My pal, Jack. Went to look for him. Nothing left. They could only bury one arm. Almost everyone killed or wounded. Bodies everywhere. Trip over bodies. Parts of bodies in the trenches. I had home leave. My parents didn't understand. I left home. Too frightened to go back to France. Too frightened. They'll shoot me when they find me. They'll find me. Soon. Soon.'

On those evenings when he became hysterical with fear, she'd put her arms round him and rock him to sleep.

It was midsummer when he started raving and shouting uncontrollably and Hetty realised that he had a high fever. She didn't know what to do with him, then. He'd take no food or water. Hetty didn't go to work, but all she could do was wet his lips and put a cold flannel on his forehead and tell him over and over again that he was safe.

One evening, when she hadn't turned up at the farm for three days, Mrs Evans called on her. Hetty let her in and took her upstairs. 'He's dead,' she said in a very calm voice. 'I tried to look after him but he died. He was a soldier. I found him in the woods. Billy Mason from Gloucester.'

She couldn't remember much of what happened after that. Mrs Evans was very kind and stayed with her while all the others came and went; Mr Evans, the doctor, the policeman, the undertaker who took away the body. 'I promised they wouldn't find him, but he's safe from them now,' she said over and over again. While Mrs Evans spent her time telling them all that Hetty was different from other people, too soft-hearted, but a good woman for all that.

They didn't listen to her. She was put on trial for harbouring a deserted soldier and was throughout the subject of great ribaldry.

'That's one way of catching a man.'

'Aye. She burnt all his clothes and wouldn't let him out of bed for three months.'

'An old maid's revenge. I reckon he'd have been better off in France.'

She was found guilty and sentenced to eighteen months hard labour, but was released a month after the armistice when she'd served only six.

During her trial, which had been widely reported, her two half-sisters from South Wales – one of them, my great-grandmother – contacted her, visited her in Swansea jail and remained in touch with her ever afterwards. 'Two sisters I never knew I had,' she told Mrs Evans. 'And so kind, you wouldn't believe.'

In the spring of 1919, she was considered strong enough to go back to work at the farm.

Later that year, Billy Mason's parents sent her a letter of thanks and a framed photograph of their son, taken when he had first joined up. He looked so young and unmarked by war, that she didn't recognise him. All the same, she kept it on the dresser for the rest of her life.

I have it now on my mantelpiece. 'Billy Mason from Gloucester,' I tell friends. 'No, not a relative. Just a soldier my great-aunt Hester picked up in the woods.'

b e l s e n

Emily Bond

Parachutes and Petticoats 1992, new edition 2010

theme: Welsh women's writing
on the second world war
non-fiction anthology

In the midst of our festivities following the declaration of peace, we were told that the whole unit of 29th BGH was going to Belsen, one of the concentration camps in Germany. We knew very little of the conditions we would find when we got there and the suffering we witnessed took us by surprise. Belsen originally had been intended as a transit camp, but during the last months of the war, as the German position weakened, thousands of Jews were moved there from other concentration camps to die.

My first glimpse of Belsen was of its enormous iron entrance gates with boards on them stating the number of people held and the number that had died up to that time. Ominous barbed wire fencing surrounded the camp. Near to the entrance hundreds of people were walking or crawling aimlessly. They were partly clothed, with heads shaven, some covered only by a grey blanket, hung over one shoulder.

British troops had liberated the camp a few weeks earlier, but still hundreds of people were dying, their psychological scars as unnerving as their physical ones.

Our tents were erected a short distance outside the wire barriers. We learnt that typhus and cholera were rife: the spread of disease worsened because of the filthy conditions, with the camps infested by lice and rats. There were no latrines and people were lying in their own excreta, sometimes inches deep. We were all sprayed daily with DDT.

Our first duties involved feeding the survivors with suitable food. It would have been easy to worsen their condition by giving them food which was too rich. At first they were allowed only nutritious fluids and vitamins, gradually working up to solid food. Often, when giving out meals, it was very difficult to allow patients only the amount of food they were medically supposed to have. They used to plead for more with a haunted look in their eyes saying that before we came they had been starved. At night some of the patients broke into the food store. One morning, attending to a dying patient in her bed, I found many tins of food neatly packed around her. How could patients believe that now there was plenty of food for all and that they would continue to get regular meals in the future? Loaves of bread disappeared during a journey of a couple of yards when being brought from the cookhouse to the wards. Once I noticed clouds of smoke coming from a site where old wooden cupboards had been thrown out. Going to investigate I found people with billy cans boiling up garbage, collected from the rubbish bins around.

As a senior Sister I was in charge of an area known as Square Eleven, which housed a thousand people, hundreds of them patients. I often felt inadequate in my capacity as a nurse to even try to counteract in any way the atrocities they had suffered. Some of the young girls on the ward had been so starved that initially they were mistaken for old women. At first, hundreds of patients died each day, including a great many from my ward. We used to write down the number of dead on a blackboard outside. It was at least heartening to notice that, as the weeks progressed, fewer and fewer died each day. As some patients were recovering they decided to leave in search of their homes and were desperate to see loved ones again. We never knew whether they reached their destinations. One case I remember in particular was a beautiful young woman who was in a ward for patients with psychological problems. Extremely intelligent, she spoke nine languages, and had been severely battered, both mentally and physically by the Germans. She was desperately malnourished and had lost all her hair. She was so thin that one day she got out of the ward through narrow beams on the window. She was never seen again.

Also under my supervision in Square Eleven was a ward full of patients suffering from Cancrum Oris – extensive ulceration of the mucous lining of the cheeks due to lack of mastication and malnutrition. The patients developed holes in their cheeks, and the tongue could be seen moving as they spoke. Even though I had learnt of this condition during nurse training, this was the first time I had encountered it. Such was the lack of control over the mouth area that feeding was made very difficult.

After each feed we also had to wash the mouth, cleanse the surrounding ulcerated areas, and spray them with penicillin, which proved extremely effective.

Some German women from a nearby village offered to come to assist us. But such was the distrust felt by the patients that if these women offered them medicine, or even a drink, it was immediately thrown to the ground or into their faces.

One of our patients, with at least three lots of numbers on her arm, had repeatedly been offered soap by the Nazis and given opportunities to be taken to a bath but had refused and thus avoided the gas chamber. Another young woman had all her teeth knocked out by her captors and now was wearing a set of teeth made out of peat.

The women were now interested in their appearance and we used to give them some of our own make-up to use. As the days passed it was evident that many patients were making rapid progress. It seemed to me that the women reacted to treatment quicker than the men on the whole.

The army had made up some wooden bed frames. The beds were paliasses filled with straw, with brightly coloured check material as covers. A sign that patients were recovering came one day when we discovered that bed covers had been removed. It did not take us long to find out that patients were busy sewing dresses. We decided to take the women to the army clothing store on the camp which we nicknamed, 'Harrods', to find suitable clothes for them. Going on duty one morning I saw a parade of women walking along in the sunshine in their new dresses. It was a wonderful feeling to contrast this to the scene when I first arrived at the camp only a few weeks earlier. We all agreed that the brightly coloured spectacle reminded us somewhat of Brighton on a summer's day!

With so many contagious diseases, certain areas of the camp had to be marked for limited access. In one such area were patients suffering from typhus. In front of their quarters was a large sign which plainly said 'Typhus – Keep Out'.

It was often sheer luck whether a person survived the horror of the camp or not. One patient explained how two hundred people were kept in one Nissen hut. Once a day the door opened and food was thrown in. The nearest to the door ate all the food, while the people at the back were dying of starvation and too weak to move forward.

A climax to the horror we witnessed came for me one evening when I visited the house that Kramer, named the Beast of Belsen, and his wife, had lived in. Here I saw a lampshade which had reputedly been made out of tattooed human skin. The attractiveness of the lampshade sickened me beyond belief.

The only sound medical care which had been administered in the camp before our arrival was in a hospital for the use of the SS troops themselves. This we took over as one of our hospital bases, naming it the Glyn Hughes Hospital, after our Brigadier Hughes, director of medical services.

Amidst all the negative experiences encountered at Belsen there were moments of excitement and celebration to remember. Such was the day when Mary Churchill, ATS Commandant, the daughter of Winston Churchill, came to visit the camp. Patients and medical staff had gone to great efforts to make the area presentable. As there were no flowers, the patients found tree branches and decorated the ward with these. I remember well the retinue arriving at Square

Eleven near the entrance to one of my wards. At first, the patients were too awed by the presence of this important lady to say anything. Then we heard the clear voice of a slightly-built Polish lady, sitting up in her bed, proudly asking Mary Churchill if she would thank her father on behalf of all the Polish people for all he had done for them. Standing perfectly still, with tears running down her cheeks, Mary Churchill said that the situation had so moved her that she could stand no more. Shortly afterwards she left the camp and, although there was disappointment that she had left so early, we knew that she would take our story back to Britain.

As the weeks progressed spirits were raised by recovery rates of many patients, and fatality rates falling dramatically from what was at first 500 people a day. Every morning a staff sergeant would come to receive the number of fatalities for the last twenty-four hours and a three-ton lorry would come around to take the dead away. The German prisoners resident with us were made to dig mass graves ready for the burial.

Belsen had been structured into three separate units – Camp 1, 2 and 3. There was soon no need for Camp 1 to be used and the major event of burning it down was planned. Psychologically speaking, this was an important ceremony for all of us. We watched the flames together, the scene of so much past horror being burnt away. It was a comforting feeling as all of us, friends of different nationalities, stood together hand in hand against Nazism. Now there was no need to use guns and violence, as the war had been won. That evening we spent hours singing and dancing around the bonfire which symbolised for us the death-knell of Nazi beliefs.

within a whisker

Beryl Roberts

Written in Blood 2009

theme: crime
fiction anthology

They say you're never more than a foot away from a rat in downtown Johannesburg. I reckon that's a conservative estimate, given that the largest city in South Africa is the mother of all cesspits, the undisputed arsehole of the universe.

The particular rat I fleetingly shared the gutter with there *was* certainly less than a foot away, its covering of hair sleek and ebony black, its eyes shining like mahogany beads, sizing me up as so many mega-bites. It had watched me hit the tarmac at a pedestrian crossing and lie stretched full out under the number plate of a metallic grey stationary car, before scuttling forward, full of curiosity, whiskers twitching, eager to identify my scent and flavour. As I eyeballed the rodent, I realised that if my plans backfired, I'd soon be reduced to tyre-tread, and the rat would get a large portion of freshly pulped nibbles.

My musing was cut short when I felt a sharp kick against the sole of my shoe and heard a cry of, 'Hoof it, *baas*! Fast! Fast!'

'Sorry, not this time, pal,' I whispered, apologetically, to the rat, 'though you were just within a whisker.' It blinked back at me accusingly, its whole face twitching with hungry disappointment.

I scrambled onto the pavement on all fours, just in time to see the grey car disappearing down the road, the two close-cropped, negroid heads of my accomplices silhouetted through the rear window. Then I became aware of the crunch of glass from a pair of broken spectacles under my feet and an anguished cry for help coming from a writhing bundle of clothes on the grass verge. I was in the middle of a crime scene and the only witness.

I sprinted half a block without stopping then I dodged up a side street and flung myself into a warehouse doorway. Sitting on the bare concrete step, waiting for my jolting heart to subside, I felt the sweat of my exertions set on my skin like a coating of lard. I had half an hour to kill. Time to reflect on our perfectly executed car-jack.

My exit-visa out of hell.

*

Hell for the last month had been a rat-infested bolt hole in the northern suburbs of Jo'burg; scruffy lodgings in an untidy ribbon development that linked the black township overspill of Berea with the downwardly mobile, white trash of Parkville. In the decade and a half since the collapse of apartheid, it had changed from a no man's land into a virtual everyman's land, a haven for drifters, drug dealers and drunks, besides attracting the usual sprinkling of do-gooders who yearned to mix and match the rag-bag of human riff-raff there and meld it into a microcosm of the new rainbow state. Quaintly described in fringe magazines as 'the sanitised squat of *les nouveaux pauvres*', the district was a ghetto of fast-food joints, pawnshop-cum-money-lenders and sleazy, backroom bars that catered for conceptions, abortions and every type of in-between sexual and narcotic pleasure-fix devised by man. It also spawned seedy boarding houses and two-star hotels, patronised by struggling travelling salesmen and those with reasons to hide.

It was in the bar of one of these, The Gold Nugget, that I had first met two recruits from Shabo township, the Kekana brothers, who had once fished a crumpled tourist map of London from a waste bin and set their hearts and sights on a single ticket to Camden.

By employing brothers driven by a dream, I reckoned I'd keep the minds of both focused. If one of them looked like screwing up, I'd threaten the other with the soup kitchen, or worse. Tribal and family loyalty among location relations is strong and binding, so I knew both would be working in unison, intent upon doing me over – though ultimately, I'd be the one wielding the spanner.

There's a thriving criminal subculture in all third world cities and Jo'burg's no exception. Deprivation and despair ensure a ready supply of raw recruits prepared to obey orders blindly, with a reckless disregard for their own skins. But however dangerous and dedicated they are, these amateurs remain cat's paws and never get to taste the cream, or to enjoy even one of a cat's nine lives. Their criminal careers are as short lived as they are squalid, because, lacking contacts, they get found in possession of hot goods or weapons they can't unload, or for concocting fanciful alibis they have to bully others to substantiate.

The Kekana brothers were typical of this breed of fall guy and I'd had no conscience about exploiting them. I'd already made certain that all the cerebral work had been done before involving them, so all one brother had to do was to act dumb, and all the other had to do was to drive fast.

The connoisseurs of sophisticated crime were the craftsmen of North Korea, sweating at their humid printing presses thousands of miles away, rolling off faultless works of art: virgin-pure rand banknotes, crackling to be exchanged for shabby but genuine dollar, sterling and euro notes.

Transported in sampans via the bustling waterways of Pyongyang, sacks full of counterfeit banknotes had already been shipped across the South China Sea and the Indian Ocean and had landed on the East African coast, disguised as safety packaging and stuffed inside containers full of cane furniture, bound for Durban's riviera hotels. Whilst the furniture was dumped unceremoniously inside dockside warehouses, the more valuable waste by-product was trucked across miles of dirt track and delivered in crates to my front door. Rotten money is easier to sell than ripe oranges.

I'd spent a month dossing down at Jo'burg's international

airport terminals, wringing from pliable luggage handlers details of where tourists were heading, then way-laying them in hotel foyers and lounges, bribing couriers, and hanging around bars and casinos, bamboozling boozers and losers with dud notes. I offered large cash loans at give-away exchange rates, swapping millions of Commie-red rands for mint-cool greenbacks, raking it in.

But success breeds envy.

Rival fraudsters registered their disapproval by torching my Chevy and threatening me with instant cremation if I tried to leave town without sharing my good fortune. The syndicate ran all the taxi and car hire companies in the city and, with copies of my photo pinned on every windscreen, there was healthy competition amongst the drivers to be the one to hand me over and collect the ransom.

Like the city's rats, I kept to the back streets and gutters after dusk and lived by night amongst filth and rubble.

During my initial business transactions, the Kekana brothers stayed physically close to me, like a pair of outsize shoulder-pads, looking menacing, but actually doing nothing. Then I needed to get myself and my money out of Jo'burg fast and, to do that, I needed a car.

Anyone would imagine a large and populous city to be full of them – there for the taking! Not so Jo'burg.

Property owners in Jo'burg live under conditions of continuous curfew and permanent siege behind the plush, drawn curtains of their urban mansions. Black, white and mixed-race upper-class residents, who want to keep what they own, are forced to live, discreetly armed, inside virtual castles, fortified by barred windows, locked doors and padlocked gates. Their cars are never parked trustingly on public roads but stand immobilised by alarms on private drives, bordered by gardens patrolled by guards and vicious dogs, and screened from the road by electronically operated gates – all major obstacles, when you need to borrow a set of wheels.

Fortunately, though, there's another phenomenon unique to Jo'burg – black 'kerb kulture'. Hawkers hang around traffic robots waiting for the red light that will bring to a grinding halt a captive market of around twenty drivers every few minutes. Then, natives swoop like ravens from the shadows to tap at driver and passenger windows, holding out bargains for sale, like economy packs of black plastic refuse bags, 'designer' sunglasses, watches, or cheap Taiwan toys.

When the lights turn green and drivers lift their hand-brakes, there's a mad rush to jump clear, because some motorists think running jaywalkers down in cold blood is fair game. Sometimes, drivers roar off clutching goods they haven't paid for but, more often, sellers deliberately fumble with customers' change and are left holding it, gesticulating innocently into the rear mirror that it's not their fault red's turned to green and they've been left with double their asking price.

I was fairly confident that my local knowledge of Jo'burg and its eccentricities would get me that car. Only the street-savvy and rats survive and thrive in Jo' burg.

D-Day – Departure Day – arrived.

The brothers met me in fading light at Smuts Street robots. Alpheus was carrying a reproduction art deco cigarette lighter, a gilt monstrosity shaped like Ali Baba's lamp, stuck unsteadily onto a fake onyx base. He seemed unsure in which hand to hold it. Right. Left. Right. Now thrown up in the air then caught with both hands. He looked anxious, nervously hopping from one leg to the other as if he wanted to relieve himself. His whole body language was arrestable. By comparison, Gladman looked confident and in full control of himself and the situation. He was chewing gum nonchalantly and even dared to wink at me. I acknowledged their presence silently then positioned myself at the kerb as if waiting to cross the busy main street. Smartly dressed and carrying my flight bag crammed tight with high denomination banknotes, I looked like any other anonymous office worker on his way home.

Suddenly, the lights blinked red and a metallic grey car with a single, elderly driver drew up alongside us. There was no car immediately behind him, which suggested that he had probably drifted mindlessly through the previous lights. I coughed and we sprang into action. While Alpheus engaged the driver's attention, pestering him to buy the 'designer' cigarette lighter at bargain price and flicking it on and off to demonstrate its working order, I dropped onto the tarmac, rolled level with the number plate, and made my brief acquaintanceship with the rat.

Gladman, as rehearsed, threw a fit, motioning to the driver that there was a suicidal maniac lying under his wheels and Alpheus joined in the rumpus. Predictably, the harassed driver left the engine running while he got out to investigate. I took my leave of the rat, scrambled onto the pavement and brushed myself down, just in time to catch sight of Gladman flooring the elderly driver with a few well-aimed body blows, before taking possession of the BMW.

*

It was time to move from my cover and rejoin the Kekanas. I felt confident that the stolen car was now safely housed in the underground car park of The Gold Nugget, where I had reserved a room for one night. Once I had settled my final debt with the brothers, and snatched a few hours' kip, Gladman could chauffeur me to the airport and take ownership of the car as his tip for a job satisfactorily completed. By avoiding using either a hired taxi or a rented car, I would have neatly side-stepped the gangland death threats, but it would only be when I was safe on board the night flight to Cape Town, that I'd be able to relax and look forward to receiving my next cargo of 'gift-wrap' for recycling. By then the Kekana brothers would probably be in custody and the stolen BMW so many spare parts. Tough.

Room 9 was basic, containing two single beds, a television, a mini-bar and a small bathroom. Once inside, the brothers, feeling dehydrated and with adrenalin levels running high, helped themselves to drinks from the mini-bar. I suggested they chilled out on the beds, or watched television, while I calculated their pay. Then, when darkness fell, we could leave from the underground car-park and join the convoy of traffic streaming to the airport and there say our fond farewells.

The hotel room lacked air-conditioning, so when Alpheus mentioned that he had a blinding headache, I gave him the aspirins I'd reserved for my flight. Then Gladman grumbled that the car snatch had made him hungry and asked if he could go out and fetch us a take-away meal. The hotel itself offered no dining facilities, because of the glut of native restaurants nearby serving exotic African dishes, like ostrich and kudu, as well as foreign food outlets, including Thai, Indian and Portuguese, that amply catered for all of Jo'burg's cosmopolitan gourmets. In addition, to satisfy the cravings of fast food junkies, there were also burger bars, hot-dog stalls and fish and chip kiosks, wafting their pungent fumes of onions, oil and spices into the air, all adding to the city's humidity and stench.

Gladman was making me nervous, sighing dramatically and pacing about the small room, so I gave him a few hundred rand and told him to get me a salami baguette and whatever he and his brother fancied.

I regretted, later, that I'd put it like that, because he took me literally.

The brothers conferred in native gibberish, to the effect

that they didn't trust me as banker, so it was proposed that Alpheus should stay with me, while Gladman went foraging around outside.

Next, Alpheus couldn't decide what to eat. He'd lived his whole life in a township, where the staple diet was *mealie pap*, a stiff maize porridge, supplemented with chunks of dry bread. What would he know of *à la carte* menus and *haute cuisine?*

Being white and carnivorous, I couldn't guess where Gladman would find *mealie pap* in the city and I didn't give a rat's rectum anyway. With his boozing, his headache and now his finicky appetite, Alpheus was getting on my tits, so I informed his brother there were umpteen vegetarian outlets nearby, including a Thai take-away, which, incidentally, employed a very tasty waitress.

Gladman left his brother watching television and me counting the money and within twenty minutes he'd returned with my baguette and two cartons of Thai Mixed Vegetable Noodles for Alpheus. I asked him what he had found to tickle his tastebuds and he said he fancied sampling a portion of the Thai appetizer who had served him the noodles. He had change in his pocket now to pay to get rid of the roe simmering in his balls like so much *dim sum*. He reckoned he'd only be gone an hour, but just in case I developed ideas of going solo, he'd take the car keys with him, as a precaution. I told him only a cynical, *kaffir* bastard could think like that.

'It only fair, *baas*,' he said, laughing. 'After all, BMW stands for Black Men's Wheels and dis car's nearly mine.' He dangled the car keys hypnotically in front of me, pocketed them and left.

In truth, I found playing for time in that cramped rat-hole more comfortable with one sweating native than two. Alpheus and I sat propped up on each of the twin beds, scoffing our snacks, him by now half-pissed with the mixture of drinks he'd been taking from the mini-bar. Then he lay back, stretched out and began breathing deeply, as if practising relaxation. Poor sod, I thought, I bet he's been used to lying on bare boards all his life. Soon he started to snore loudly, so I took the flight bag of money into the bathroom, locked the door and shat, showered and shaved to save me valuable time later. When I emerged after thirty minutes, I felt de-toxed as well as decriminalised. I could even feel the Jo'burg jitters evaporating through my pores and a perverse nostalgia for the godforsaken place seeping through me.

Alpheus was still lying on the bed, surrounded by the empty food cartons but now I noticed that he was breathing irregularly and jerking his skinny limbs, as if re-enacting a nightmare. To ignore the convulsions, I switched on the television – just as the Bafana-Bafana Premier League striker headed a winning home goal into the back of the net – but I had to turn it straight off, distracted by the gasping and rhythmic twitching coming from the adjacent bed.

Did I have an epileptic on my hands?

Whatever happened, I resolved not to give him the kiss of life in case he enjoyed it.

Suddenly, Alpheus, draped in a white sheet like a reviving corpse, jackknifed into a sitting position, frightening the shit out of me. His whole body heaved violently and his mouth gaped open, as if he was going to scream at the top of his voice. Instead, khaki-coloured vomit spouted from deep in his throat, down his clothes and onto the bedding. He gasped and coughed, struggling for breath, his arms flailing about wildly. I ran into the bathroom and grabbed the wet towel. When I reached Alpheus with it, I found him groaning, and retching, his torso overhanging the bed and his head hovering limply above the pool of congealing, mottled vomit on the floor.

'What's up with you, man?' I yelled. 'Are you out of your

tiny mind? Look at this fucking mess. The place smells like a sewer! I've paid big money to have a few hours' shut-eye in here, you selfish sod.'

As Alpheus groaned, tears streamed from his bloodshot eyes and fell in cascades down his face. Then, he lay back, exhausted. For the first time in my life, I realised that negroes can turn ashen. Better let him sleep it off, I thought. My mind raced up several blind alleys. Where the hell was Gladman? What would he do when he came in and saw this stretcher-case? What if he took it into his devious mind that I'd been manhandling Alpheus and turned savage? Even worse, how could I rely on this pair of rats' arses to get me out of here tonight in time to catch a plane?

As Alpheus' panting subsided, it was my turn to hyperventilate. Even if I bolted and survived a taxi journey to the airport, Gladman, as designated chauffeur, knew my flight details. He'd follow for his cut, perhaps even involve the police and convince them that I'd assaulted his brother. Bunking off would confirm my guilt, lead to my bags being searched and get me arrested. I had no choice but to sit it out.

The smell of the acrid vomit was unbearable. Just how many exotic Thai dishes was Gladman getting stuck into?

There came a light tap on the door. I dashed to open it, half suspecting that it was Gladman trying to tease me into a temper, but it was a young chambermaid standing there, her hair sleek and black, her eyes glistening like mahogany beads.

'I'se come to turn over yo' bed covers,' she said.

'I don't think it would be wise to disturb my friend when he's sleeping,' I answered, preparing to close the door. 'But thank you, anyway.' Then an idea struck me and I called after her retreating figure. 'I don't suppose you'd have a vacuum cleaner handy, would you?'

'It's in de cupboard at de end of de corridor,' she said returning. 'Why? Has you spilt somet'ing?'

'My friend's been sick,' I said. 'I tried mopping it up but I've probably made it worse. I've got to stay here for a few more hours, before catching a night flight. If you're not doing anything else now, I'll pay you to clean up the room.'

The maid nodded and bustled off.

I picked up the brothers' pay packets and my flight bag and laid them, for maximum security, under and alongside Alpheus's lank body, tucking the heavy coverlet underneath and all around, so that man and money were enclosed in a tight cocoon of padded cloth.

The maid returned, dragging a vacuum cleaner and holding fresh bed linen.

'Bless you,' I said, handing her a fifty rand note.

'T'ank you, sir,' she said, obviously taken aback by the sum.

I pointed to the mess on the bed and floor, embarrassed, and glanced back at her to gauge her reaction. Her beady eyes glistened and her nose twitched as she breathed in the vile stench.

'Now, you jus' keep out of de way, sir.'

Relieved, I disappeared into the bathroom and sat on the loo with the door open. I could hear the portly maid grunting as she bent to pick up the food cartons and soiled tissues and expressing disgust when she found the sick-encrusted towel. I heard her muttering, probably incanting a tribal curse, as she sorted out the vacuum heads, before plugging the machine into the wall socket.

She knocked on the bathroom door and peeped in.

' Your frien' has a fever, sir. I t'ink he needs a doctor.'

'Doctors take hours to answer a call. I'm just waiting for his brother to come back then we'll all push off.'

'He don't look good, sir.'

'That's his brother's problem,' I said. '*I've* paid for the room.'

Despite the generous tip I had given her, a day's wage in current terms, the maid looked reproachfully at me under drooping eyelids and shook her head.

'There'll be extra, if you're quick,' I urged.

The maid hurried into the bedroom and I returned to the loo seat. I could hear she was making a thorough job of cleaning the room; the mechanised nozzles buzzing as they penetrated the carpet fibres, sucking up all the fetid food particles. I decided the filthy job was worth another twenty rand, when she'd finished.

Suddenly, the bathroom doorway darkened with the sinuous profile of Gladman. He looked down at me sitting tensely on the loo seat, his skinny fingers twitching the crotch of his shapeless trousers suggestively, a silly grin spread across his face.

'What de fuck's been goin' on in 'ere?' he asked. He sounded cocky and looked refreshed. It was obvious how he'd spent the last hour and I hated him for getting one up on me.

'Your brother's been honking his guts up non-stop, since you left,' I said cuttingly. 'The maid's clearing up the mess he's made. I'll deduct her hundred-rand fee out of his pay packet.'

I rose from the toilet seat and went to examine Alpheus. He was where I had left him an hour before, in deep sleep, motionless. But the coverlet I'd wrapped tightly around him had been loosened and thrown back, as if in a feverish frenzy, and the flight bag and the two envelopes of money had gone.

Near the door, the abandoned vacuum cleaner lay roaring with life on the carpet, unmanned and sucking away noisily at nothing.

'Where's the maid?' I yelled.

'I pass her outside, climbing in de taxi wit' bags, *baas*. I t'ink she go on holiday. She wave to me an' smile.'

'I bet she did,' I said, between clenched teeth. 'The cunning ratbag's cleaned us right out.'

I explained to Gladman where I had hidden the money. Of course, being a cynical primitive, he didn't believe me. Thought I was cheating him. Accused me of being in cahoots with the maid, who was obviously waiting for me at the airport. When he said that, it occurred to me that it would have been a brilliant idea – if he hadn't confiscated the car keys. Now, besides being broke and being in possession of a stolen car, we had a casualty on our hands.

Someone knocked on the bedroom door and, for one crazy moment, I thought the chocolate-eyed charmer had scuttled back, racked with guilt at chiselling a punter, who had paid her over-generously for work she hadn't even done.

Instead, a thin, wiry-haired Jew stood in the doorway, clutching a Gladstone bag.

'You called a doctor?' he asked, sliding through the doorway, like an eel. 'Hotel reception contacted me minutes ago. Fortunately I had my cell phone on and I was passing. Where's the patient?'

He seemed to know the layout of the room and, by the time I had checked the corridor for snoopers and closed the door, he had glided past Gladman and was struggling to rouse Alpheus, by first tapping his face, then pounding his chest. I moved into the bathroom to think and Gladman followed me.

'How we go pay a real doctor wit' no money, *baas*?' he whispered, his eyes rolling.

'The same way we're going to pay the hotel bill,' I answered, out of the corner of my mouth. 'By doing a runner.'

The doctor called out, 'What's this man eaten recently?'

'Thai noodles, sir,' Gladman shouted.

'With meat?' yelled the doctor.

'No, sir. Just veggies,' yelled back Gladman.

'Definitely Thai?'

'Def'ni'ly, sir.'

I pushed Gladman into the bedroom to stop the shouting, in case the management arrived to complain. Walls in these doss houses are as porous as sponges and some clients expect to sleep during evenings, to prepare them for their nocturnal activities.

'And drink?'

'Plenty,' I said, indicating the waste bin full of discarded bottles and cans.

' Drugs?'

'A few headache pills.'

'Headache pills?' the doctor queried.

'Aspirin.'

'Hm. As I suspected. The classic lethal cocktail,' said the doctor. 'Alcohol, aspirin and peanuts.'

'Peanuts?' I echoed, convinced everyone was going ape. '*Peanuts?*'

'A staple ingredient of Thai cooking,' said the doctor. 'I'm afraid there's nothing I can do for this young man, beyond issuing him with a death certificate. The cause of death is peanut anaphylaxis. With more time, I could have tried epinephrine injections, but there's a good chance he'd have died of respiratory failure anyway. Chronic TB is a natural hazard of living in a township and a post mortem is certain to prove that his lungs were about as useful as a pair of lace doilies inside his chest.' The doctor snapped his bag shut. 'I'll leave my bill at reception to be added to your tab. Would you like the mortuary contacted?'

Tears and sweat mingled on Gladman's contorted face.

'No, t'anks, sir. I take my *brudder* home,' he said weakly. 'No money for dead parlours, or t'ings like dat. I go take him home.'

I nodded my agreement and showed the doctor out.

Gladman looked broken, so I put my arm around his shoulders.

'No money and no brudder to go to Camden wit', *baas*,' he murmured thickly. 'And all dat work for nuttin'.'

'Within a whisker,' I said in a daze. 'We came just within a whisker. It was nothing *we* did wrong, Gladman. Blame the Jo'burg jinx. *And* the local rats. The female ones are real mean killers.'

the return

Brenda Chamberlain

A View Across the Valley 1999

short stories from women
in Wales c 1850 to 1950
Honno Classics, fiction anthology

It isn't as if the Captain took reasonable care of himself, said the postmaster.

No, she answered. She was on guard against anything he might say.

A man needs to be careful with a lung like that, said the postmaster.

Yes, she said. She waited for sentences to be laid like baited traps. They watched one another for the next move. The man lifted a two-ounce weight from the counter and dropped it with fastidious fingers into the brass scale. As the tray fell, the woman sighed. A chink in her armour. He breathed importantly and spread his hands on the counter. From pressure on the palms, dark veins stood up under the skin on the backs of his hands. He leaned his face to the level of her eyes. Watching him, her mouth fell slightly open.

The Captain's lady is very nice indeed; Mrs Morrison is a charming lady. Have you met his wife, Mrs Ritsin?

No, she answered; she has not been to the Island since I came. She could not prevent a smile flashing across her eyes at her own stupidity. Why must she have said just that, a ready-made sentence that could be handed on without distortion. She has not been to the Island since I came. Should she add: no doubt she will be over soon; then I shall have the pleasure of meeting her? The words would not come. The postmaster lodged the sentence carefully in his brain ready to be retailed to the village.

They watched one another. She, packed with secrets behind that innocent face, damn her, why couldn't he worm down the secret passages of her mind? Why had she come here in the first place, this Mrs Ritsin? Like a doll so small and delicate, she made you want to hit or pet her, according to your nature. She walked with small strides, as if she owned the place, as if she was on equal terms with man and the sea. Her eyes disturbed something in his nature that could not bear the light. They were large, they looked further than any other eyes he had seen. They shone with a happiness that he thought indecent in the circumstances.

Everyone knew, the whole village gloated and hummed over the fact that Ceridwen had refused to live on the Island and that she herself was a close friend of Alec Morrison. But why, she asked herself, why did she let herself fall into their cheap traps? The sentence would be repeated almost without a word being altered but the emphasis, O my God, the stressing of the *I*, to imply a malicious woman's triumph. But all this doesn't really matter, she told herself, at least it won't once I am back there. The Island. She saw it float in front of the postmaster's face. The rocks were clear and the hovering, wind-swung birds; she saw them clearly in front of the wrinkles and clefts on his brow and chin. He coughed discreetly and shrugged with small deprecatory movements of the shoulders. He wished she would not stare at him as if he was a wall or invisible. If she was trying to get at his secrets she could till crack of doom. All the same. As a precautionary measure he slid aside and faced the window.

Seems as though it will be too risky for you to go back this evening, he said; there's a bit of a fog about. You'll be stopping the night in Porthbychan?

— and he wouldn't let her go on holiday in the winter: said, if she did, he'd get a concubine to keep him warm, and he meant —

A woman was talking to her friend outside the door.

You cannot possibly cross the Race alone in this weather, Mrs Ritsin, persisted the postmaster.

I must get back tonight, Mr Davies.

He sketched the bay with a twitching arm, as if to say: I have bound the restless wave. He became confidential, turning to stretch across the counter.

My dear Mrs Ritsin, no woman has ever before navigated

these waters. Why, even on a calm day the Porthbychan fishers will not enter the Race. Be warned, dear lady. Imagine my feelings if you were to be washed up on the beach here.

Bridget Ritsin said, I am afraid it is most important that I should get back tonight, Mr Davies.

Ann Pritchard from the corner house slid from the glittering evening into the shadows of the post office. She spoke out of the dusk behind the door. It isn't right for a woman to ape a man, doing a man's work.

Captain Morrison is ill. He couldn't possibly come across today. That is why I'm in charge of the boat, Bridget answered.

Two other women had slipped in against the wall of the shop. Now, four pairs of eyes bored into her face. With sly insolence the women threw ambiguous sentences to the postmaster, who smiled as he studied the grain in the wood of his counter. Bridget picked up a bundle of letters and turned to go. The tide will be about right now, she said. Good evening, Mr Davies. Be very, very careful, Mrs Ritsin, and remember me to the Captain.

Laughter followed her into the street. It was like dying in agony, while crowds danced and mocked. O, my darling, my darling over the cold waves. She knew that while she was away he would try to do too much about the house. He would go to the well for water, looking over the fields he lacked strength to drain. He would be in the yard, chopping sticks. He would cough and spit blood. It isn't as if the Captain took reasonable care of himself. When he ran too hard, when he moved anything heavy and lost his breath, he only struck his chest and cursed: blast my lung. Alec dear, you should not run so fast up the mountain. He never heeded her. He had begun to spit blood.

By the bridge over the river, her friend Griff Owen was leaning against the side of a motor-car, talking to a man and woman in the front seats. He said to them, ask her, as she came past.

Excuse me, Miss, could you take us over to see the Island?

I'm sorry, she said, there's a storm coming up. It wouldn't be possible to make the double journey.

They eyed her, curious about her way of life.

Griff Owen, and the grocer's boy carrying two boxes of provisions, came down to the beach with her.

I wouldn't be you; going to be a dirty night, said the man.

The waves were chopped and the headland was vague with hanging cloud. The two small islets in the bay were behind curtains of vapour. The sea was blurred and welcomeless. To the Island, to the Island. Here in the village, you opened a door: laughter and filthy jokes buzzed in your face. They stung and blinded. O my love, be patient, I am coming back to you, quickly, quickly, over the waves.

The grocer's boy put down the provisions on the sand near the tide edge. Immediately a shallow pool formed round the bottoms of the boxes.

Wind seems to be dropping, said Griff.

Yes, but I think there will be fog later on, she answered, sea fog. She turned to him. Oh, Griff, you are always so kind to me. What would we do without you?

He laid a hand on her shoulder. Tell me, how is the Captain feeling in himself? I don't like the thought of him being so far from the doctor.

The doctor can't do very much for him. Living in the clean air from the sea is good. These days he isn't well, soon he may be better. Don't worry, he is hanging on to life and the Island. They began to push the boat down over rollers towards the water. Last week Alec had said quite abruptly as he was stirring the boiled potatoes for the ducks: at least, you will have this land if I die.

At least, I have the Island.

Well, well, said the man, making an effort to joke; tell the Captain from me that I'll come over to see him if he comes for me himself. Tell him I wouldn't trust my life to a lady, even though the boat has got a good engine and knows her own way home.

He shook her arm: you are a stout girl.

Mr Davies coming down, said the boy, looking over his shoulder as he heaved on the side of the boat. The postmaster came on to the beach through the narrow passage between the hotel and the churchyard. His overcoat flapped round him in the wind. He had something white in his hand. The boat floated; Bridget waded out and stowed away her provisions and parcels. By the time she had made a second journey Mr Davies was at the water's edge.

Another letter for you, Mrs Ritsin, he said. Very sorry, it had got behind the old-age pension books. He peered at her, longing to know what was in the letter, dying to find out what her feelings would be when she saw the handwriting. He had already devoured the envelope with his eyes, back and front, reading the postmark and the two sentences written in pencil at the back. He knew it was a letter from Ceridwen to her husband.

A letter for the Captain, said the postmaster, and watched her closely.

Thank you. She took it, resisting the temptation to read the words that caught her eye on the back of the envelope. She put it away in the large pocket of her oilskin along with the rest.

The postmaster sucked in his checks and mumbled something. So Mrs Morrison will be back here soon, he suddenly shot at her. Only the grocer's boy, whistling as he kicked the shingle, did not respond to what he said. Griff looked from her to the postmaster, she studied the postmaster's hypocritical smile. Her head went up, she was able to smile: oh, yes, of course, Mrs Morrison is sure to come over when the weather is better. What did he know, why should he want to know?

It was like a death; every hour that she had to spend on the mainland gave her fresh wounds.

Thank you, Mr Davies. Goodbye, Griff, see you next week if the weather isn't too bad. She climbed into the motor-boat and weighed anchor. She bent over the engine and it began to live. The grocer's boy was drifting away, still kicking the beach as if he bore it a grudge. Mr Davies called in a thin voice ... great care ... wish you would ... the Race and ...

Griff waved, and roared like a horn: tell him I'll take the next calf if it is a good one.

It was his way of wishing her God-speed. Linking the moment's hazard to the safety of future days.

She waved her hand. The men grew small, they and the gravestones of blue and green slate clustered round the medieval church at the top of the sand. The village drew into itself, fell into perspective against the distant mountains.

It was lonely in the bay. She took comfort from the steady throbbing of the engine. She drew Ceridwen's letter from her pocket. She read: if it is *very* fine, Auntie Grace and I will come over next weekend. Arriving Saturday tea-time Porthbychan; Please meet.

Now she understood what Mr Davies had been getting at. Ceridwen and the aunt. She shivered suddenly and felt the flesh creeping on her face and arms. The sea was bleak and washed of colour under the shadow of a long roll of mist that stretched from the level of the water almost to the sun. It was nine o'clock in the evening. She could not reach the anchorage before ten and though it was summertime, darkness would have fallen before she reached home. She hoped Alec's dog would be looking out for her on the headland.

The wind blew fresh, but the wall of mist did not seem to move at all. She wondered if Penmaen Du and the mountain would be visible when she rounded the cliffs into the Race. Soon now she should be able to see the

Island mountain. She knew every Islandman would sooner face a storm than fog.

So Ceridwen wanted to come over, did she? For the weekend, and with the aunt's support. Perhaps she had heard at last that another woman was looking after her sick husband that she did not want but over whom she was jealous as a tigress. The weekend was going to be merry hell. Bridget realised that she was very tired.

The mainland, the islets, the cliff-top farms of the peninsula fell away. Porpoise rolling offshore towards the Race made her heart lift for their companionship.

She took a compass-bearing before she entered the white silence of the barren wall of fog. Immediately she was both trapped and free. Trapped because it was still daylight and yet she was denied sight, as if blindness had fallen, not blindness where everything is dark, but blindness where eyes are filled with vague light and they strain helplessly. Is it that I cannot see, is this blindness? The horror was comparable to waking on a black winter night and being unable to distinguish anything, until in panic she thought, has my sight gone? And free because the mind could build images on walls of mist, her spirit could lose itself in tunnels of vapour.

The sound of the motor-boat's engine was monstrously exaggerated by the fog. Like a giant heart it pulsed: thump, thump. There was a faint echo, as if another boat, a ghost ship, moved near by. Her mind had too much freedom in these gulfs.

The motor-boat began to pitch like a bucking horse. She felt depth upon depth of water underneath the boards on which her feet were braced. It was the Race. The tide poured across her course. The brightness of cloud reared upward from the water's face. Not that it was anywhere uniform in density; high up there would suddenly be a thinning, a tearing apart of vapour with a wan high blue showing through, and once the jaundiced, weeping sun was partly visible, low in the sky, which told her that she was still on the right bearing. There were grey-blue caverns of shadow that seemed like patches of land, but they were effaced in new swirls of cloud, or came about her in imprisoning walls, tunnels along which the boat moved only to find nothingness at the end. Unconsciously, she had gritted her teeth when she ran into the fog-bank. Her tension remained. Two ghosts were beside her in the boat, Ceridwen, in a white fur coat, was sitting amidships and facing her, huddled together, cold and unhappy in the middle of the boat, her knees pressed against the casing of the engine. Alec's ghost sat in the bows. As a figurehead he leaned away from her, his face half lost in opaque cloud.

I will get back safely, I will get home, she said aloud, looking ahead to make the image of Ceridwen fade. But the phantom persisted; it answered her spoken thought.

No, you'll drown, you won't ever reach the anchorage. The dogfish will have you.

I tell you I can do it. He's waiting for me, he needs me.

Alec turned round, his face serious. When you get across the Race, if you can hear the foghorn, he said quietly, you are on the wrong tack. If you can't hear it, you're all right; it means you are cruising safely along the foot of the cliffs . . . When you get home, will you come to me, be my little wife?

Oh, my dear, she answered, I could weep or laugh that you ask me now, here. Yes, if I get home.

Soon you'll be on the cold floor of the sea, said Ceridwen.

Spouts of angry water threatened the boat that tossed sideways. Salt sprays flew over her.

Careful, careful, warned Alec. We are nearly on Pen Cader, the rocks are near now, we are almost out of the Race.

A seabird flapped close to her face, then with a cry swerved away, its claws pressed backward.

Above the noise of the engine there was now a different sound, that of water striking land. For an instant she saw the foot of a black cliff. Wet fangs snapped at her. Vicious fangs, how near they were. Shaken by the sight, by the rock death that waited, she turned the boat away from the Island. She gasped as she saw white spouting foam against the black and slimy cliff. She was once more alone. Alec and Ceridwen, leaving her to the sea, had been sucked into the awful cloud, this vapour without substance or end. She listened for the foghorn. No sound from the lighthouse. A break in the cloud above her head drew her eyes. A few yards of the mountaintop of the Island was visible, seeming impossibly high, impossibly green and homely. Before the eddying mists rejoined she saw a thin shape trotting across the steep grass slope, far, far up near the crest of the hill. Leaning forward, she said aloud: O look, the dog. It was Alec's dog keeping watch for her. The hole in the mist closed up, the shroud fell thicker than ever. It was terrible, this loneliness, this groping that seemed as if it might go on for ever.

Then she heard the low-throated horn blaring into the fog. It came from somewhere on her right hand. So in avoiding the rocks she had put out too far to sea and had overshot the anchorage. She must be somewhere off the southern headland near the pirate's rock. She passed a line of lobster floats.

She decided to stop the engine and anchor where she was, hoping that the fog would clear at nightfall. Then she would be able to return on to her proper course. There was an unnatural silence after she had cut off the engine. Water knocked against the boat.

Cold seeped into her bones from the planks. With stiff wet hands she opened the bag of provisions, taking off the crust of a loaf and spreading butter on it with her gutting knife. As she ate, she found that for the first time in weeks she had leisure in which to review her life. For when she was on the farm it was eat, work, sleep, eat, work, sleep, in rotation.

I have sinned or happiness is not for me, she thought. It was her heart's great weakness that she could not rid herself of superstitious beliefs.

Head in hands, she asked: But how have I sinned? I didn't steal another woman's husband. They had already fallen apart when I first met Alec. Is too great happiness itself a sin? Surely it's only because I am frightened of the fog that I ask, have I sinned, is this my punishment? When the sun shines I take happiness with both hands. Perhaps it's wrong to be happy when half the people of the world are chain-bound and hungry, cut off from the sun. If you scratch below the surface of most men's minds you find that they are bleeding inwardly. Men want to destroy themselves. It is their only hope. Each one secretly nurses the death-wish, to be god and mortal in one; not to die at nature's order, but to cease on his own chosen day. Man has destroyed so much that only the destruction of all life will satisfy him.

How can it be important whether I am happy or unhappy? And yet it's difficult for me to say, I am only one, what does my fate matter? For I want to be fulfilled like other women. What have I done to be lost in winding sheets of fog?

And he will be standing in the door wondering that I do not come.

For how long had she sat in the gently rocking boat? It was almost dark and her eyes smarted from constant gazing. Mist weighed against her eyeballs. She closed her eyes for relief.

Something was staring at her. Through drawn lids she felt the steady glance of a sea creature. She looked at the darkening waves. Over an area of a few yards she could see; beyond, the wave was cloud, the cloud was water. A dark, wet-gleaming thing on the right. It disappeared before she could make out what it was. And then, those brown beseeching eyes of the seal cow. She had risen near by, her mottled head scarcely causing a ripple. Lying on her back in the grey-green gloom of the sea she waved her flippers now outwards to the woman, now inwards to her white breast, saying, come to me, come to me, to the caverns where shark bones lie like tree stumps, bleached, growth-ringed like trees.

Mother seal, seal cow. The woman stretched out her arms. The attraction of those eyes was almost strong enough to draw her to salt death. The head disappeared. The dappled back turned over in the opaque water, and dived. Bridget gripped the side of the boat, praying that this gentle visitant should not desert her.

Hola, hola, hola, seal mother from the eastern cave.

Come to me, come to me, come to me. The stone-grey head reappeared on the other side, on her left. Water ran off the whiskered face, she showed her profile; straight nose, and above, heavy lids drooping over melancholy eyes. When she plunged showing off her prowess, a sheen of pearly colours ran over the sleek body.

They watched one another until the light failed to penetrate the fog. After the uneasy summer twilight had fallen, the woman was still aware of the presence of the seal. She dozed off into a shivering sleep through which she heard faintly the snorting of the sea creature. A cold, desolate sound. Behind that again was the bull-throated horn bellowing into the night.

She dreamt: Alec was taking her up the mountain at night under a sky dripping with blood. Heaven was on fire. Alec was gasping for breath. The other islanders came behind, their long shadows stretching down the slope. The mountain top remained far off. She never reached it.

Out of dream, she swam to consciousness, painfully leaving

the dark figures of fantasy. A sensation of swimming upward through fathoms of water. The sea of her dreams was dark and at certain levels between sleeping and waking a band of light ran across the waves. Exhaustion made her long to fall back to the sea-floor of oblivion, but the pricking brain floated her at last on to the surface of morning.

She awoke with a great wrenching gasp that flung her against the gunwale. Wind walked the sea. The fog had gone, leaving the world raw and disenchanted in the false dawn. Already, gulls were crying for a new day. Wet and numb with cold, the woman looked about her. At first it was impossible to tell off what shore the boat was lying. For a few minutes it was enough to know that she was after all at anchor so close to land.

Passing down the whole eastern coastline, she had rounded the south end and was a little way past Mallt's bay on the west. The farmhouse, home, seemed near across the fore-shortened fields. Faint light showed in the kitchen window, a warm glow in the grey landscape. It was too early for the other places, Goppa, Pen Isaf, to show signs of life. Field, farm, mountain, sea, and sky. What a simple world. And below, the undercurrents.

Mechanically she started up the engine and raced round to the anchorage through mounting sea spray and needles of rain.

She made the boat secure against rising wind, then trudged through seaweed and shingle, carrying the supplies up into the boathouse. She loitered inside after putting down the bags of food. Being at last out of the wind, no longer pitched and tumbled on the sea, made her feel that she was in a vacuum. Wind howled and thumped at the walls. Tears of salt water raced down the body of a horse scratched long ago on the window by Alec. Sails stacked under the roof shivered in the draught forced under the slates. She felt that she was spinning wildly in some mad dance. The floor rose and fell as the waves had done. The earth seemed to slide away and come up again under her feet. She leant on the windowsill, her forehead pressed to the pane. Through a crack in the glass wind poured in a cold stream across her cheek. Nausea rose in her against returning to the shore for the last packages. After that there would be almost the length of the Island to walk. At the thought she straightened herself, rubbing the patch of skin on her forehead where pressure on the window had numbed it. She fought her way down to the anchorage. Spume blew across the rocks, covering her sea boots. A piece of wrack was blown into the wet tangle of her hair. Picking up the bag of provisions, she began the return journey. Presently she stopped, put down the bag, and went again to the waves. She had been so long with them that now the thought of going inland was unnerving. Wading out until water swirled round her knees she stood relaxed, bending like a young tree under the wind's weight. Salt was crusted on her lips and hair. Her feet were sucked by outdrawn shingle. She no longer wished to struggle but to let a wave carry her beyond the world.

I want sleep, she said to the sea. O God, I am so tired, so tired. The sea sobbed sleep, the wind mourned, sleep.

Oystercatchers flying in formation, a pattern of black and white and scarlet, screamed: we are St Bride's birds, we saved Christ, we rescued the Saviour.

A fox-coloured animal was coming over the weedy rocks of the point. It was the dog, shivering and mist-soaked as if he had been out all night. He must have been lying in a cranny and so missed greeting her when she had landed. He fawned about her feet, barking unhappily.

They went home together, passing Pen Isaf that slept: Goppa too. It was about four o'clock of a summer daybreak. She picked two mushrooms glowing in their own radiance.

Memories came of her first morning's walk on the Island. There had been a green and lashing sea and gullies of damp rock, and parsley fern among loose stones. Innocent beginning, uncomplicated, shadowless. As if looking on the dead from the pinnacle of experience, she saw herself as she had been.

She opened the house door: a chair scraped inside. Alec stood in the kitchen white with strain and illness.

So you did come, he said dully.

Yes, she said with equal flatness, putting down the bags.

How sick, how deathly he looked.

Really, you shouldn't have sat up all night for me. He stirred the pale ashes; a fine white dust rose.

Look, there's still fire, and the kettle's hot. He coughed. They drank the tea in silence, standing far apart. Her eyes never left his face. And the sea lurched giddily under her braced feet. Alec went and sat before the hearth. Bridget came up behind his chair and pressed her cheek to his head. She let her arms fall slackly round his neck. Her hands hung over his chest. Tears grew in her eyes, brimming the lower lids so that she could not see. They splashed on to his clenched fists. He shuddered a little. Without turning his head, he said: Your hair's wet. You must be so tired.

Yes, she said, so tired. Almost worn out.

Come, let us go to bed for an hour or two.

You go up, she answered, moving away into the back kitchen; I must take off my wet clothes first.

Don't be long. Promise me you won't be long. He got up out of the wicker chair, feeling stiff and old, to be near her where she leant against the slate table. One of her hands was on the slate, the other was peeling off her oilskin trousers.

He said: don't cry. I can't bear it if you cry.

I'm not, I'm not. Go to bed please.

I thought you would never get back.

She took the bundle of letters out of the inner pocket of

her coat and put them on the table. She said: there's one for you from Ceridwen.

Never mind about the letters. Come quickly to me. She stood naked in the light that spread unwillingly from sea and sky. Little channels of moisture ran down her flanks, water dripped from her hair over the points of her breasts. As she reached for a towel he watched the skin stretch over the fragile ribs. He touched her thigh with his fingers, almost a despairing gesture. She looked at him shyly, and swiftly bending, began to dry her feet. Shaking as if from ague, she thought her heart's beating would be audible to him.

He walked abruptly away from her, went upstairs. The boards creaked in his bedroom.

Standing in the middle of the floor surrounded by wet clothes, she saw through the window how colour was slowly draining back into the world. It came from the sea, into the wild irises near the well, into the withy beds in the corner of the field. Turning, she went upstairs in the brightness of her body.

He must have fallen asleep so soon as he lay down. His face was bleached, the bones too clearly visible under the flesh. Dark folds of skin lay loosely under his eyes. Now that the eyes were hidden, his face was like a death-mask. She crept quietly into bed beside him.

Through the open window came the lowing of cattle. The cows belonging to Goppa were being driven up for milking. Turning towards the sleeping man, she put her left hand on his hip. He did not stir.

She cried then as if she would never be able to stop, the tears gushing down from her eyes until the pillow was wet and stained from her weeping.

What will become of us, what will become of us?

mistaken identity

Jo Mazelis

Power 1998
second fiction anthology

Committee rooms. Committee rooms that are big and blank and impersonal. With tables arranged in a square, circle or rectangle. Chairs with leather seats all placed just so. All facing inwards. All facing each other. Each placed one foot from its neighbour. Twelve inches, very precise.

This is where the world turns. Men and women in suits sit here. They say yes, no, nod sagely. They make amendments, think, talk, jot notes. The walls that surround them are white and bare except for one large portrait which watches them. A man in a suit done in oils. How did he find the time in his busy schedule to pose? Did his wife suggest the green serge suit? Or was it debated on by the committee? And the tie? That's surely the old school tie? Or the Honourable Member's tie? None but the initiated will recognise it. For them it marks him. Points to his importance in the world.

Every time the cleaner comes into this room she bows to the picture. She does this because she can. Because no one is looking. Because no one would care. For her it's become like touching wood to stop bad things from happening. Like throwing spilt salt over her left shoulder to blind the devil. And besides that he looks a bit lonely up there on the wall. His eyes, she thinks, look sad.

The cleaner is eighteen years old and has long blonde pony-tailed hair and a pretty face. She wears jeans, trainers, an old sweater that belonged to her brother and a shapeless overall of baby-blue nylon which she hates. Everyone recognises the overall. It marks her out. Shows her place, just as the man's suit shows his. But the cleaner doesn't make the world turn, she just cleans it.

She squirts the world with polish, rubs it with a cloth until it shines. Removes its ashtrays and empty coffee cups, vacuums it, empties its waste-paper bins. Places its chairs in their regimented positions, twelve inches between each. One foot. Just so. She doesn't water the plants, that's someone else's job. She doesn't rearrange the tables. Doesn't open or close the blinds. Doesn't touch the picture, except to carefully run the feather duster across the frame. Of the last, she is certain she is doing right, as the supervisor was clear on that point. 'Don't polish this,' she had said, 'and don't scrub it with Vim either.' As if. How stupid did the woman think she was?

When the cleaner comes here at night, after all the committee members and the managers and personal assistants and secretaries and word processors and receptionists have gone home, the room is hers. She wheels her trolley up the corridor, unloads the vacuum, the cans of polish, the dusters and the black plastic bags, then carries it all into the committee room and lays it out in readiness. Sometimes the room looks just the same as when she left it the day before. It looks just as if no one had been in there at all. She peeps in the waste-paper bin nearest the door. It's empty. Not even an illicit cigarette end or a suspect tissue, and she's seen plenty of both. So the room is spotlessly clean. That would please her if she could knock off early, but she can't and so she glances at her watch in order to judge how much time she has to kill.

Instead of vacuuming the floor she runs her eye over it. She finds one tiny fleck of lint, probably from her duster last night, and picks it up between thumb and forefinger and drops it in her rubbish sack. Next she decides to polish the table. This is partly so that the room will smell freshly cleaned, but mostly because she actually enjoys doing this. Sometimes, when she is in a particularly indignant mood, she sprays words in large letters across the table. Words like 'WANKERS' or 'ARSEHOLE'. Today she's in a gentler frame of mind so she sprays a large heart and inside it writes 'Olivia loves . . .' She hesitates then – who does she love? – and settles for a question mark.

Olivia. What a name to be stuck with. She blames Olivia

de Havilland for this indignity. Olivia de Havilland, Gone With The bloody Wind and her mother's over-romantic imagination. She gets her duster and draws it over her words in large sweeps, turns her love into a beautiful shine. A shine that will reflect the faces of the committee members. A shine which will mirror their eloquent frowns, their expensive shirts. Their ties will make a river of colour with their stripes of blue and emerald and scarlet and gold. As if they'll notice. But it passes the time. Offers a little variation, a stand against the tedium.

Olivia does corridor Q which consists of one committee room, five offices, two public toilets, male and female, and two private 'washrooms', also male and female. She does the corridor itself which is the most boring part, being straight and long. The equivalent, she thinks, of motorways for long-distance lorry drivers. This work takes three hours out of her life each evening from Monday to Friday. On Saturday she works in the market selling bread, a job she's had since she was fifteen. On Friday and Saturday night she works in the Quayside Nitespot as a barmaid. Olivia's friend Sue works in the casino and says she'll try to get Olivia work there. The pay's not much better but the tips are good. 'Oh,' says Sue, 'the tips. You wouldn't believe it.' Olivia does believe it, but all she can do is wait and hope . . .

Olivia's been cleaning corridor Q since she started this job back in June. It's now the beginning of December and she no longer wonders what the rest of the building is like. She no longer yearns to see corridors A, B, C, D, E, F, G, H, I, J, K, L, M, N, 0 and P leave alone clean them. All she wants to do now is get a better job. Get a better job and fall in love.

More than any other, the big committee room with its floor-to-ceiling windows and its starkness makes her aware of the changes in the weather and the seasons. In June she watched the sun sink while she cleaned the room and went home in the last of its light. Now it's dark when she arrives and the windows, with only blackness behind them, have become enormous mirrors. Out there, beyond the brightly lit room, another room hovers like a twin world. The cleaner can see herself, a little figure in a blue overall. A nobody. It reminds her of that poem about nobody which the teacher had read aloud at school. It had been the first time she'd been touched by words in the alien language of poetry. She remembered how she'd felt a sweet lilt of recognition in the pit of her stomach, and breathed an involuntary sigh, and then Ed Thomas had said, in his belligerent, full-of-it way, 'Yeah, but she's not nobody, is she, Miss? She wouldn't be in the book if she was no one.' The teacher – one of those new young hopeful ones – had just wilted into silence, while Ed Thomas had given the class an evil leer and rocked his chair back, his arms resolutely folded, proud to be an angry zero who could see through all the lies.

This December the weather is mild, but in the office black heat blasts from the radiators regardless. Olivia's feeling uncomfortably hot. She hasn't been sitting still, coolly talking, calmly shuffling paper, she's been pushing around an industrial-size vacuum. She's been rubbing and lifting and shifting and lugging and scrubbing, and she's hot.

The overall is sticky so she unzips it and takes off her jumper. She takes off her shoes and socks, hopping about to keep her balance. She was going to keep the overall on over her T-shirt, but that's even more uncomfortable. The clammy nylon sticks to the skin of her arms and neck, so she throws the hated garment through the door where it lands near her trolley. Now that she's just in her jeans and T-shirt she feels much better. Not only cooler but also much more herself.

She checks her watch. There's still time to kill. She goes to the corner of the room and stands, back erect, head and arms held high as if she were about to dive into a pool. She's aware of the carpet hot and bristling under her feet. Of her breathing and her stillness. Then she throws the top part of her body down and forward. Her hands reach the floor and her legs arc upward and for a moment she hovers there like an acrobatic toy. Then she flips down into a crab, but she can't quite lift herself into the standing position again, so she collapses instead. Next she throws herself into four perfect cartwheels, one after another, which bring her to within inches of the window.

Momentarily dizzy, Olivia faces her reflection, remembers that this glass is not a mirror, but a window, imagines reports of gymnastic goings on. Imagines the supervisor's sarcasm, her own humiliation. She frowns, then cups her hands around her eyes and presses her brow on the cold glass and stares out. The town is spelled out in a constellation of street lights. Over the far hills patterns of yellow dots traverse the night. Nearby four towers of bright white light illuminate the football ground and closer still, across the car park and the dual carriageway, the prison offers its broken rectangles of half-light to the stars, to her eyes.

Unlike the little terraced houses with their downstairs glow and flicker of blue TV, and unlike the flats with their patterns of occupation and emptiness, the prison has only two states. There, all the cell lights are uniformly either off or on, regardless of the occupants' needs or desires. Olivia stares at the curtainless windows and wonders who lives beyond them, what men they imprison. She doesn't imagine rapists or murderers. She knows that they are there, but thinks instead about the beaten men, the half-innocent, the young, gone-wrong, never-given-a-chance men. Men like her brother Jake. But Jake is in Strangeways in Manchester. If he was here she'd be able to visit him. She'd be able, maybe, to wave to him.

She counts the windows. There are ten across by five

down. Fifty windows. Fifty souls. Fifty narrow beds. She imagines a man like Jake. He's probably in there for drugs, like Jake. Probably only sold stuff to his friends. Then found he suddenly had a lot of friends, like Jake. Then no friends, also like Jake. She'd been to see Jake once since he'd been inside. The journey took four and a half hours and someone on the train, an insipid woman in a pink shell suit with three screaming children, had sat with her and attempted a conversation. 'Visiting friends?' she'd said. Olivia had just said 'No,' and turned away.

Olivia looks away from the main block of old grey stone to the newer red-brick extension and counts the windows again. Eight across and only three down. And then she sees him.

He's standing on the second floor at the third window from the left. His arms are outstretched, holding the bars at shoulder level. She can't see his face, the light behind him makes him a silhouette. But she can read his sadness in that pose. He's a crucifixion of misery. He doesn't move.

Does he see her?

Tentatively, she raises one arm and makes a slow arc at the night. And slowly, like a strange mirror which responds only after a mistimed delay, like a star whose light reaches earth long after its last flicker has died and given way to endless night, the figure raises its arm in an echoing arc.

In the prison, the guard, who has been standing by the window in the staff room, yawns and, as is his habit, fingers the heavy metallic bulk of the keys that hang from his belt. He smiles as he thinks of the girl in the office block opposite.

The night hangs between them, a curtain of blackness. Far away and long ago, unnoticed by either of them, a nameless star gives its last violent pulse of light, shrinks down to the volume of zero and becomes a black hole that swallows everything within its pull.

poor players

Rhian Thomas

Luminous and Forlorn 1994

first fiction anthology

The third of October was the wrong time to visit the town. All along the promenade, the hot-dog sellers and deck chair merchants and seashell women had boarded up and gone away, leaving the salt to pick at their paintwork through another long winter. In the first sullen streaks of morning newspaper clung damp in doorways as if waiting, the coming day still uncertain. The houses grasped the last shreds of night while a milk float hummed in a side street. He stopped at the end of the promenade, hesitated for a moment with his hand laid tentatively on the wet railing, then moved quickly down the gritty steps.

At the bottom, he paused again, momentarily dismayed to think how the coarse sand would claw his shoes, but he left the last step behind him with resolve. Beneath the sea wall the beach was empty and long and bleak, stretching out in a wide grey curve behind him where the town washed over it. He moved on, away from the dead eyes of the kiosks and guesthouses, with the cold, ringing emptiness of the sea thrashing in his ears. Recoiling inside his drab anorak, he threw a watchful eye over the sea, glad to see that the tide-table, specially purchased and stored away months beforehand, had not let him down. The waves were moving back, leaving a bright layer of water across the flat sands. It would be hours before the expanse up ahead was cut off again. He breathed slowly into his upturned collar, feeling the knuckles wrapped around the heavy spade handle stiffen with cold and blocked circulation. He stopped and swung the spade up to rest across his shoulder, where the wind snapped at the black bin liner wrapped around it. Blinking, he gazed round, suddenly dwarfed against the vast, sweeping sky, wondering what in the world he was doing here. No walls to keep things in place, no lines; only the heaving sea that reaches out and takes what it pleases. But he'd let go of the railings. The last of his safe lines was left behind.

*

He had had no trouble finding a room for the night. The road from the station was littered with bed-and-breakfast signs, swinging from verandas, hanging in windows. Number seventy-eight, Park Mount, boasted neither a park nor a hill to stand on. Its steps led directly from the front door to the pavement. A single window-box hung by gritted teeth somewhere on the second floor. Cramming misgivings into the very back of his mind, he'd allowed himself to be scrutinised in the cold hallway, pouring out hopeful flattery until Mrs Worth's eyes lost some of their edge.

'I've always thought it was such a lovely town.' His arms ached. He wanted to put his bags down, but didn't dare. 'I travel through every day – on the train, on my way to work.' She waited, arms folded stiff across a chest strong enough to stand up to any number of unruly holidaymakers. 'I've always wanted to – to spend some time here.' She was almost satisfied. 'I've always said to myself, why bother trekking across the country for a holiday when there are such lovely places just on the doorstep, as it were?'

She had nodded, her short, brittle eyelashes blinking rapidly. He breathed, grateful for her approval. 'And so,' he finished, 'as I've got a week's holiday to visit my sister, I thought, why not make it a real holiday? So I wondered – do you have a room, just for one night?'

Of course she had a room. Mrs Worth led him up the stairs, congratulating herself on her discerning clientele. This one, for instance, could be retiring before long, and might be good for no end of weekends. She gave him the front room and watched proudly as he hid his dismay and said politely, 'What a lovely view.'

As his ears started to ache with the cold, he repeated to himself, this is now. I am not dreaming. His heels sank with every step, and sand crept in over the edges of his shoes. He crossed the last of the blackened, half-buried breakwaters, and then he was out on the long stretch of unbroken sand where even in summer only the least sociable holidaymakers ventured. He was further from the town now; he saw that the headland was reinforced with concrete to support the road above. The muted roar of the waves and the slow-crying gulls filled his head from one direction, and the dull, echoing hum of the coast road from the other, and he picked his tedious path somewhere in between. This is real, it is happening.

He glanced at his watch, his last ticking prop of reality, gripping his wrist. Almost half-past seven. The bay was awash with shades of blue, the sky, daubed across with great wet watercolour clouds running at the edges, split here and there with puddles of bright light. Ten more minutes. Now the sand was less even, twisted into gouged curves by the retreating waves, with streaking pools of water left behind. There was a salty tidemark across his leather shoes. Looking up, he saw the words 'Kevin loves Julie' scrawled in a barely convincing heart shape on a convenient slab of concrete, and wondered where his indignation had gone. He pictured himself under painted walls at the station each morning, a little man with no surprises, neck hunched into his shoulders, unflinching against the world. Hooligans. Why did they suddenly have his sympathy? They just wanted to leave their mark somewhere, something to show that they'd lived that moment. They'd be forgotten soon enough. They'd forget ... He shook himself. At seven-thirty on any ordinary Tuesday morning he would be sitting on the train, shoes polished, trousers pressed, hair combed smooth, surrounded by men who avoided sitting next to each other. Already, he could feel his peppery hair flying wild. As for the anorak – goodness only knows how it had survived his sweeping tidiness and stayed in the house so long. The tight skin of his knuckle was white where he held the spade, shot through with red in the cracks. No one would have recognised him.

*

As the interminably cosy evening at Park Mount wore on Mrs Worth had run out of questions. His life could only be stretched so far in polite conversation. She had already turned back to her faded magazine when he summoned the nerve to ask,

'I was hoping to take a walk along the beach in the morning. Would you – I mean, I don't suppose you might have a spade I could borrow?'

Mrs Worth's eyes were on him immediately, scouring his face for an explanation, and he withered. In this weather? She turned to her husband. Mr Worth watched him, and then said, with some doubt,

'You must be a bit of a biologist, then?'

'Yes, that's right,' he nodded, clutching at his lifeline gratefully, 'yes, I'm very interested in ...'

They waited. He fumbled in his mind for snapshots of himself as a child on the beach. 'Sandworms,' he whispered. They looked away. The gas fire hissed.

Mrs Worth turned back to her magazine, and mumbled something about the outhouse. Her husband gazed at him and said, 'I'm sure we can find something.'

He returned to his white room, but was afraid to sleep in case the dismal walls swallowed him up. He left the bedside light on and slept, and dreamed that the door was locked, and that the spade couldn't break it down.

The railway line ran along the beach only for a short way, but for a few seconds passengers could see right out across the sands. Strange, it was all so different from this angle. It was silent from inside a train window, where all the world was inside the glass shooting towards city streets and offices in straight, reliable lines. Now, as he lifted his face, the wind beat about his ears, rattled his trouser legs, and stung his eyes. He could taste the salt on his lips, and the air wouldn't leave him alone. He could feel it all over, driving through layers of clothing, cold and clean. They had no idea, those men on the train. To them it was only a picture, an empty picture. How often had he seen it flash by himself?

Stepping off the train in the early afternoon, at the wrong station, had been like walking in a sick dream. He had felt guilty, moving along the platform with housewives and pensioners, constantly reminding himself that there was no reason to hurry. He forced himself to stop and buy a magazine, then stuffed it into his overnight bag, knowing that he would never read it. The autumn afternoon was sodden, and threatened fog. At the station entrance the housewives and pensioners left him behind.

He looked at his watch again. Almost time. At seven forty-two the train would run by on the headland and into the town, and men in pressed trousers and polished shoes would gaze at the sea and then look at their watches to check they were on time. Once, he had looked out of the window and seen a man alone on the beach, folded over by the wind, his back turned to the world; and even as he'd dismissed him as an eccentric and looked at his watch again, he'd envied him. To be out of that train, not to care whether it ran or not … he sighed deeply. The clouds were dragging their torn hems across the sky and the sun spilled scattered shafts of light over the waves. He scanned the headland, then turned and walked towards the water's edge, leaving shaky, flooded footprints in the wet sand. The full force of the wind caught him in the face, taking his breath, and he walked slowly, the cold air inflating his throat. His steps threw shining beads of water off his shoes. This is real, he thought. I am here. A cold silver stream of sunlight crept along the horizon, and the last trickle of the waves' onslaught washed safely around his feet. Very soon now. He tightened his eyelids against the sun, and threw his gaze all around. They would be able to see him here. A corner of the black bin liner had worked itself loose from the spade, and the wind tugged and swept it like a banner, an emblem. His shoulder ached. Not long ...

From somewhere in the distance the railway tracks rang with the rush of a train. He drew himself up straight and as tall as he could. The wind froze his face, and he could feel the colour on his cheeks. The sound grew stronger, mingling with the persistent traffic and the numb fire of the waves. Louder. It would almost be in sight now; but he stood straight, facing the sea, feeling the wind laugh at his thinning hair. His ears were burning with cold, and the freezing air ached inside his head. The thundering rattle of the train rang out over the beach. Were they watching? Little men with no surprises, little men whose eyes he avoided every morning; he wanted them to watch. The sound was brimming through the clouds, beating at him with the wind, and he swayed and stood his ground. Look: there's someone on the beach. And – something over his shoulder? His hands ached with ice in the bone. Were they watching? Did they see him stand?

The roar died away as the train wound its way into the town, echoing under the bridge and between the quietly waking houses. He lifted the spade from his shoulder, bending slowly to let it rest on the sand. The gulls spiralled dolefully overhead, crying for the unrest of the sea and the sky. Pressing his fingers to the warmth of his neck, he felt the slow tingle of blood moving beneath the skin. There was a dark ship waiting beneath the shadowy horizon. He could make out its angular outline against the grey sea; so far away. The cold, bright glare of the early sun retired, and the day began. The rumble of traffic on the coast road grew more frequent as he stood, the waves a little further down the sand. The bin liner clung about his wet feet. It was a long walk back to town.

the madness of winifred owen

Bertha Thomas

Stranger Within the Gates 2008

Honno Classics, fiction anthology

The Old Face

'Not from an old face will you ever get the same fine effect as from an old house.' The old saying was brought to my mind by the sudden sight of an exception to the truth of it in the person of Mrs Trinaman, landlady of the Ivybush, at Pontycler, in the heart of South Wales.

It was in the summer of 1899, when the cycling fever was at its height in all spinsters of spirit. I and my 'Featherweight' had come three hundred miles from our London home, nominally to look up the tombs of forgotten Welsh ancestors in undiscoverable churchyards; more truly for the treat of free roving among strangers in a strange land. So much I knew of the country I was in – that Wales, the stranger within England's gates, remains a stranger still.

At Pontycler, a score or so of cottages dumped down round a cross-roads tavern in a broad green upland valley, I thought to halt for the night, but was met by objections. The accommodations at the Ivybush was not for such as myself. So the striking-looking woman above named – plainly intimated.

A woman well on in the fifties, stout and grey, form and features thickened by years and the wear of life; a woman substantially and spotlessly clad in black stuff skirt, white apron and cross-over, and crowned by a frilled cap as awe-instilling as a justice's wig. Yet, to look at her was to feel that there, once, stood a beautiful girl. There was power in the face, there was mind; but it held you fast in girl's fashion by some indefinably agreeable attraction.

'Board and lodging that are good enough for you are good enough for me,' I thought, and said so.

At that she fairly laughed, and agreed to house me, for one night only.

The Old House

While the room was preparing I strolled out on foot. Led by a habit of avoiding the beaten track, I presently left the road for a lesser lane; the lane for an approach to a farm; the farmyard for a rough upward track between pastures screened from view by hedgerows so tall as nearly to meet overhead.

On a sudden break in the left bank I saw, close by, on higher ground, an old house looking down on me as if it were in surprise at the intrusion. A small, grey-stone, slate-roofed house, in a curious stage of dilapidation. The sash windows, carved wooden porch, broad grass-plat in front shaded by a lofty ilex and dense foliaged yew, also some handsome wrought-iron gates beyond, marked it as a dwelling-place of another class to the snug thatched farm just passed, or the jerry-built Pontycler cottages. Some steep stone steps in the hedge-gap led me up to the little green; and through the broken front windows I saw inside – saw solid mahogany doors and marble mantels, but ceilings coming down, floors falling in, and no sign whatever of present or recent occupation.

An elderly shepherd, escorting a few sheep up the track I had left, told me that Cilcorwen – so the house was named – belonged to distant folk who, unable to agree as to its use and upkeep, let it go thus to decay.

I remarked that it bore traces of better keeping at some time or other.

'Ah,' he said meditatively, leaning on his pitchfork, 'that was when Dr Dathan had it, twenty, thirty years back, when I was a lad. Twelve years or more he was living there.'

'Rather an awkward, out-of-the-way residence for a medical man,' I let fall.

'Ah, well, but he – Dr Dathan – was not one who went doctoring the sick, unless in some sudden great need,' said my informant. 'He was always at his books – *and other things* – studying – studying – all the time. A man who knew a lot more than others. Too much, they used to say.'

'Oh, a witch doctor, was he?' said I jokingly, but catching at the notion like a trout at the fly. It suited the weird little place so well.

'I do not know. Some would call him a conjurer, and feared him like a ghost,' the Welshman admitted, adding, with a sour smile, 'As a boy I wasn't afraid of no ghosts, nor anything, unless it was a mad dog or a bull, and that one man, Dr. Dathan. And I thought he *was* a ghost! He looked like one.'

'What became of him?' I asked.

But my frank curiosity made my friend cautious and suspicious. He shook his head, repeating it: 'It is all long ago. I was a lad. There are those here who could tell you more than I.'

'Mrs Trinaman, at the Ivybush, perhaps?' I hazarded, explaining that I was stopping there this night.

'Winifred Owen? She at the Ivybush?' His eye – his tone – woke up. 'Yes, indeed,' he said, nodding gravely and mysteriously. 'She should know. She should remember. I believe he did cure her once, when she went clean off her head – crazed, as you say; and was given up by the regular doctors.'

'What?' I exclaimed, startled. Here was a fact stated, more unexpected, more inconceivable than any tale of demonology or witchcraft. For if ever woman stood up looking like sanity in thick shoes, it was surely my landlady at the Ivybush.

'Aye. It was the talk of the parish! She was keeping house then for her father, Evan John David Owen, at his farm, away down yonder by Pontycler bridge. She went from here after that, rather sudden; and we never saw her no more till two – three years ago she came back to her people, and set up at Pontycler Inn, to be near her old home.'

His sheep were bleating to him to come on; we exchanged courtesies after the custom of the courteous country, and went our opposite ways.

At the Ivybush

The vision of the old house, posed there as if for a picture, stayed in my mind's eye as I retraced my steps to the Ivybush, there to find, to my dismay, that my hostess had vacated her own bedroom to give it up to me. It was too late to remonstrate. Nay, later on I encroached still further, forsaking the cold comfort of the 'parlour' for a snug corner of the oak settle by the kitchen hearth, watching Mrs Trinaman step to and from the bar serving many comers – greybeard village chatterboxes, tired quarrymen, beer carters, pert cyclists, and tramps; customers very various, but all impatient and out of temper, for a wild wet evening had set in, threatening worse. Half the conversation being carried on in the local dialect – elusive as a secret code – was to me unintelligible; but only to listen and watch her was to perceive she found the right word, way, and tone for each.

No need to teach man or boy how to behave in her presence. By-and-by they ceased to come; the storm had burst forth on a heroic scale.

She closed the door, observing, 'Wherever a man is now tonight, there, if he can, he'll stay.'

Ten minutes later she was sitting opposite me with her knitting, and we were having a friendly chat. Her remarks, her questions, showed a knowledge and understanding of men and things acquired in a wider world than Pontycler; and she readily resumed touch with it, opportunity offering. She obviously believed in class distinctions, accepting these as a social fact, without attributing to the fact such sinister importance as to resent its existence. She neither proffered her company and conversation, nor refused them when invited and welcome. But never have I been more conscious of personal and mental inferiority than in the presence of Mrs Trinaman. She simply towered – not by dint of any self-assertion – but by the sheer sense she conveyed of force of character.

Demented? She? Never! Her part in the shepherd's tale I dismissed as a fable. But I spoke of Cilcorwen and the gossip I had picked up by the wayside concerning its sometime occupier.

'Dr Dathan,' she said, quite freely. 'Yes, I knew him.'

'Was he a pretender to magic, pray; or only a quack?'

'Certainly not a quack,' she replied. 'He – he – never put his hand to cure any one if he could help it. For the rest – well, they said he practised black magic. But, I, for one, should be sorry to believe any harm of him, since to him and his "sorcery" I owe my life.'

'How could that be,' I asked, 'if, as you say, he left the healing of the sick to others?'

'Not "my life" in that sense.' She smiled enigmatically. 'Yet in more senses than one.' Her grave eyes seemed taking a long view – a backward sweep; her strong, expressive face told of deep and lasting emotional experience undergone – yet not of the sort that corrupts or warps the soul. 'It's an odd story,' she resumed. 'One that wouldn't be believed here even now – *as it happened* – which is why I never tell it.'

But as we sat there over the smokeless, glowing hearth, with the storm-wind howling round, she told it me, as follows.

The Tenant of Cilcorwen

'I was a little girl of ten when I first remember him. I think he had not long come to Cilcorwen, but wonderful tales went abroad about him from the first. A doctor who took no patients, yet who was not taking his ease and his leisure but toiled hard all day; some said, all night! Ned the poacher, whose habits took him out and about mostly at bedtime or in the dark hours, vowed the light was always burning at Cilcorwen. Two of the lower rooms were kept locked, and not even the old woman, lodging in the lean-to hovel attached, who cooked and so on for him, was permitted to meddle with them. We children used to take to our heels if we saw his figure coming down the road. I don't know why. It was odd-looking, and seemed not to belong to these parts. He wasn't of a tall make, but spare and flexible; and he wore his black hair longer than is customary. He dressed carelessly, but always like a gentleman, a London gentleman – in black, not squire or sportsman fashion as they all do here. He was sharp-featured, with eyes like two burning fire-devils; his skin wrinkled and white – yellowish white, like a buried thing dug up again, as they say.'

'And they took him for a ghost,' I said.

She laughed.

'More than likely it was the natural effect of a life spent poring over books; and breathing the unwholesome fumes and vapours of the chemicals in his laboratory. Only the pure, keen air of our Welsh hills kept him alive. Perhaps that was why he had settled down here. But the boys said it was because Pontycler being so out of the way and behindhand he could practise his forbidden unholy arts there without risk of being found out.'

'What sort of arts?'

'Nobody knew; but they whispered he spent his time

making experiments on living animals – besides dissecting dead ones; studied poisons; could cast spells; knew incantations that would poison your food. Another story said he was an anarchist and made bombs, but I think that was only because he always wore a crimson tie! Oh, there was no end to their tales. Pat Coghlan, an imp of an Irish farm-hand, boasted that, spying round Cilcorwen one winter evening and seeing the blind awry and the light burning, he climbed up on the windowsill, peeped in and saw ...'

'Saw what?'

'Dr Dathan in his shirtsleeves raising the devil. So he assured us; but it's my belief he was too scared to see anything. For the doctor turned his head, and Pat dropped away and ran for his life.

'"Corpse candles was a-burning in the garden," he told us. "If he had set eyes on me it's a dead boy would be telling you this now!" We believed every word.'

'Did he make no friends, no acquaintance, here?'

'He avoided company, never cared to see the neighbours, rich or poor, unless on business. But he was in correspondence with great doctors and learned professors all the world over; the letters he posted and the stamps on those he received showed that. Sometimes a visitor from town would come down for a few nights – someone in his own style; and now and then he went there himself for a week, always leaving Cilcorwen securely locked up. Yes, though he harmed no one, he was a mystery, and something of a terror; but no one molested him, and he stayed on so long that we got used to him and forgot to wonder or to pry. He never took the faintest interest in anything or anybody here, but was always civil-spoken and always paid his way.'

The Man in Blue

'One evening father sent me on a message to the Ivybush. A handyman had been repairing the roof there, and I was to urge him to come tomorrow to make good some damage done at our farm by a heavy gale the night before.

'Finding no one at the bar, I walked straight into the kitchen, and was taken aback at the sight there of two men – foreigners – Englishmen, that is. One was a little redcoat, and one was babbling in the foolish, rambling way of a man who is the worse for drink. The other wore a plain dark-blue uniform, and I took him for his mate, but he had such a pleasant, open face and quiet, determined look that I was not afraid to stay waiting. I noticed the tact and judgement with which he treated his companion, keeping him from making a worse fool of himself than could now be helped. In a few minutes the innkeeper came back and told me that the handyman had gone off to another job, a day's journey from Pontycler. I was very much put out, for skilled labour here is scarce. So I stood bemoaning our predicament, and the landlord shaking his head and chiming in "What a pity!" when the man in blue, who had been lending an ear, spoke – I seem to hear his voice – saying: "Now, if you'll listen to me, I'll tell you how you can do what you want done yourselves."

'And he described very precisely and clearly how the thing could be managed. But I could not follow him; I had learnt English and thought I knew it, little knowing then how much there was to know. He soon saw I was puzzled outright.

'"Well," said he, with a funny side-glance at the little redcoat slouching sleepily on the bench where you are sitting now, "I'm stranded here for tonight. You live near, you say. If you like I'll step over first thing tomorrow and do it for you myself."

'I was shy and suspicious of strangers – as we all are here –

but somehow I never once thought of refusing his offer, or even asked myself whether I could trust this man, so knowing he seemed, and yet so simple spoken! My head was full of what seemed to be quite a little adventure as I ran home. But I remember my father scolded me sharply for giving the job without bargaining for a price, and I was vexed to death that he, when the man called next day, began by haggling with him about the charge. He laughed outright; he was no journeyman tinker, and wanted no pay for lending a helping hand to a fellow-Christian. That so hurt father's pride that he walked off in a huff. The other turned to me with a sort of merry appeal in his eye. "Come, there's no pleasing you Welsh!" he complained. -

"'Don't say that!" The words slipped from me without thinking; then I felt overcome with confusion – hot and red. Our eyes had met for a moment, and I turned away, my heart beating fast.

'Well, he made short work of half a dozen jobs – leaks, broken panes, and what not; refused payment, but stayed to take a cup of tea at our table.

'He told us he was a seaman in the Royal Navy, and that he and the soldier-man had first met in the train yesterday afternoon. He had managed to keep his half-tipsy fellow-passenger quiet, till, on nearing Pontycler, the booby tried to pull the communication cord, then wanted to fight the stationmaster, who turned him out of the train as unfit to travel. Just to save him from further scrapes, the sailor threw in his lot with the culprit, piloted him to the safe shelter, for the night, of the Ivybush, and had packed him, sad and sober, off to Cardiff that morning.

'All the time I was thinking, "presently it will be thank you and goodbye – and all over!" sadly. For I liked him. Then, just as he was taking leave, he told us how, last night, Dr Dathan had come to the inn on exactly the same errand as myself, and persuaded him to stay and help patch up the roof at Cilcorwen. And (father had been called off for a moment) though he didn't say so, he let me know he was glad to be detained, because of the chance offered of seeing me again; and my heart gave a thump of rising joy.

'So we did meet, once or twice; but along with the gladness of it I was sorely, sorely troubled. He seemed very far off; and if he and his speech and ways gave me a chink view into a new life and world, it was one with which I had and could have nothing to do. For one thing, he was a servant of war. War was wicked, and all fighting men servants of sin; so said every teaching and preaching man I had ever heard. A stranger too, one of an alien race; while I, born and reared at Pontycler, belonged body and soul to the little Welsh world of my fathers. Add to that I was as good as promised to another man – Vaughan Hughes of Bryngolau, who had been courting me for some time – and father had made up his mind he was to have me. He was a farmer in a larger way than ourselves; and said spiteful things about the power of the pretty face. And though I hung back, feeling shy of the man, no one believed my bashfulness would last long. We were not brought up to consider our fancies, for father was a very masterful man. I knew that with his old and confirmed prejudice against the English and his heart set on the marriage with Vaughan Hughes, he would be frantic if he knew how I was feeling now.

'Well, a sailor's wooing is short. The fourth time we met – very gravely, very quietly, very tenderly, Walter – that was his name – asked me to be his wife.'

The Struggle

'Then the whole trouble of it plumped like a shower of stones upon me. Walter would not and could never understand why, since he had won my heart, he should not have my hand for the asking. There was no stopping him. He went straight to my father for his consent, startling him out of his wits, poor father! He went into a violent rage; then, as Walter persisted, unmoved, he broke into taunts and abuse, shouting out that all sailor men drank, had a wife in every port; loudly treating the offer as an affront to an honest Welsh girl. Walter, stupefied, turned silently to me. I stood up to my father, for the first and last time, said that I loved and wished to marry the man who had spoken; and that, come what might, I would never marry Vaughan Hughes.

'Then father broke out in the old Welsh tongue of his forefathers. Oh, he could use it and make it work, in ways Walter could never conceive of. He reproached me as treacherous and unfeeling – a girl who, for a light passing fancy for a foreign vagabond, could be false to ties of home, country, kindred, religion – every holy thing.'

'What? Can you mean that he considered that for you to marry an Englishman would be a disgrace?' I asked in wonder.

'Well, no,' she half smiled. 'I won't say. Perhaps had there been money or advantage in the match he might, though not liking, have thought it his duty not to forbid it. He knew as little about the English as you – pardon my saying it – do of Welsh people; and he judged them from the worst sort that come here because they have gone wrong in their own country. Walter's quiet assertion that he was in a position to support a wife, he scouted. Here, he had made up his mind, was a tippler, an unbeliever, a spendthrift, whose dupe I should never be if he could help it. Oh, you might just as well have tried to move the Black Mountain yonder as to reason with father on the point. The difference of language rose up suddenly like a wall between them, and father seemed to lose his power of understanding or expressing himself in any but his mother tongue. Even Walter was discouraged; felt it was hopeless to argue or to pray.

'He had to join his ship; but made me take heart, hold firm, and in a few weeks he would come back for my final answer. It was with a sinking heart I saw him go. But he wrote, he wrote!

'The next fortnight felt like a year of torment. Father was confident I had given in, and tried his best to hurry on the affair with Vaughan Hughes, who had heard about Walter and his suit, but was not jealous – not he! – refusing to take it seriously. "What, an impudent English sailor rascal from who knows where to steal his little girl?" Father, now that Walter was out of the way, had calmed down; but his pleading was hard, too terribly hard for me to resist. When he stood up and spoke you were moved and awed as by one of the prophets or patriarchs in the Old Testament. How could I want to break his heart and bring shame on the family by giving him the godless English vagabond for a son-in-law – I, the only daughter left? My head had been turned for an instant – he could forgive that. But so heartless, so undutiful, as to mean it – he couldn't believe it of me.

'I felt somehow he saw things in a wrong light and would never see them in any other. He was old, too. There was no help anywhere. I was bound to go under. My appointed place in life was here with my people, while Walter, far off in the busy world, would presently forget me. It was bitter, and yet I might have yielded but for the dread of being drawn into the other marriage. After that, no hope in this world for Walter and me – none! My brothers, the neighbours, every one were against me, and full of hard words for him who in passing by had broken, if not destroyed, the peace of our hearth.'

A Critical Interview

'There came the yearly grand fair day at Llanffelix, three miles off. Every one was starting for the town, all the girls in holiday clothes. I was in no humour for sports, and stayed to mind the house. Then, left alone with my trouble, it so possessed me and became so unbearable I half wished I had gone with the rest.

'There were butter and eggs to be taken up to Cilcorwen, and later in the day I went over with them myself. And as I went, thinking of father, of Vaughan Hughes, but mostly of Walter, whom I must give up – desperate, and at my wits' end what to do, it crossed my head, not for the first time, to consult Dr Dathan!'

'Did you really look on him as a magician?' I asked.

'Well, I won't say that I did not. And only some superhuman power, I thought, could come to my relief. It seemed a wild notion, yet as I walked on in the loneliness – every human creature was at the fair – the determination grew. I knocked at the house door, and receiving no answer, wondered if he too had gone to Llanffelix. The blinds were drawn, but the door opened to my hand, and the passage door into the sitting room stood ajar. I peeped in. Dr Dathan sat facing me at the table that seemed lit by magical stars. He was so absorbed in watching something in the glass that he never heard me on the threshold. The room, all misty and queer smelling, was full of strange things whose nature and use were to me beyond conception – mysteriously shaped bottles, tubes, glasses, and scientific instruments; but the strangest object of all was Dr Dathan, with his peaked, pallid face and lanky hair, under a red smoking-cap. Coming into that sickly smelling little den straight from the open, the simple fields and feeding cattle, it knocked me stupid. At the moment I believed all the fairy tales I had ever heard of him.'

'Were you frightened?'

'I felt cold; but something seemed pushing me on. Then he looked up at me standing there, and I spoke. "Dr Dathan, I am in dreadful difficulty. I want to consult you ..."

'"I never give medical advice," he said, sharply.

'"Nor do I need that," I answered.

'I had broken up some precious bit of study, and he was impatient and annoyed. But – I was not bad to look at in those days – he hesitated a moment to order me off, and out I came with my story. I made it short. Something warned me not to talk to his pity, but to his power, his wisdom and experience. He knew something of my father and Vaughan Hughes, and had seen Walter and me. Still, having said what I had to say, I felt – oh, so miserably foolish! Unless he were a real wizard, what could he do for me in such a pass?'

'"You mean that you cannot hold your own," he said, "Well, in this world the weakest must go to the wall."

'"If I am parted from Walter, what my father wills I shall do in the end. He upbraids, he talks of my dead mother, he beseeches, then he cries and sobs. If I defy him, and go off with Walter, it might be his death. With fury and excitement he will work himself into a fit." My own feelings were getting out of hand, and I broke out helplessly, "Oh, tell me some way to safeguard myself from being over-persuaded into this other marriage at least. I read once of a girl who disfigured herself – spoilt her good looks – to get rid of a suitor. I thought it something too terrible to be true, but feel now that I could do it myself!"

'"That would be a pity," he said, and I heard him mutter as if thinking aloud, "Girl of an uncommon stamp – in more ways than one!" Then he levelled his fire-devils of eyes at me searchingly – suddenly – with an expression so outspoken, I seemed to read it off like writing. It said: "Shall I or shall I not?"

"'You can do something for me,' I said hastily. "I see it in your face!"

'He was put out and silent for a moment, glanced down at some papers lying before him, then shot another look at me, as keen as one of his own blades.

"'So you think you would face anything that offered you a chance?"

"'I would face death,' I said.

"'Death ends all chances,' he said grimly. "Besides, there are worse things than loss of life or lover.'

"'What things?' I asked shakily. His manner had changed from one of indifference and become earnest, and he was watching me now as carefully as the chemicals in the glass when I came in.

"'I dare say you have heard horrible things told of me,' he began – "that I make a study of the things of darkness – poisons, and so on.'

'I assented in silence.

"'It is a necessary part of the physician's art. Disease is a poison they have to deal with, and that we men of science are occupied in tracing to its origin. You or anybody can understand the principle of what we call the 'anti-toxin treatment', namely, that by introducing a small dose of some particular poison into the system we bring about a mild attack of the particular complaint, which secures immunity from all danger from it in the future. The extension of this principle is bringing us to the verge of discoveries of tremendous importance. Now I have in this glass a certain liquid," he laid his hand on a small tube. "Were I to use it on you it would hurt neither you nor your beauty, yet it might bring about, in the natural course of events, all that you desire. Say that I were to inject a drop of it into your veins ..."

"'What will happen?' I asked, all of a tremble.

"'Ah!' The smile on his face made me shiver! "Since the

experiment is one I cannot make usefully on myself, and no other human subject is forthcoming, I can only tell you what I *believe* will happen. It will affect one organ only – your brain. After a few days you will probably suffer from definite mental derangement. You will think, act, and talk absurdly, just as in a dream."

"'Do you mean that I shall go mad?" I asked, scarcely believing my ears.

"'Well, your memory, your reason, will be temporarily disordered. The disorder will pass away. But you will find farmer Hughes will have cooled in his suit. A man like him thinks twice before wedding a girl who has been out of her mind. Ask yourself! What passes here would of course remain our secret."

'I shrank, scared at what I thought a demoniacal offer. "Oh, Dr Dathan, I cannot."

"'Well, well, in that case there is no more to be said," he replied, his tone changing quickly. "Go home! I was only joking, you little fool!"

'Never joker looked and spoke as he had done! I knew better. "Why, they would put me away, shut me up in an asylum," I stammered out.

"'Even if they did, you would be released soon. But I think I can prevent that. I shall interest myself in the case, and will talk to any other doctor they may summon, and provide an attendant for you at home if necessary. No special treatment will be needed, and in three weeks I say you will be well – and rid of Vaughan Hughes' attentions."

'His urgency and confidence were gaining ground on me. "But say I consented," I faltered, "there is Walter. What of him?"

"'Oh – he – the navy man – leave him to me. In any case you will be relieved of what you tell me you dread most. To your lover I will – well, I'll tell him something; not all – but enough. Think now. Will you or will you not?"

'I was agitated, as never in my life before. But the excitement, the eagerness that seemed to devour him, and heaved under his ordinary manner, was a thing I couldn't describe or ever forget.

'"Mind," he said, pulling himself up, as it were, "the only certain risk is mine. I have gone further into these studies than most; and it may be long before certain processes of protective treatment I would advocate are recognised as safe and proper. I am defying law, public opinion – endangering private and professional standing by proposing this to you. And if you consent, you must speak of this to no one – not even to Walter – until my death. Observe, I am trusting you, as you will trust me."

'His audacity and zest caught and clutched me like a hawk, and carried me away. "Yes," I said, "I am willing. Will it – will it – hurt much?"

'His whole person lit up with elation and excitement. "Oh, a pin-prick," he said, with the laugh of those who win.

*

'A pin-prick, and it was done.

'Then, from an evil spirit tempting me, he seemed to become a human being; and talked to me kindly and cheeringly, as to one who has rendered you a service. I went home palsied inwardly with fear, but repeating over to myself his last words: "Don't think. Don't worry. Wait. Let what will happen; hold on and trust to me. All will be well at the last."

The Hidden Hand

'The blessed, blind trust we put in doctors helped me to do as he said, at the first. Soon, awful tears came like big waves to swallow me up. He seemed to know – for sure. But suppose he was mistaken – had miscalculated; and the effect were to destroy my mind – make of me a madwoman for life! Had I perhaps committed a sin, though unknowingly, in consenting to let him try the experiment? I perhaps deserved this most terrible punishment. I had seen in his face that it would be nothing to him what became of me. All he cared for was to study the effect on me of the treatment.

'In the long after-years I have been in lands where they still offer up human sacrifices to their gods. I thought once or twice then of Dr Dathan.'

'Well, what did happen?' I asked, deeply curious.

'For a few days – I don't know how many – I went about my work as usual. Then one morning I was smitten by an awful headache; could scarcely see or speak. As by chance, Dr Dathan looked in at the farm that very day, spoke cheerfully to me, and advised me to keep very quiet.

'It's little or nothing I can tell you from my own knowledge of anything after that. They say I went completely off my head; talked and behaved just as he had foretold, as senselessly as in a dream; persuaded that impossible things were happening; persons there who were not; one thing changing, melting into another. I was incapable of understanding what was said to me, or of making myself understood. My father and brothers were as scared as if I had turned into a goblin or a ghost. They fetched Dr Dathan in a hurry – he being so near. He managed to quiet them a little, till the Llanffelix doctor came, who was perplexed, and not particularly hopeful. Dr Dathan professed to leave me in his hands, but let him know that he held a different opinion. He offered to watch the case for the other, and was as kind as could be, coming every day; and, while confessing he had never seen an attack like it before, predicted that in due time I should recover.

'And so it happened; gradually – as I was told – but to myself it seemed as if in one happy hour, I shook off a nightmare – a heavy cloud; and my wits became clear again, though I was weak as a little child. "Patience," Dr Dathan whispered to me. "You will soon be as well and strong as before."

'And so it came to pass!

'But the whole parish knew I had been off my head, and some whispered, since Dr Dathan gave no pills or draughts, that he had cured me by a charm. Vaughan Hughes behaved just as the doctor had foretold. There must be madness in the family, he supposed. Certainly I seemed to be Winifred Owen herself again; but the attack might recur. He had inquired, and heard how rare it was that patients, though discharged from asylums as cured, remained permanently sane. I don't see that he was to be blamed for his caution, but he offended father by his plain-speaking, and they had some words. Just then Walter came back; and Dr Dathan took a lot of trouble – got hold of him and talked to him in private, in the first place.'

'What did he tell him?'

'That he felt certain mine had been a case – a rare case – of blood poisoning, and that there was not the slightest danger of a relapse. To father he hinted that a thorough change of scene and circumstances would be a desirable thing for me on all accounts. Other admirers might behave like Vaughan Hughes; while here was Walter, with a bundle of badges and testimonials from his superior officers, ready and eager to wed me. Father gave in; Walter Trinaman was married to me three weeks later, and away with me to England – to Plymouth – to the fleet.'

The Tree Of Knowledge

Five-and-thirty years ago she went out with him into a new and complicated world, the world of infinite good and evil, from which Pontycler prudently still keeps its face averted. Yet had she been blessed in her deed. Walter Trinaman proved of the good leaven, one of the best in a line of life where all must be of the better sort. His officers, his mates, knew it; and his Winifred came to know.

'And when I said I owe my life to Dr Dathan, I mean Walt's life and mine that we led together!'

Much had she seen, 'places and men'. Sorrow she had known, 'our little son – we lost!' And that sorrow, I felt, was unhealed. 'But we had two other daughters.'

Both married young, she told me; and two years ago Walter Trinaman, then in the coastguard service, was one of the six lives lost in rescuing others from a memorable wreck on the coast of South Devon.

'My own life seemed ended and lived out. Of my girls, one was settled in Canada; the other in Glasgow. My heart turned suddenly – so strangely and unexpectedly – to Pontycler and the old country, and I came over, to find father still living, though going on for ninety years old. My brothers carry on the farm. The people at the Ivybush were leaving, and so it came to pass that I took it.'

'And Dr Dathan,' I asked, 'what became of him?'

'It was about three years after I went away that I read a notice of him in the paper. He was found dead in his bed at Cilcorwen by the caretaker who brought up his breakfast one morning. At the inquest the doctor said his whole frame was wasted and perished, and that it was a miracle he had lived so long, not ailing, apparently; as he might have dropped off at any moment the last twelvemonth. There are those here like Caleb Evans, whom you met today, who still half believe that the devil came for his own and fetched him away. That is not fair. What became of his researches I never heard; nor do I think he cared to be famous – only to find out, and to know.'

On leaving the Ivybush regretfully the next morning, I suggested enlarging and improving the inn, since so pleasant a halting-place as Pontycler could not fail to attract numerous summer visitors of a better class. Surely it would be worth while.

'If you mean that it would be more remunerative,' said Mrs Trinaman plainly, 'I, or any one who knows anything about it, can tell you this kind of thing pays much better!' And that, I felt, was the proper answer to my commonplace, middle-class suggestion. But her last words were in another key, as, standing before her door, a serving hostess to every passing wayfarer, to the fit and unfit alike, she wished me good speed. 'So long as I stay,' she said wistfully, 'it shall stay as it was when I first met Trinaman – I've told you where and how!'

the first alien

Marianne Jones

Even the Rain is Different 2005

theme: Welsh women's experiences of travel
non-fiction anthology

Four men were waiting for Non at the provincial airport: the head of English and three members of his staff. They fussed her into the university's limousine, which bumped down a dusty road into flat countryside. A glossy orange fruit on a leafless tree against a blue sky – in November – was her first image of Japan.

'Persimmon,' the head of department explained. 'One left for God to give sank for harvest.'

The limousine stopped to let out two of the men, in smart Western suits, so that they could relieve themselves by the side of the road. After this, the car left the trunk road and went down a lane lined with weeping-willow trees to the house where she would be a lodger. It was on the edge of a village near some ricefields and you could see the mountains in the distance. Strings of drying persimmon hung from its eaves.

When they were about to enter the house, the wife of the family got down on her knees and bowed her head to the floor in greeting. From signals too subtle to define, Non sensed it would embarrass them if a guest copied this behaviour and instead smiled awkwardly in the doorway. She was invited to take her shoes off and step into the house, but the head of department was leaving and his staff – including Mr Kumamoto, the head of the house – were going back to work with him. Non was left with Mr Kumamoto's mother and wife.

She felt lost: broken English and embarrassed laughs were replaced by silence. Wondering how they could communicate, she got out photographs of her family and pointed at the people in them. The wife supplied her with words for what must have been 'father', 'mother' and 'sister' and she repeated them and tried to fix them in her memory.

In the evening Mr Kumamoto came home, but he was tired. They ate a silent supper in front of dinosaurs spewing out their guts. This was the favourite TV programme of the six-year-old son who had come home from school, stared at her, and then started drawing cartoon heroes. Mr Kumamoto, in a navy *yukata*, relaxed a little after the meal and did some interpreting for her. She gathered that his mother, called 'grandmother' by the whole family, had been trying to communicate with her during the afternoon by simplifying her Japanese. She had repeated, 'Japan – island. England – island. Japan – king. England – king. Our country – friend. I fan of Royal family and can I have English stamp?' but the only answer she had received was 'father – mother – sister'.

Mr Kumamoto put vinegar in his coffee – to give him strength against the winter, he said. He was reserving moxification and mantrifying 'I feel warm' for later, when it got colder. He translated the question which had been bothering the grandmother all day: 'What are you doing here, Nonna? Shouldn't you be getting married?'

It might cause scandal if she told them about Takeo. 'I want to see the world,' she said.

'You're not scared?' the grandmother asked through Mr Kumamoto. She looked perplexed and asked how people got married in Britain. Her parents had chosen a husband for her early. She had not seen him until her wedding day. 'Then I peep sideways,' Mr Kumamoto translated, 'and I see.'

'Weren't you scared?' Non asked, and they smiled at one another.

The smile reminded Non of her grandparents sitting in front of their coal fire on winter evenings. Their 'young people these days ... not in my day' remarks burnt like paper in the affection they felt for her and she for them. There was no uncrossable divide between people, not even when there was a language barrier.

'What if he'd been ugly?' Non asked, enjoying the flare of the stove as it was lit and then noticing grandmother's look of shock to her son. Was it so outrageous to refer to what men were like physically? In which case, why had grandmother peeped sideways on her wedding day? 'Or incredibly handsome, of course,' she added politely

'I learn to love him later.' Grandmother's last sentence was translated as she blew her nose on the sleeve of her kimono.

'Nowadays you see each other first,' Mr Kumamoto added with a grin.

'What would you do if your parents arranged an interview for you to meet suitable young man?' grandmother wanted to know. 'Isn't it a good idea at your age?'

'I'd be cross with them,' she answered.

Grandmother hissed disapprovingly, didn't speak to her for several minutes and sucked down a cup of green tea.

At breakfast the next day, the sides of the house – wooden sections on runners – were pushed open because it was warm. Non knelt on her flat cushion trying to enjoy bean soup with seaweed; it tasted medicinal. She contemplated the raw egg in a lacquer bowl but felt that it was too early in the morning to adapt to her new life. The TV was on and grandmother's eyes were full of tears. A young man in uniform was giving a fervent speech to his community before leaving home for the war. His eyes were raised to the flag of the Rising Sun. 'Banzai!' he yelled. Here she was, twenty-five years after these events, eating breakfast on a sunny morning with 'the enemy' and feeling sympathy for the tears in grandmother's eyes. What had happened to her husband?

Going to work on the back of Mr Kumamoto's scooter, swinging round corners, rattling along miles of country roads, was the best part of her first day. Her spirit rode high on sun in winter. As they reached the university city, Mr Kumamoto shouted something to her about the castle moat containing lotus. The roots were harvested and they could have some for supper that week. Non wondered if she would then forget her home and become part of this new country.

That evening, however, Mr Kumamoto had to tell her that his wife was not happy about him giving a young woman like her a ride on the back of his scooter and please could she find her way to work by bus in future. He laughed awkwardly. They were not worried but they feared gossip. She had to understand that.

Over the next few weeks the images of the persimmon tree and the ride on the bike were replaced by those of eyes staring and strangers following her in the street shouting 'Foreigner!' Feeling lonely, she went for long walks along the banks of the willow-lined river. She saw women stitching quilts at the open sides of their houses, and stared across the ricefields at the mountains.

Mr Kumamoto had to warn her that people found her peculiar because she went for long walks by herself. They could see that there was no purpose to her walks; she was not shopping or going to the bus-stop. Non found this hard. She was used to walking in the mountains or down to the beach: fresh air at the end of the day, a chance to be alone with her thoughts. If only Takeo were nearer.

She did not mention problems of loneliness in her letters to him; the winter break was coming and it would cure everything. He was flying down to see her then. She knotted all her strength together and waited. At least she was learning some Japanese.

One morning she received a small parcel and recognised the italic writing of her best friend at home. She tore off the stamps, gave them to grandmother, and ripped open the parcel. It contained a letter and a 'Silver Fountain' firework to celebrate her arrival on Japanese soil. She saved it so that she could light it with Takeo.

Then suddenly he was there, commenting on the mildness of the weather. It was snowing in Tokyo.

The Kumamotos were impressed by being called upon by

a scholar from the great city, by the perfection of his manners and his obvious intelligence and learning. They asked his opinion, bowed, and nodded their assent.

Non walked along the river bank with him and he translated ancient poetry for her: poems about princesses gazing out into the darkness at the moon and waiting for the lover from whom they had been parted, or about life floating like leaves on a river and vanishing like a deer into the forest. She remembered the firework – if life was going to be fleeting, let it be full of sparks!

'What firework?' he asked with concern. 'They're very dangerous. We must get rid of it.'

In the end he agreed that he would not stop her lighting it and she agreed to do it at once and not wait for the night. After the silver sparks fizzled out, he apologised to the Kumamotos for their strange behaviour. Naturally, they would not normally light fireworks like this.

'We have firework,' said grandmother, 'in summer, of course.'

'We have them in winter, ' Non said.

Grandmother smiled. 'Not cold?' she asked.

'Very cold! You need a scarf in bright colours to keep you warm.'

They went for more walks in the slightly chill air. Then, as suddenly as he had come, Takeo was gone. It would be spring before she had another break and enough money to visit him.

After he left, as she was sitting alone in her room trying to hold onto the warmth of being near him, there was shouting at the front entrance. She heard Mr Kumamoto's reasonable voice, followed by the raised voices of two or three men and then quiet Mrs Kumamoto shouting hysterically. She was out of her room before she realised she could not help. One of the three men stared at her; another nodded brusquely.

Raised voices broke out again. The word 'foreigner' was repeated. Mr Kumamoto's soothing remarks were interrupted. Grandmother looked at her in obvious distress, said something to Mrs Kumamoto and they both retreated into the living room. There was an awkward silence. One of the three men softened, smiled at her and said something to his companions. The one who had nodded brusquely protested but gradually calmed down and the three bowed deeply and left.

Mr Kumamoto explained that this delegation from the village, led by the headman, had come to criticise her for walking around on her own with a man who was obviously no relative of hers.

Non retreated to her room and gazed at the moon rising over the distant mountains. Could she really stay here? Even worse thoughts, about whether her love for Takeo was an illusion or a poem she had read somewhere forgetting the author, she brushed aside. He seemed distant, beyond the moon.

At some time during the night she must have lain down on her mattress and fallen asleep in her clothes. She was woken by chill light and a touch of frost in the air. Startled, she got up to wash and change into fresh clothes for work.

She was called to breakfast and handed her soup in silence. She fixed her attention on the sound of the boy slurping. Grandmother muttered something and walked into the kitchen.

Mr Kumamoto translated: 'She says it is not necessary to make so much criticism.'

Non relaxed slightly and felt warmth returning to her face and hands. Mr Kumamoto switched the TV on, irritably.

Silence continued, punctuated by short bursts of speech from the television as Mr Kumamoto switched from channel to channel. He finally turned it off.

'Oh yes,' he said. 'We have to go to the town hall tomorrow.

They not know what to do. So they take time and get excited. They even write to Tokyo to ask what they should do!' He laughed and turned up the oil-stove.

'What do you mean?' she asked, dreading some worse development.

'They ready to give you alien registration card,' Mr Kumamoto said. 'They need your sign and fingerprints.'

She released the breath she was holding so tightly. It was only about a card. 'Fingerprints?' she queried.

'You have to forgive them so slow – already two months,' he said. 'But you first alien who ever lived here.'

sex in a
strange city

Siân Melangell Dafydd

Laughing, Not Laughing 2004

theme: women's experiences of sex
non-fiction anthology

Something, deep down was wrong. The deepest you can get in a woman is her womb, because men don't go there. And there, I felt something was missing.

Think for a second. There's a reason why I'm typing away at my laptop about the most passionate subject in my heart and bones, in a language that isn't my own. Again, I ask, what's a 'womb' in Welsh? Here lies the problem. Apparently it's 'croth' but I thought that was something biblical that only Mary had. 'Vagina', now that's another matter. We Welsh, you know – we call our vagina by all sorts of things. When my friend, Sara was eleven, she got terrified when hairs started growing on her 'Jemima' – and I thought 'Puddleduck' – your Jemima should have feathers, not hairs. Then she showed me. We had just been swimming in the lake, and tried to get changed in the passenger seat of our fathers' cars. She wanted to know that everyone else's was growing too, and wouldn't believe that mine wasn't. Considering that I'm older and all. So she said we should both show, together. There she was, sat on the leather, with her flowered knickers to one side, and me stood behind the open door of the car, hiding from everyone else in the direction of the lake. So we stuck our naked vaginas out, facing each other and wondered at our differences. Her knickers were prettier. Behind my knickers, I had smooth skin, and she had a balding head look, with just the few dark hairs. We both got embarrassed at our difference and covered up, in case someone found out what we were sharing. I started to understand. When she was sixteen, her Clint (Eastwood) gave her an 'Orange' for the first time, when she was in the bath. Figure that one out if you can.

We might complain if someone has 'chips' for dinner instead of their rightful Welsh name, or 'baked beans' with a plateful of other, Welsh-named food, but when it comes to making love – we justify doing that in English. After all, sex is such an 'Ych a Fi', disgraceful thing, we couldn't possibly face each other over cornflakes if we did it in our mother tongue. 'Vagina' is something that goes by the name of 'Red Sleeve' because, you see, we women are terrifying creatures that truly belong on the film set of *Aliens*. Hang around too close and an extra arm will reach out of our deep, mysterious 'hole' and aim for your throat, punch you, leave slime all over you. Or maybe this name is the linguistics pennyworth for the cause, to make all women more like men, and give them too – a dangly thing between her legs. Don't you think that she would be easier to understand if she had at least a pretend penis, even if it's a knitted sleeve thing?

I hate to dispel the myth, but just for the record, vaginas are not knitted. So let me tell you about one man who made me look for a corner in this world where women, or me specifically – this woman here – I – am worth touching. This man was only sixteen, so call him a man only if you feel that it's a fitting description. He was named after a king, and liked it. He had stubble, and liked that too, though he complained about the constant shaving, and scratched his chin, to point out that he was a man. He never touched any part of me other than my lips and made sure he took out his chewing gum before doing that. After a week of this body-avoiding, he turned around to me, on the back seats of a town hall, the night of the Young Farmers Eisteddfod, and said, 'I want to sleep with you,' twice, aloud.

I pretended not to hear, but a few people around us heard, twice, made big eyes at him whilst he just sank into his seat and squeezed his cock tight to pretend it was never there. Then he pretended not to see me for a while until I got the message and I saw him touching lips like a well-engineered bridge, bums apart with another girl, woman – whatever – who obviously wasn't worth touching completely either.

That was the beginning of the relationship my bum had with mid air, since sex you see, isn't about touching. It's about isolating pieces of yourself like pebbles off a rock, and giving those away to be juggled by someone whilst keeping the rest of yourself cool, calm and collected. When I ate a mango in the bath, it was more like what I wanted sex to be, licking the juice from my elbow to my little finger, ripping lightly at the flesh and licking the core stone. My tongue knew it so well, I thought I could mould it if I was blind. Maybe my Mango was one step from being one of Sara's 'Oranges'. I let the Mango slip, cold along the hot water on my skin, but I wasn't quite fulfilled.

I went away. You could call it running away, but I'll say this much – it was to a hot city. I didn't know this until I landed. I found myself in a place that had an entire new language, one that covered greetings, bread buying, rail ticket buying and sex. As the aeroplane was about to land, I wondered, how on earth do the people of this country earn a reputation for being such passionate beings? The fields were exact squares. It was a maths paper with shy grass, and I had nothing but a sudden understanding of Welsh mountains, like voluptuous naked sleeping women. The 'passionate' place seemed just limp. We landed into heat. That was the key. Looking at the amazing jigsaw of people, buses, junk stalls, exhaust fumes, me, and sticky ice cream holding the whole picture together, I wondered how it all fitted into one public square. Sitting on a bus, waiting for water, my skin started to change, open to the heat. Do you have a favourite word, for the sound of it, I mean? Say it slow – isn't 'heat' entrancing? It feels as if you are breathing out heat as you say it, and that's how I felt. Not until then did I remember where these people's passion came from. It's heat. And so I sat on my luggage in a ball, resting my lips on my arm and looking over it like over a hill. The feeling of being on the road like that is the same as feeling undressed, bare to the minimum – nothing left but the jewellery that won't come off my fingers, even in cold water, just me. So, in the heat, I felt my own tongue in my mouth. The alien air around me made me feel everything much closer, as if every nerve ending bud had just opened, and I was being kissed, always, over and over, constantly.

It was in this city that I met a man, who I've decided, should remain nameless. So let's call him 'September', since that's when it was. It's a strange time of year, when the buildings stubbornly hold onto the summer heat from the odd cold-ish day attempting to drag it out of them. For the most part, the buildings win the day, and heat seems to radiate out of the city's edges. People still wear a look of exhaustion, as if they've collapsed into the street after having just finished making love to summer, still wearing next to nothing and glowing with an ice-cream-smelling sweat. It was with strawberry and pistachio stickiness on my lips I met September in a tall and narrow street after watching a film I wouldn't otherwise have watched.

The film was *Priscilla, Queen of the Desert* and I loved, loved and stayed fascinated by it, knowing that there were people in the audience getting plenty of Sara's 'Oranges' from it. It was all a mistake. There was a man whose name I never knew imitating a mosquito and insisting on pinching my bum in the street, so I sneaked into this nice airy cinema to escape. I had sunk into my seat successfully, the little Methodist beast in me dragging even my split ends into the lumpy cushion of the seat whilst whispering 'you're not really here, and nobody will see you here, in a place like this', drag, drag. But it was all too late, because I still watched. It was the same little beast who Tippex-ed all the sexy words out of the Welsh dictionary, but was failing miserably at making me invisible, because I had to walk out of the cinema, on two feet somehow, and I'm a visible 5'7". It was at that exact moment September's voice made me turn around.

He was a clean and dirty man, all in one. He looked clean and scrubbed, but with the odd scratchy lump of clay hardened onto him, clinging. I thought straight away of my attempt at love with the man named after a king, and our failure to *cling.* This man had got it. It was lunchtime, and just outside the cinema hall, there was a food stall. We ate in the street. He was a sculptor. He moulded a piece of bread between the thumb and finger of his right hand, at the same time moulding another piece with his tongue. I think back, and I think, 'I do not, under any circumstance, trust strange men; I do not take sweets from strangers. What were you thinking, girl, you idiot!'

But I didn't take anything from him, and I was travelling so there somehow wasn't a concept of not moving on. We rambled, we ate, and in a small public square round the corner he had a studio with big glass doors onto the street that seemed to let the breeze in and not the heat, which was by then at its height, at midday.

Men on bikes slowed down to see inside. I can tell you that because I spent enough time in there. On the far wall there was a chaise longue smelling of toasted sunflower seeds, and which made puffs of dry clay clouds every time I rearranged myself on it. It started clinging to me. September was working on something marble and I just read and wrote letters, and noticed the world going by from left to right and right to left through the doors in front of me. That didn't last long.

Mid carving a delicate finger, September threw a blanket on top of the marble and said that something was wrong, that something was missing. Well I knew that! I knew that there was more to kissing than touching lips, that my whole body should be in it, not left untouched and empty. September started touching it. He got hold of a dollop of clay and got stuck into it until I could almost feel my fingers turning into clay to finger his – but I was turning the pages of a book, peering up at him and watching.

'You have inspired me!' he said. I translate of course. 'I must make something else.' His finger gave the lump of clay a sort of belly button and I stayed there, lounging, wondering how he could sculpt my belly button, being that it was hidden under a vest top. But it was mine. You could only just make me out, but it was me, my belly, the turn of it, and he was stroking it into place, going in and out, reaching right in there into where my womb would be and stroking even that. I grew in front of my eyes, and he held me, he held all around me to sculpt the back of my shoulders as if that was the only way he could make them, by feeling them, as if he were used to holding around me like that. His finger trailed up the centre of my back, tickling that little dip all the way up. At a glance, he had known my body well enough to sculpt me, without sight. It was scary, and seductive. When he leaned away from moulding my back, my body's clay left dark red stains on his T-shirt and arms. He was holding me so close, and did everything by pressing against me.

I made myself more comfortable and lay watching, book dropped, spine upwards. I swear he didn't have to keep sculpting me, that I was looking all right the first time, but he kept on caressing me, making sure. It might not have been necessary, but it was fun anyway. He smiled from behind my bum and smoothed it over with eight fingertips, playing a cheeky peep-bo.

I wanted him to get to my breasts. I wanted him to stroke my collar bone from right to left as light as a necklace, as light as the jewellery that won't come off my body even in cold water. And finally, he did it, he cupped clay in one slow movement, and I appeared from under his palm, one and two breasts, erect after wanting to appear for so long. That was not enough. I knew that this body he was attending to, the whole body was mine, but he still worked at it. With every movement I could almost, and I say almost because I tingled, I almost felt his sliding fingertips around, and then pulling my nipples up and hard, into shape.

The torso he created had no head. He hadn't created lips. The sculpture could not kiss. Four hours passed too quickly. I felt like he was playing a game, and had no idea where it was leading. Checking my belly button again, inspecting it, he bumped his cheek against my breast and a piece of me was left there, clinging to him. Was he gay? Was he just not turned on by what he had in his fingers, beyond me being more interesting than an apple and orange? I pressed my vagina against the clay of the 'chaise longue' just to keep myself still. Then, after inspecting my clay belly button, he looked up at my eyes behind his image of me, and with no warning, without looking at the sculpture, created in two quick swoops, my vagina and inner thighs, so I nearly bit my lower lip off with, oh I don't know – such maddening pleasure, and failure to keep it for more than a milli-second. Go back there!

But he was done. The sculpture was a finished piece. He left only one fingerprint on me – and that was on a curl of hair that he moved out of my face's way to say goodbye, and thank you for the inspiration. He hugged me closer than anybody had ever kissed me, and I had found what I was looking for. I had found being with someone in my entirety, touching every surface of my body with his – but I was still waiting to feel it! Jealous of a sculpture of myself, I left and clay stuck a clump of my hair into a curl.

Back in an empty youth hostel above a cafe, early evening and a roomful of white beds, with breeze and open shutters, my legs separated, my arms separated, my hips yearned upwards, and I had one thin white sheet over me. I felt myself as if my fingers were September's, and moulded away. Okay, so sometimes I thought that I might be interrupted.

But really, I stopped being shocked and forgot being silly and found that right where September had last stroked the sculpture of me, my vagina had more moulding needing. There, pressing my body right against September's heat I mixed the sweat that we created like clay and clung to him. Again, I could feel him holding me like he held my image, all around, bums in, crutches tight. No Oranges here, no Mangoes, only Orgasms, and sweeter! There, with the sour smell of coffee from downstairs dying, I wondered at how sweet the sex of one woman could smell all by herself.

home is where the heart is

Brenda Curtis

Mirror, Mirror 2004

theme: the other woman
fiction anthology

'Home is where the heart is.' Doris repeated the phrase to herself as she swept the path. It gave a rhythm to her sweeping as she brushed vigorously and methodically towards the front gate. Reaching it, she stood for a moment, resting, and a vague worry returned to nag her. Something about moving – holiday – she couldn't quite remember. 'Home is where ...'

Her reverie was interrupted by a car that drew up at the kerb opposite. A woman stepped out and waved. After retrieving her bag and locking the car, the woman crossed the road. Doris felt joy and apprehension as her daughter approached.

'Mum, how are you?' The two women embraced and kissed. Doris noticed that Christine was wearing shiny black trousers and that it was a scarlet-nail day. She'd better mind her 'ps' and 'qs'.

'Mum, your hands are icy.'

'Cold hands, warm heart,' replied Doris, as Christine swept past her in a breeze of perfume.

Doris followed her daughter into the house, thinking how strange it was that she felt so vulnerable, so childlike, in the slipstream of this crisp, efficient younger woman. Christine hung her jacket on the back of a chair in the kitchen and put her bag on the floor.

She started saying, 'That looks heavy, dear, what on earth have you got in it? You look as if you're going on holiday,' but seeing Christine give an impatient shrug, added, 'Lovely to see you, dear. Cup of tea?'

While Christine went upstairs to the bathroom, Doris stood looking out of the kitchen window at her little garden, nervously fingering the carefully prepared tea tray. Where was George? He would have known Christine was coming. He was usually the first to greet her. She turned as Christine walked briskly back into the kitchen, saying she was dying for that cup of tea, and watched as her daughter crossed over to the kettle.

'But, Mum, you haven't switched it on.' Doris' heart sank as Christine's lips tightened, as she bent to check the water level before flicking the switch. Not a good beginning. Doris felt stupid and helpless.

'Mum. Why have you put out three cups?'

'George should be here any minute now.'

Doris stopped speaking, going hot and cold as memory flooded back. She felt herself folded into her daughter's arms.

'George is dead, Mum. He's gone.'

Doris remained for a moment in her daughter's embrace, then, releasing herself, sat down at the kitchen table, hands clenched, biting her lip.

'He's still alive to me.' She stared at her fists, trying to make sense of her confused thoughts. 'Silly me. I keep forgetting. How could I forget a thing like that?' She relaxed her hands and looked up at her daughter. 'Christine, when did he die?'

The kettle was bubbling and blowing out plumes of steam and, with a sigh, Christine set about making the tea. 'Last January, Mum. Remember? He was in hospital. We visited him.'

They fell silent.

After a moment, Christine said, 'What month is it now, Mum?'

Doris gave a short laugh. 'Well, if you don't know, there's the paper.' She indicated a newspaper on another chair. Christine returned her attention to the tray and Doris watched as her daughter inspected one of the cups, took it to the sink and rubbed it with a scourer under the hot tap.

'Let's take the tea outside, shall we, while the sun's shining.' It was more of a command than an invitation, thought Doris, but, picking up the newspaper, she followed Christine into the garden. She was glad to get out of the kitchen. She knew her memory wasn't what it used to be but she got by, didn't she? Again she felt that flicker of worry nagging her, biting at the corners of her mind, something about home – a holiday – going away.

Doris sat down on the garden bench and, letting the worry go, prepared to pour tea, while Christine wandered off to inspect the topiary bird that her father had nurtured over the years in the hedge between the gardens. As Doris lifted the jug it slipped, and she watched in dismay as milk poured in a stream on to the lawn, disappearing between blades of grass, soaking into the ground. 'Bugger.'

She coughed, but saw that Christine had heard and turned with a worried frown. Doris stood up, laughing, 'No use crying over spilt milk,' and made a hasty retreat back to the kitchen.

Christine did not laugh.

When they were finally settled and drinking their tea, Doris asked after the children.

'Oh they're fine. Always out and about, you know. We all are.'

Doris dearly wanted to hear all about her family, her grandchildren, her son-in-law, their lives, all of it. 'What is ... How is ... Is it football or ...?'

'Yes. Football. Always.'

But try as she might, Doris could not remember their names to ask after each one personally. And Christine wasn't going to help her.

'I saw Mrs ... um ... one of my neighbours the other day and ...' She stopped when she saw her daughter's face was a mask of boredom. The conversation faltered and stalled. It was obvious that Christine's mind was elsewhere. She's doing her duty, thought Doris in a panic, desolation shooting through her. She looked down at her hands, fingers crooked with arthritis. She rubbed and flexed the joints to ease the ache, thinking how much more painful were the hurts you couldn't see.

For a while they drank their tea in silence, until Doris caught her daughter staring at her with a frown. Taking both her mother's hands in her own, Christine opened her mouth to say something. Then, changing her mind just as quickly, she rose and walked over to the garden border where she broke off a sprig of mint, held it to her nose and breathed deeply.

Doris returned to her newspaper. 'It says here that some fishermen in Australia caught a giant cod and when they opened its stomach they found a man's head inside! Isn't that extraordinary?'

'Bizarre. What a shock.'

Christine seemed interested, so Doris continued, 'They think it was the head of another fisherman who disappeared the week before, after falling from the deck of his trawler.'

The younger woman didn't comment. Doris read on in silence until Christine returned to her seat.

'Christine, listen to this.'

'What?' said Christine, toying with the mint.

'It says here that when some fishermen ...'

'You've just told me that.'

'No, I haven't.'

'Yes, you have. Just a minute ago.'

'You must have read it yourself then.' Doris felt sure her daughter was mistaken but she didn't argue. She wanted to enjoy this afternoon with her.

Tense, Doris got up, walked to the hedge and looked over to see if she could see anybody. No, no rescue there. On impulse, she took a swipe at the privet bird, pretending to knock it off its perch, but then, stroking it gently, said, over her shoulder, 'A bird in the hand is worth two in the bush.'

She turned in time to catch the flicker of a smile that crossed her daughter's face.

Christine patted the seat next to her. 'Come and sit down, Mum. More tea?'

Doris sat down.

'Well, Mum. I've got to "mother" you now, haven't I? What about a holiday? I know a nice place by the sea. You'd like a change.'

'Oh, I don't think so. I like it here. I don't need a holiday.' The nagging memory returned, just out of reach.

Christine raised her arm and glancing at her watch, jumped up, 'Look, Mum, I'll make us a quick lunch and then I must go. I've got some work I must catch up on before tomorrow.'

She picked up the tray and walked briskly back through the garden to the kitchen. Doris followed, feeling unsure of herself, disadvantaged. She was overwhelmed by a need for George's strong presence, for protection, security. Where was he when he was wanted? He should be home soon. Then she remembered: he was gone, buried. Christine was all she had now.

In the kitchen, Christine was at the fridge taking out a bag of salad, a rather shrivelled cucumber and some tomatoes. Doris busied herself at the sink, but out of the corner of her eye, saw her daughter throw a packet of cheese and half a loaf into the waste bin. Oh dear, she thought, nothing is right today. She gave her hands a quick wipe, went over to the dresser, took out a knife and started to slice the tomatoes. She bent down to reach a plate from the bottom cupboard and the whole pile slid to the floor with a clatter. Laughing, before Christine could speak, she said, 'More haste less speed. Butter fingers,' and she dived for the dustpan and brush at the same moment as Christine. They collided. Doris, still laughing merrily, gasped, 'Too many cooks spoil ...' and, bending to sweep up the broken china, saw Christine give an exasperated shrug. She felt she'd made a fool of herself again but the thread of mirth that had started within her was unstoppable. She remembered the muddles that she and George had got into as they struggled to manage the tasks of everyday living, how they had screamed at each other and then laughed at their own incompetences. Christine was still a child, didn't know anything yet. Thinking this made her feel stronger and wise and she felt a rush of love for her only child.

Christine laid out the salads and they sat down to eat. Doris saw Christine bend forward, peer into her food and say, 'There's a ladybird on my lettuce. Well, let's hope it ate all the greenfly.' Without waiting for a response, Doris rose quickly and took the lettuce leaf, with the ladybird, to the back door, where she gently placed them amongst the branches of a rose bush.

Their meal finished, Doris told Christine to leave the plates. 'I've got lots of time to do that. Your time is more precious than mine.'

Christine remained hunched over the table, her gaze concentrated on her fingers which she laced and re-laced. 'You know, Mum, don't you think this house is too big for you, now that Dad's gone?'

'No, no. This is my home. George and I came here just after we were married, before the war.' But she knew Christine wasn't listening and thought, how stupid of me, she's heard all this before, she doesn't want to hear it again. Then the worry surfaced. That's what had been hanging about in her memory. Christine wanted her to move. To go into a flat? A home? Not likely. No, she would not be talked into that. She felt far too young and fit for that yet. No wonder she had pushed the idea into the recesses of her memory. She didn't want to remember the suggestion that she now knew Christine had made several times. She took the dirty plates over to the sink and rattled them about under a fast-running tap, singing, 'Run rabbit, run rabbit, run, run, run'.

Becoming aware that Christine was gathering up her jacket and bag, Doris stopped the tap, dried her hands carefully on a towel, and hurried into the middle room. She wanted desperately to give her daughter a present before she left. Clutching the bureau for support, she went down on her knees and scrabbled about in the bottom drawer, finally pulling out some knitting and crochet patterns.

'Here, Christine, would you like these? I've made them up and they work very nicely.' Slowly easing herself back on to her feet, she saw Christine try to hide a grimace.

'Thanks, Mum, although I don't get much time to sit and knit.' But she put them into her bag. 'Must go now.'

They walked together to the front door, halting briefly before their twin reflections in the hall mirror. Doris saw her own face haloed by a frizz of white hair with watery blue eyes swimming behind the magnifying discs of her spectacles and Christine's face, pale, red lipstick now vanished, her eyes two deep, anxious pools and hair, sleek auburn, the colour that her own had once been. At the door the two women embraced and kissed.

'I'll ring you this evening, Mum.'

Although Doris felt herself again under scrutiny, she thought her daughter now seemed rather upset and unsure, no longer bullying and impatient. Doris gave her a reassuring pat on the arm and said, 'Take care of yourself. George will be home soon and I must get his tea.'

She waved as Christine drove away and continued waving until the car turned the corner and was out of sight, before she gently shut the front door.

making perfume

Laura Morris

Safe World Gone 2007

theme: the turning point
fiction anthology

We've been making perfume, Lucy and me. Lucy's my cousin. She has strap marks on her back from where she's been wearing her bikini. You wouldn't know that today because her vest covers them, but I know it.

The smell isn't very strong but I reckon if we leave it for a bit then it will get better. We thought that we could sell it to the old ladies who live in my street. Mrs Clarke might like some. She looks like the kind of lady who wears perfume. So, after we have ridden around the block a few times, and I have timed Lucy and Lucy has timed me, we decide to go to Mrs Clarke's house. Simon from next door is out in the street kicking a ball up against Mr Jones' garage door. Mr Jones doesn't mind because he is deaf.

'Where are you two going?' he says, staring at Lucy.

'We're going to Mrs Clarke's house,' I say, 'to sell her some perfume we made.' I unzip the bag on the back of my bike to show him.

'I heard she killed her husband,' he says, 'and buried him in the garden.' I don't take any notice of him, but before we knock on Mrs Clarke's door I say to Lucy that we should have a look in the garden just to check that there's no sign of any funny business going on. We put the stands down on our bikes and balance on the pedals so we can look over the wall. Only we're still not tall enough to look over it. So we come down and lean our bikes up against a tree and I take two bottles of perfume out of my bag and follow Lucy up the path. I notice how good she walks, like someone off the television. When we get to the front door we have to push each other to knock because neither of us wants to, but neither of us wants to say that we don't want to. In the end, after Lucy says that Mrs Clarke is my neighbour not hers, it's me that steps forward. I knock the door, quite quietly, but it's a knock. We wait. Nobody comes. I peep through the window to see if I can see anybody. *Countdown* is on the television and there are three or four cats crawling around. Maybe she fell over or something. After all, she is a very old lady and I know that my grandmother fell down the stairs once. I go to knock the door again, but stop because I hear somebody coming. I turn around and see Mrs Clarke walking towards me. I've never seen her this close up before. Although I'm trying to be polite and look at her face, something on her hands makes me want to look at them. I look down: her hands are old and thin like the tissue paper we wrapped the perfume in and they're covered in earth.

'Why were you looking over my wall?' she asks me. Then she turns to Lucy. 'What were you hoping to see?'

I think carefully about my answer, but decide it's better to go with the truth. 'Simon told me that you killed your husband and that you might have buried him in the garden.'

She raises her eyebrows at me and blinks slowly. 'Did he now? And how on earth would Simon know that? Perhaps you should come and have a look in my garden.'

I look at Lucy: she doesn't move, breathe, anything.

'Come along,' says Mrs Clarke.

I fiddle with my shorts, leaving dirty marks on the turn-ups. Then I take a long, hard look back at our bikes. She must notice because she says, 'You can bring your bikes with you.'

Without speaking, we get our bikes and push them up the path and follow her round to the garden. When I see her garden, I swear to God, I almost stop breathing. There is just a long green lawn and some pathetic flowers. I am gutted.

'You can leave your bikes here and come in for a cup of tea,' she says.

Her house smells of cats, like the way my Aunt Mary's house smells, and everything looks a bit yellow, like the old films that my mother lets me watch when she's doing the ironing and my father's in the office and I can't sleep. She says that I shouldn't tell my father or anyone that she lets me watch these films. Mrs Clarke looks a bit yellow herself. She takes us into the living room and tells us to make ourselves comfortable while she washes her hands and makes some tea. I feel funny, but Lucy looks okay. She brings the tea in on a silver tray, with a jug full of milk and sugar in a bowl like they have in the restaurant in Debenhams when I go and have dinner with my mother. I sip it, trying not to make a noise, because my father often tells me that I eat and drink far too noisily. It tastes a bit funny and I think for a minute that she must have poisoned it. But then I realise that the tea that she's drinking came from the same teapot as ours, so she couldn't have, otherwise she must have poisoned herself as well.

She shows us a picture of her husband meeting Prince Charles. She points at the scarf that he is wearing and says that she knitted it for him. Then she takes a cigarette out of the packet on the table and offers us one. I say no because I wouldn't know what to do with it, but Lucy takes one, although she doesn't smoke it, she just sits there turning it through her fingers. Mrs Clarke tells us that her husband died. She says that he used to be a teacher and asks us what we want to be when we're older.

'An actress,' says Lucy straight away. She always says actress. I always say different things, depending on how I feel.

'An actress?' Mrs Clarke looks at Lucy for a long time. Then she tells us to sit still while she goes upstairs. While she's away I ask Lucy for a go on the cigarette, but she won't let me, so I don't talk to her and we sit and watch *Countdown* in silence. I'm making words in my head. I don't know what Lucy's doing and then I hear Mrs Clarke coming back down the stairs. She walks very slowly, like the way Lucy's mother walks. I run up and down the stairs unless I'm trying to be quiet. The nights I come down to watch films with my mother and eat bread and butter and drink tea on the settee,

I walk very, very slowly and carefully so I don't make a noise and my father doesn't hear me. I have to open the living-room door really quietly or he'll hear.

Mrs Clarke comes into the room with her arms full of bags and a vanity case. She takes a purple shawl out of the bag, looks at it and sighs. It's got lots of beads and sequins on it. She wraps the shawl around Lucy and ties it at the front. She stands and looks at her for a moment, like she is thinking about something. She opens the vanity case. There's loads of stuff in it, much more than my mum has got, and all different colours in tubes and jars and bottles. She puts pink lipstick on Lucy's lips and some blue stuff on her eyes. Lucy looks at me. She doesn't look embarrassed or anything. In fact, she looks lovely. Mrs Clarke is enjoying herself too. She tells us about the first time that she met her husband. His name was Alan. She says that they had been at different schools. She was at the girls' school and he was at the boys' school. Every Christmas, she says, the two schools joined together and had a dance, and that's where she met Alan.

'When I first met him, I didn't really like him. I thought that he was cheeky. But then I saw him smile and ...' She stops, remembering it. I try and catch eyes with Lucy but she isn't looking at me.

'I was wearing my hair like this,' says Mrs Clarke. She scoops up Lucy's hair and twists it in close to her head, holding it there with hairgrips. 'Yes, just like this. I had long hair once,' she says, 'just like yours. You must never cut your hair short.' I feel my hair, and wish that it was long like Lucy's.

She asks if we've got boyfriends. Lucy says yes and tells her about Will, a boy that she met on holiday while she was in France with her father. She told me about him before, but I don't like listening. She knows that I don't like it. I hum a tune in my head, a tune I made up myself.

Mrs Clarke gets up and goes over to her record player. She flicks through her records, deciding which one to play. She says that she'll teach us to dance. She shows me how to hold Lucy. I have to put one hand on her shoulder, then one on her waist. She comes behind me and shows me how to move my feet. She tells us to take our sandals off. We dance barefoot on her carpet. The carpet is really thick, and feels nice and warm under my feet. I think about how funny it would look if someone was spying on us through the window now and saw us dancing there in her living room, and I think that it is possible someone is watching us right now. But I'd feel bad if I stopped dancing. Mrs Clarke is having such a good time. Once we get the hang of it Mrs Clarke sits down on the settee and watches us dance. She sings to the music and claps along. Then there is a slow song and Lucy's face goes all serious and she is concentrating. I look at Mrs Clarke and see that she has stopped singing. Her eyes have gone still and she's staring and whispering sorry over and over again. She starts crying. It's horrible. I've never seen such an old lady crying before. She says sorry, but she misses Alan and that he shouldn't have died when he did. She says that she has enjoyed us being at her house, but that it's late now and is time for us to go home. 'You must come back and see me though, any time you like.'

Lucy gives back the shawl and the hairgrips, and we leave her house. When we come outside it's like we have come back into a new street. It's quiet and still. The other children have gone in. When we get in, my mother doesn't even mention Lucy's make-up, or ask us where we've been, but she says that the hospital phoned and that she has some good news: Lucy's mother is nearly well enough to come home and soon Lucy will be able to go home.

I can't look at Lucy. I go into the kitchen. I feel hot, like I want to cry. I take my nightie from the pile of ironing next to the fridge and change into it. I don't even care if anyone walks in. I know it's wrong to think it, but I didn't want Lucy's mother to get better. I thought that Lucy could just live with me in my room.

I take off my shorts and then remember about the perfume in my pocket. What with Mrs Clarke scaring me, and the lawn and drinking tea and dancing I'd completely forgotten why we had knocked at her door at all. I unwrap the tissue paper and ribbon and have a look at the perfume. I hold it up to the light. The water is beginning to go brown and sludgy. I take the lid off and sniff it. It doesn't even smell that nice any more. It all seems like such a waste of time.

I kiss my mother goodnight and run upstairs to bed. I call goodnight to my father through the keyhole of his office door then rush back to my room thinking that it'll be too late, but it's okay because Lucy is still in her shorts and vest. I can hardly bear to watch as she undresses and slips into her satin pyjamas.

I close my curtains and notice that the light is still on in Mrs Clarke's house. I click my lamp on and turn the big light off. It doesn't make much of a difference because it's still light outside, although I know that it will start to get dark again soon. I close my bedroom door and get into bed with Lucy. She lies face down on the mattress. I push up her pyjama top and stroke her back with the tip of my nail until she falls asleep. I won't be asleep for a long time yet.

I think about things. I think about Mrs Clarke, and realise that I too will soon be alone. I think about my mother, my bike and going back to school in September, and then Lucy. I think about Lucy. As I'm about to sleep, I hear my father opening his office door and the sound of his footsteps as he crosses the landing.

sleeping with the enemy

Molly Parkin

Changing Times 2003, new edition 2010

non-fiction anthology

M y life exploded in the sixties. It was as if I had been on strangulated hold until then, trying to subdue my soaring spirit to the hushed confines of the Welsh chapel, gratifying a devout grandmother to whom I was devoted. Embracing strict conventions espoused by my highly strung mother and the academic impositions of two orthodox aunties, the headmistress and the schoolteacher, I was in thrall to their collective female power; always the people pleaser and failing miserably.

My older only sister fitted their bill perfectly throughout our childhood. The stark contrast in our school reports summed it all up. She was the well-behaved little lady, the pleasant and friendly pupil. Mine carried the terse comment, 'a disruptive influence'. Much of my scholastic career was spent in the school corridor, banned from class for general bad behaviour. It was to prove, however, a fertile preparation for the painter and writer to be, left alone for long hours with that most inspirational companion, my own imagination. I came effortlessly top in English composition, and art.

We laugh now about how different we were as children, Sally and I, but we always shared the same sense of humour. Though resentment of this universal approval for my perfect sister simmered in me for years and gave me the role model to kick against, she says she envied my naughtiness, my nerve in questioning everything and answering back, and generally being an uninhibited, exuberant pain-up-the-arse.

But the sixties gave me the opportunity to mix with kindred spirits, all those other pain-up-the-arses who had never quite fitted into their families. Round pegs being forced to fit into square holes, now leaping from conformity with blood-curdling relish. At last we could be ourselves and let our creativity rip, full strength.

I'd just come out of the English upper-class marriage, which had always been my mother's ambition for me. My father's too, but he died before enjoying the exalted circles which they'd both aspired to and which my smart marriage would provide. They willed with all their might that I should 'better myself'. A heavy burden. But their marital plans for my future bore confusing messages for a child reared between the coalmining Garw Valley of industrial South Wales and the seedier suburbs of London.

In both places the upper classes, so-called moneyed swankers and wankers, lived on another planet far beyond us lesser mortals. Though my parents voted Liberal because of Lloyd George being Welsh, we were socialists, who saw to each other. All toffs were Tories, who looked out for themselves. We were Labour, who believed in progress and opportunities for all. They were Conservatives, opposed to change, dedicated to preserving the status quo. They were Ancient. We were Modern. They were the enemy.

And in South Wales, in Pontycymer, which was always my most favourite place in the world (and remains so) the rich and privileged meant the English and they really were the enemy, not just the class enemy, but the actual enemy, a tribal thing to do with race. It boiled down to a question of national identity. We had fought them in battle and lost, for God's sake! They had stolen our land and destroyed our language. They had driven us to the hills and underground to hack out a living in the coalfields. They had forced us to crouch like animals for our daily bread. And the bitterness and the bile at the very thought of the English was something apart. This was what united all Celts.

We were told that when we emerged from the womb in Wales, back in the 1930s, where racism ran rife and the English were reviled as no other race, save for the Germans during the war. So why would my parents want to elevate me to their midst for the sake of their own social pretensions, sacrifice me to the enemy? And not just my parents, my granny too. When I answered, using my mother tongue, in this Welsh-speaking household, she was the one who reprimanded me, 'Speak in English, bach. You are the one going to England for us, to find the fame and the fortune, isn't it.'

Why couldn't I be allowed to stay in Pontycymer with my granny in chapel and my tadcu (Welsh for grandfather) Noyle, tending his roses? And my tadcu Thomas, Sam the Post, tramping the mountains and sucking on toffees and seeing to the world. And sitting by the fire toasting bread on a wire fork with my other aunties, not the headmistress or the schoolteacher, but my favourite ones, Auntie Eunice and Emily, school cleaners, who kept chickens for boiled eggs to go with the toast. And their sister two doors away, Auntie Maggie, who knitted and had three different kinds of Co-op cake on the table for breakfast – jam sponge, ginger, and iced fairy with silver balls. I loved it up in the valley. I never wanted to leave.

My background has been described as Welsh working class, and we did all have outside lavvies at the top of the garden, if that proves anything. I'm proud to claim it all as my own, but the facts are more complicated than that. Like most valley families, mine is all of a mixture. We boast teachers, preachers and miners. I can add commerce because of Auntie Bess, Wool shop, and Auntie Lizzie, Cats, who sold kittens. My cousin Miriam, who died in childbirth barely an adult, had gone to England as a downstairs scullery maid, which was thought a step up. My paternal grandfather described himself as a civil servant: he was Sam the Post. When asked in interviews if I descend from a literary line, I answer truthfully that my grandfather was a man of letters.

But my own father, son of Sam, was a frustrated writer and painter, and that is the truth. I have actually led the life that he had envisaged for himself. It didn't make things easy between us and there had always been tension: ours was a deeply unhealthy relationship. Beatings to break my spirit. Fondlings to tie me to him. Secrets which had to be kept from my mother ...

But he couldn't break my spirit, nor obliterate my creativity. He watched me write and paint effortlessly, win a five-year scholarship to Art School and whilst there the coveted travelling scholarships which would take me on a tour of Italy: the Sistine Chapel, the canals of Venice, Michelangelo's statue of David, the frescoed murals of Giotto. He listened morosely and took refuge in the pub. Most parents are proud of their children's achievements, but not always. Not if they've ached for the same themselves and been denied the chances. He claimed that writers and painters, like musicians and poets, can cross any class barrier, that social opportunities would never be denied them, that they transcend forbidden circles and choose their own company. Creativity brings its own rewards.

Now, in the wisdom of age, my heart goes out to my dead father.

Each fresh sketch of mine as a child, each scribbled line as a teenager, later (mercifully, death spared him this) my published novels, poetry and journalism and public exhibition of paintings, would have been as salt to the wound. I wonder how many such blocked artists must endure this pain from their children, trapped as they are in their own adult years of abject conformity, denied the glorious release of self-expression and never succeeding in being true to themselves. I would have been like that if I hadn't broken free. If the sixties hadn't happened for me.

I recently watched a television documentary on the late Anthony Eden, former Conservative Prime Minister, and I finally had a true glimpse of what my mother wanted for me. Urbane, sophisticated, suave, as handsome as a god, beautifully shod (shoes were always important to my mother), fanatically well groomed, with exquisite nails. He was the kind of man she felt she should have married. He must have been what she glimpsed as a young girl, sent away to boarding school from Pontycymer (unusual then) by my grandmother. For my grandmother had begun life in a real Welsh castle, Craig-y-nos Castle in Abercrave, and had been part of the good life and inherited wealth. Her family had owned the surrounding hills as far as the eye could see, only for my male forebear to lose it all through alcohol and gambling. She remembered waking up on the next dawn in the humblest dwelling on the edge of the estate no longer theirs. The shame and humiliation never left her.

Her mother married three times and ended up in the Garw Valley, with my grandmother and her four sisters. They all married, my granny to my grandfather, who was known as John the Bump because his mordant sense of humour raised a laugh when he lowered the cage of miners down into the pit, bumping them on the final stage. He earned a top wage for that position of responsibility, but had worked from the age of ten in the mines for it.

My granny, with the zeal of lost land-owning in her blood, scrimped and saved to buy up most of her street of miners' cottages. When pit catastrophes came or strikes with no pay, she was able to tell the tenants not to worry about the rent. She put her religious faith into acts of kindness. She is an example of generosity to me still, long after her life is over, and she was a shining beacon in the valley.

My mother was the only one to survive of her twelve children. In one month alone she lost three babies under the age of six. So she saved enough money to send my mother away to school, away from the rain-soaked valley where TB was rife, to the Vale of Glamorgan, where the climate is less harsh. There my mother mixed with the cream of society, gazed at the fathers and grandfathers who arrived at the end of term to whisk their daughters away to luxuriant mansions, whilst she went back home for the holidays in Pontycymer. Some contrast. The charming gentlemen must have fanned a fascination for the likes of Anthony Eden, a predilection which ruled the rest of her life. And mine.

Meanwhile, my father was storing up similar malcontent for himself. Having successfully lied his way into obtaining a commission in the Royal Flying Corps, the equivalent of the air force then, he adapted easily to the life of a young officer. The very best years of his life, he always claimed. He'd sworn he was of age, though he was only fourteen, and that he was as a skilled horseman as if a country boy. The only ponies he'd ridden had been the wild ones at the top of the mountain, hanging on for grim life, bareback. But his charm would always get him through and the twinkle in his eye. And the way he looked just like Cary Grant with a dimple in his chin – and this was when Cary Grant was still Archie Leach in mid-England, before Hollywood got to him. My father invented the mould.

So, after school at Miss Culverwell's Academy for Young Ladies in Cowbridge, my mother went back home to become the chapel organist in Tabernacle, Meadow Street, Pontycymer, with nothing to look forward to. And after the good life of a young officer, with the fine taste of fiery liquor still on his tongue, and smooth leather brogues caressing his toes, my father returned to Park Street, overlooking the tennis courts in Pontycymer. His cousin invested his service annuity funds training to become a doctor in Cardiff. My father spent his cash on solitary boozing up the mountain, unsuccessfully trying to write poetry. Then descending to boast of the good times. There was nothing else to look forward to. My parents were perfect for each other. Their circumstances had designed it to be so. They fell in love and were wed from an aunt's house up in Watford. From there they fled to London, where they really believed that the streets were paved with gold. They were a mirror image of each other's dreams and fears and frustrations. They planted their mutual ambition in me.

My own marriage was a whirlwind affair, following closely upon the death of my father. I was unhinged by this loss and wasn't thinking straight when I met my future husband. My mother was desperate for a male in the family to replace her husband, even if it meant the man would be mine and not hers. She beseeched me to follow the rules laid out for me in earlier years. That he should be a public schoolboy. That his university should be only the very best, either Oxford or Cambridge. That he would have been a commissioned officer whilst doing his National Service (an obligatory two-year stint in the armed forces for all eighteen year olds then).

My first husband supplied all the requirements. But I must add that we did fall passionately in love. Now, almost fifty years later, the bitterness of divorce long forgotten, I have to admit that I see why I fell for him. We are friendly. We meet at grandchildren's events and sometimes in the Chelsea Arts Club, to which we both belong. We have a genuine fondness for each other and a mutual respect, and we still laugh at the same things. He has been a warm and loving father; his daughters adore him.

He is English, very, and when I met him he voted Conservative. We quarrelled about this, but I married him anyway. He was exactly what my mother had ordered. My father would have genuflected at his largesse and the note of natural command, and writhed with pleasure at his cultured voice. I know he would. I did myself. He was blond, with blue eyes and a chiselled, cherubic mouth. He loved classical music and good literature, and fine wines and expensive tweed and polished shoes, and money and breeding and friends with vast estates and titles, and castles in Scotland.

And this is how and where we spent our time together. We went to the continent before the masses did. And stayed in Manhattan, the first of our lot to do so. We honeymooned in Paris and cruised the South of France. Breakfast in Nice, supper in Cannes, and a trip over to St Tropez for a glimpse of Brigitte Bardot, big at that time, the sex-goddess of the world.

We lived in the very centre of Chelsea, off the King's Road, with our two delicious daughters, half English of course, who attended private schools (the greatest anathema to me, a grammar schoolgirl). I was now a highly successful landscape painter, in the abstract expressionist style. Our home was a Mecca for all that was upper class and fashionable, until the permissive sixties poisoned my very own domestic idyll. I kicked my husband out for flagrant infidelity and sued for divorce, viewing his behaviour as a betrayal of our wedding vows before God. Beneath it all, I had remained a child of the chapel. My granny would have been proud of me.

So there I was, mother of two and still in my twenties, at the start of the sixties, single again and about to explode. Ready to blossom into being myself – immaculate timing. The first thing to go was my affected accent, the strangulated vowels of Margaret Thatcher, which I'd adopted and strived to maintain for the seven years of my marriage. I'd had to speak very slowly when I gulped too much champagne, for fear of losing my 'h's, as in ''appy', and my endings, in case 'dancing' became 'dancin'', for instance. When you've affected a posher accent than the one you used in childhood, there are many ghastly pitfalls. A pal of mine in similar circumstances said she always got unstuck at 'sprouts'. And another said that it took her ages to cancel out the 'ov' in 'getting a book off ov the shelf' (which probably should be 'from the shelf' anyway!). Added to which I was not only aiming for an upper-class accent, but an upper-class English one – come to think of it, is there any other?!

So I could relax, not fearing any more that I would be letting my husband down by revealing my origins. Instead, it was time to flaunt them. The lower orders were rising, they were finding their true voice, like me. After all, we had Harold Wilson at the helm, the socialist government was in power again. With the impact of the Beatles, screen stars like Albert Finney and Rita Tushingham, and sirens like Shirley Bassey from Cardiff, it was considered fashionable to sport a provincial accent: the voice of the people. Even young Etonians affected a twang and took to dropping their 'h's just to be part of things.

Cockney models like Twiggy were photographed by East End fashion photographers: the famous trio, Bailey, Duffy and Donovan. Cockney hairdressers like Vidal Sassoon gave hairdressers a social kudos, dictating the shapes of heads for each season. His simple cuts for straight, shining hair swept the world, and did away with the discomfort of sleeping in curlers and following in your mother's permed footsteps. Carnaby Street revolutionised clothes for young men, with the camp and casual designs of a young man from Glasgow, John Stephens. I dressed my own moppets in scarlet leather minidresses and knee-high boots from Kids in Gear, Carnaby Street. Mary Quant ruled King's Road before moving to Knightsbridge. I'd been at Art School with Mary Quant, the first to dress in her youthful designs. And now I embarked on my life-long, still-enduring friendship with Barbara Hulanicki, who, with Fitz, her husband and partner, launched the wildly successful, groundbreaking fashion emporium, BIBA. This was where the daughters of duchesses really did do battle with the daughters of road-sweepers, stars such as Bardot, and teenyboppers from the typing pool, all equal, tearing the latest batch of backless mini and maxi-dresses from the rails, trying them on in the frenzy of the communal fitting rooms. Democracy, indeed.

It was in the world of fashion then that I made my name in the wider sense, though I was already known in the art world. A vast canvas of mine, an abstract oil painting in cadmium yellows and lemons, called 'Spring in New York', had been purchased by the Contemporary Arts Society and was then housed in the bowels of the Tate Gallery in London.

But when I kicked my husband out, my painting muse left with him and I was traumatised by the double loss. I didn't paint again for another twenty-five years, not until the late 1980s, when the muse returned in my new-found sobriety. I'd given up drink, drugs, nicotine and rampant promiscuity. Those destructive habits, which had afforded me such delights in the sixties, had become such dangerous addictions by the end.

So, having earned so much from my painting, I now had no income as a newly divorced single parent. I light-heartedly turned to what I could do with ease and very little involvement of the heart and soul. I needed money for me and my children. I did the first thing that came along. I supplied BIBA with hats and bags before opening my own boutique off the King's Road in Chelsea, one of the very first boutiques to open in London. It was an instant success and within a few months I sold out for a sizeable sum. News of my boutique had travelled. I mixed in exciting circles of people doing their own thing.

At one of the celebrity-strewn parties that I was constantly invited to now, this one was at Len Deighton's – author of *The Ipcress File*, a novel to be made into a film starring the young cockney actor, Michael Caine – I met a publisher from IPC. He was seated beside his pal David Frost and listened intently to my piss-take of the fashion trade, on how to start and sell a boutique and make a bomb in a matter of months, no sweat, as I'd just done. He subsequently confided that he'd been impressed by my attitude, my get-up-and-go, my lack of neurosis, so rare around fashion circles. And the undoubted fact that I looked so, so good in what I was wearing, which, in fact, was simply my usual kind of outfit: everything hurled on bar the kitchen stove, with strategic items removed just before leaving the house to enable normal mobility. Lashings of Elizabeth Taylor black eyeliner, of course, and a fringe or a hat drowning any suggestion of eyebrow. It's the look I have affected all my adult life and it has never let me down. Enough said.

The following day, he rang up and invited me to lunch, then on to meet the editor of the revolutionary new glossy magazine for women, *Nova*. They offered me the position of fashion editor on the spot. There was no way that I could have turned down the salary. Several years later, I moved to be fashion editor at *Harpers & Queen*, then became fashion editor of *The Sunday Times* in 1969. It was a meteoric rise in the effete world of fashion journalism, especially for a fashion maverick like me. My training as a dedicated painter had nothing to do with Parisian haute couture. The frivolous aspect of vast amounts spent on a single glove-and-handbag set stuck in my gullet.

My only previous job, until marriage when I was enabled to paint full-time, had been serious and profoundly satisfying to the soul: teaching art to deprived children at a secondary modern school at the Elephant and Castle. At Art School we students of fine art, such as sculpture or painting, were taught to despise 'the commercial crew', those students of fashion and design and illustration: we found them superficial and therefore contaminating. We worshipped at the ethic of 'Art for Art's sake'. Hard cash and making a living didn't come into it. Our talent was God-given and as such had to be nurtured in its purity. I swooned at the high concept. It could have been my granny talking.

Yet here I was in this despised world of fashion, garnering just about every covetable award for my work, culminating in Fashion Editor of the Year for my pages on *The Sunday Times*, when I left in the early seventies to become a novelist. I was a legendary figure in fashion journalism, irreverent in the extreme, because at rock bottom I just didn't care. In truth, I was faintly ashamed. I knew that my granny would have said that I was squandering my talents. So would those tutors from college. The conscience is an uncomfortable companion. It wasn't a proper occupation. It wasn't a calling, a career. It wasn't a compulsion, not like painting was to me. I couldn't treat it seriously. But the sixties provided the backdrop for that attitude – take the money and run – and I was surrounded by people who felt the same. We were all only there for a laugh, and the drink helped that. I wasn't ruled by the normal anxieties and fear of management or the editor. I could take risks and work on instinct, always ahead of the latest trend. In fact my pages caused trends to happen, though I was blithely unaware, or too busy having fun to care.

And this was where the sixties were important to me. They were irreverent times, like the twenties. There was a lot of laughter in the air, drug or drink induced, no matter. Everybody was in employment, there was no housing crisis, we were not at war, though concerned with America and the Korean conflicts. But that war wasn't ours. We demonstrated but we didn't fight. We cried bitterly over the assassination of Kennedy, but it didn't happen here. Our own ship was in order. We were safe and everybody was swinging.

I had no abiding interest in the world of fashion, never had and still don't. My own bizarre style of dress is still actually merely that of a post-menopausal art student, nothing more or less. Apart from Barbara Hulanicki, I have no friend from that world. My chosen companions are from the literary and visual world, other artists or poets and writers. The world of fashion has always felt too superficial for me and yet it was that that made it the perfect vehicle on which to ride with the wind in the sixties. It supplied me with the wherewithal, the power, the prestige, the opportunities and the contacts, to surf the excitement, to satisfy my hedonistic appetites, to fly my kite until my feet left the ground. I was the sparkling hostess of a party which lasted the entire decade. It almost killed me.

Many of my friends and lovers never survived the sixties. They perished in a sea of alcohol. They overdosed on drugs. They died of disappointment by their own hand, preferring suicide to financial failure. There were many victims of that time.

Looking back I wonder sometimes if the sixties weren't a total waste of time for me, in terms of my development as a serious artist. The spurious fame that it and subsequent years in the limelight brought me, feels meaningless now, an empty aftertaste. I know for certain that I would have painted more paintings, probably better ones, if I had continued throughout the sixties, up until now, uninterrupted. I'm doing them today instead. Even so there's a gap which can never be filled.

Maybe my real error was marrying out of my race and background under pressure from my mother, believing her when she said it would bring me happiness and a better life. People-pleasing.

But that charming, courteous, cultured Englishman gave me the devoted daughters of our mixed marriage. And for the profound blessing of them alone, and the infinite joy of all our sweet grandchildren, it was well worth this wise Welsh woman sleeping with the enemy. I can forgive myself now.

author
biographies

Elin ap Hywel is a poet and translator and is a former editor and development officer with Honno. Her translations of some of Menna Elfyn's poems have appeared in *Cell Angel*, *Cusan Dyn Dall/Blind Man's Kiss* and *Perfect Blemish/Perffaith Nam* (all from Bloodaxe). She is also editor of *Merch Perygl*, an anthology of Menna Elfyn's selected poems in Welsh (Gomer, 2011). Her own work has been widely anthologised and translated into Czech, English, German, Galician, Italian and Japanese. According to Robert Minhinnick, her work 'finds the dreamlike in the domestic ... below this [are] the strata of the sinister and the desperate.' As a brief respite from the domestic (not to mention the sinister and the desperate) she enjoys collaborating with other creative artists, most recently with Stuart Evans and Anna Davies on the multimedia project 'We Spirited Creatures' at Aberystwyth Arts Centre. 'The Food of Love' is one of the few short stories she has written.

Elizabeth Andrews Born into a poor mining family, from these humble beginnings Elizabeth became a self-educated and motivated individual with a keen interest in politics. Elizabeth fought tirelessly to improve the working conditions for miners and the health and wellbeing of the community. In 1948, for her services as a Justice of the Peace in Ystrad,

Rhondda, Elizabeth was awarded the OBE. Elizabeth died in 1960, following complications after a fall on her way to a meeting, active to the end.

Emily Bond Born Mary Emily Jones at Alltwen, Pontardawe 1912, she trained at Hatfield as a nursing sister before the war, joining Queen Alexandra's Royal Army Nursing Corps at the outbreak. She saw service in field hospitals in France, Belgium and North Africa, and also on the hospital ship *Atlantis* where she met, and in 1943, married Cardiff-born RAMC officer Haydn Bond. They remained in the army after the war, stationed in Singapore and Northern Ireland, eventually retiring to live in Caerphilly. Emily died in 1998.

Paula Brackston has an MA in Creative Writing from Lancaster University, and is a part-time Visiting Lecturer at the University of Wales, Newport. In 2007 she was shortlisted in the Crème de la Crime search for new writers, and in 2010 she was shortlisted for the Mind Book Award (writing as PJ Davy). Her first novel, *Book of Shadows*, has just come out in the USA as *The Witch's Daughter*. She is currently working on her next book. Paula lives in the Brecon Beacons with her partner and their two children.

Brenda Chamberlain was born in Bangor in 1912 and trained as a painter at the Royal Academy Schools in London. During the second world war, while working as a guide searching Snowdonia for lost aircraft, she temporarily gave up painting in favour of poetry and worked, with her husband John Petts, on the production of the *Caseg Broadsheets*, a series of six which included poems by Dylan Thomas, Alun Lewis and Lynette Roberts. In 1947, her marriage ended, she went to live on Bardsey Island, where she remained until 1961, a life she describes in *Tide-race* (1962). Her book of poems, *The Green Heart* (1968) reflects her life in Llanllechid, on Bardsey and in Germany; the latter is also portrayed in her novel *The Water Castle* (1964). After six years on the Greek island of Ydra, where she wrote *Rope of Vines* (1965)(Library of Wales 2009), she returned to Bangor. She died in North Wales in 1971.

Brenda Curtis has made her home in west Wales since 1985. Originally practising as nurse/midwife, she then became wife, mother, grandmother, and, in 1998 gained an Open University degree. Brenda enjoys writing prose and poetry. Honno has published four pieces of her work; two autobiographical and two short fiction. 'Home is where the Heart is' was her first published short story. As a member of 'The Word Distillery' poetry group, Brenda has read her poetry at Aberystwyth Arts Centre and is a founder member of the local branch of the University of the Third Age, where she is convener of the Poetry Appreciation Group.

Patricia Duncker is the author of five novels and two collections of short fiction including *Hallucinating Foucault* (1996), winner of the McKitterick Prize and the Dillons First Fiction Award, and *Miss Webster and Chérif* (2006) shortlisted for the Commonwealth Writers Prize 2007. Her fifth novel, *The Strange Case of the Composer and his Judge* (Bloomsbury, 2010), was shortlisted for the CWA Golden Dagger award for the Best Crime Novel of the Year. Her critical work includes a collection of essays on writing, theory and contemporary literature, *Writing on the Wall* (2002). She is Professor of Contemporary Literature at the University of Manchester. She has lived in Aberystwyth for over twenty years. www.patriciaduncker.com

Christine Evans has published seven collections of poetry, several landscape pieces and *Bardsey*, a personal history of Ynys Enlli, the island where she lives for half the year with her fisherman husband and family. Her most recent collection is *Burning the Candle: Writing Observed* (Gomer).

Jan Fortune (originally published as Meg White) read theology at Cambridge and has a PhD in feminist theology and an MA in creative writing. She has taught creative writing for a wide range of organisations and is the founding editor of Cinnamon Press. Her books include novels, *A Good Life, Dear Ceridwen, The Standing Ground* and *Coming Home*, and poetry collections, *Particles of Life* and *Stale Bread and Miracles*. She is currently working on a poetry sequence exploring emotions through the landscape and architecture of an abandoned slate mining village, and a novel that ranges across three generations and two continents, exploring issues of metamorphosis and identity. Jan lives in North Wales.

Christine Harrison has written many short stories and has won national prizes, notably the *Cosmopolitan*. She has published other fiction but is especially drawn to the short story.

Sarah Jackman was born in Berlin and has lived variously in England, Germany and France; she moved to South Wales in 2004 and now lives near Neath. She has published four novels: *Summer Circles* (2010), *Never Stop Looking* (2009), *The Other Lover* (2007) and *Laughing as they Chased us* (2005) all by Simon & Schuster UK. Sarah also works as the Arts Administrator for the fine arts organisation, Swansea Print Workshop and coordinates creative arts projects for artists and community groups. Sarah is currently working on her next novel as well as developing a nature writing project. More details on Sarah can be found at: http://sarahjackman.com and her nature writing blog: http://writeaboutnature.com.

Siân James has written thirteen novels and two books of short stories. Her first two novels each won a Yorkshire Post prize and her first book of short stories *Not Singing Exactly,* published by Honno, won the Welsh Arts Council Book of the Year in 1997.

Marianne Jones grew up on Anglesey. After graduating she taught English at a Japanese university. Before moving to Tokyo she lived in an area where no foreigner had ever lived before. She learned Japanese and helped to translate Contemporary Japanese Literature (1972). She has also lived in Canada, England and Wales and has taught Japanese and Creative Writing. An earlier version of 'The First Alien' appeared in *Cambrensis* magazine.

Jo Mazelis (originally published as Jo Hughes) was born and lives in Swansea, though she has also lived in London and Aberystwyth. She has been awarded a prize in the Rhys Davies Award five times, but never the big one. Her first book, *Diving Girls* was shortlisted for Commonwealth Best First Book and Welsh Book of the Year. Her second book, *Circle Games* was longlisted for Welsh Book of the Year. She was an RLF Fellow at Swansea University from 2009 to 2011.

Siân Melangell Dafydd is an author, poet, translator and co-editor of *Taliesin*. Originally from Llwyneinion, Merionethshire, she studied History of Art at St Andrews University and worked in galleries in London and Europe before completing an MA in Creative Writing at the University of East Anglia. Her novel, *Y Trydydd Peth* (*The Third Thing*), won the 2009 National Eisteddfod Literature Medal. She has published in many anthologies in Wales and abroad. In 2010 she won a Translators' House Wales–HALMA award and held residencies in Finland and Germany. A collaborative work with poet, Damian Walford Davies and photographer, Paul White will be published in spring 2012, *Ancestral Houses: The Lost Mansions of Wales / Tai Mawr a Mieri: Plastai Coll Cymru*.

Catherine Merriman is the author of five novels and three collections of short stories. Her first novel won the Ruth Hadden Memorial prize for best first work (1991) and many of her stories have been broadcast on Radio 4. She currently lectures in creative writing at the University of Glamorgan and is creative editor for the Welsh Books Council's Quick Reads series. She lives near Abergavenny in Monmouthshire and is a Fellow of the Welsh Academy.

Laura Morris Having completed an MA in Creative Writing at the University of Wales, Bangor, Laura Morris now works as an English teacher. She lives in Penarth and enjoys walks to the pier and drinking hot chocolate.

Fiona Owen writes fiction and poetry, teaches literature and creative writing for the Open University and lives on Anglesey. Her books of poetry include *Going Gentle* and *Imagining the Full Hundred*, and she is currently finishing *The Green Gate*. She has a collection forthcoming by Cinnamon co-written with Meredith Andrea, and has recorded two CDs of songs with Gorwel Owen.

Molly Parkin was born Molly Noyle Thomas in Pontycymmer, near Bridgend in the Garw Valley in 1932. She is a painter, poet, TV personality, novelist, mother and grandmother. She has worked as an art teacher, painter, boutique owner, milliner for BIBA and fashion editor for the magazines *Nova, Harpers & Queen* and *The Sunday Times*. She has published ten comic erotic novels, and two autobiographies: *The Making of Molly Parkin* and *Welcome to Mollywood*, and is currently adapting her latest poems into songs with top Welsh jazz musicians, Ian Shaw and Simon Wallace, towards staging 'Mollywood the Musical'.

Beryl Roberts is a feisty seventy-year-old deputy head teacher with three university degrees, feminist sympathies and a wicked sense of humour. She has recently published her debut novel, a romantic comedy called *A Discerning Woman's Guide to Manhunting*, in which her heroine, Geri Jones, champions the cause of multi-tasking middle-aged women. Following from this, she starred on *The Jamie and Louise Show* and Rhodri Morgan's *Guide to Life after Work* programme on BBC Radio Wales in 2011.

Her short story, *A Touch of Gloss*, was broadcast twice on BBC Radio 4 and can be read in her ebook anthology of short stories, *Opportunity Mocks,* published by Cambria Books in 2012. She has also had travel articles published in the South African *Weekend Post* and in *The Sunday Telegraph*.

Beryl lists her hobbies as working out in the gym, solving cryptic crossword puzzles and travelling. Between hobbies, she is currently working on a sequel to her novel.

Bertha Thomas (1845-1918). The daughter of a Glamorganshire clergyman, Bertha Thomas moved from her childhood home in Wales in 1862 when her father was made Canon of Canterbury Cathedral. In the early 1870s she started to contribute articles and stories to English literary magazines. *Proud Maisie*, the first of her eleven novels, appeared in 1876. Many include reference to the political topics of her day and demonstrate her interest in the suffragette movement and early socialism. She was a popular writer in her lifetime, publishing on both sides of the Atlantic.

Irene Thomas born in Ebbw Vale in 1930, was an art teacher and a freelance artist, designer, poet and writer, also a dance teacher and a spiritual healer. She has published four volumes of poetry, mainly on life in the valleys. In 1986 and 1988 she won the Wales Writer's Prize at the Cardiff Literature Festival. She was a Radio Wales broadcaster and has performed readings and workshops for schools.

Janet Thomas is a freelance editor, living in Aberystwyth. She has published several short stories, her children's picture book, *Can I Play?* (Egmont) won a Practical Pre-school gold award, and her children's story *Button Owl* was featured on the BBC's *Driver Dan's Story Train*.

Rhian Thomas hails from Anglesey, and most of her writing is inspired by the island itself. She has studied for a degree in Russian and French at Nottingham University.

Eloise Williams was born in Cardiff in 1972, and lives in Tenby with her husband, artist Guy Manning. She has recently completed an MA in Creative and Media Writing at Swansea University and was awarded a distinction. Her poetry and short stories have been published in various publications, including Honno's anthology *Cut on the Bias* (2010) and she has had success in The Marches Literary Prize, the Welsh Poetry Competition, Leaf Books Poetry competition and *Undercurrents*. In addition to her short stories and poems she also writes plays for Wales-based companies.

honno anthologies

On My Life (1989), ed. Leigh Verrill-Rhys, non-fiction, essays

Luminous and Forlorn (1994), ed. Elin ap Hywel, fiction

Not Singing Exactly (1996), by Siân James, fiction

Of Sons and Stars (1997), by Catherine Merriman, fiction

Silly Mothers (1997), by Catherine Merriman, fiction

Power (1998), ed. Elin ap Hywel, fiction

Catwomen from Hell (2000), ed. Janet Thomas, fiction

Getting a Life (2001), by Catherine Merriman, fiction

A View Across the Valley: Short Stories by Women from Wales 1850–1950 (2002), ed. Jane Aaron, Honno Classic

The Woman Who Loved Cucumbers (2002), ed. Patricia Duncker & Janet Thomas, fiction

Laughing not Laughing (2004), ed. Catherine Merriman, autobiography

Mirror, Mirror (2004), ed. Patricia Duncker & Janet Thomas, fiction

Even the Rain is Different (2005), ed. Gwyneth Tyson Roberts, autobiography

My Cheating Heart (2005), ed. Kitty Sewell, fiction

A Woman's Work is Never Done: political writings by

Elizabeth Andrews (2006), ed. Ursula Masson, Honno Classic

Safe World Gone (2007), ed. Patricia Duncker & Janet Thomas, fiction

Strange Days Indeed (2007), ed. Lindsay Ashford & Rebecca Tope, autobiography

The Very Salt of Life: Welsh Women's Political Writings from Chartism to Suffrage (2007), ed. Jane Aaron & Ursula Masson, autobiography

Coming up Roses (2008), ed. Caroline Oakley, fiction

In Her Element (2008), ed. Jane MacNamee, autobiography

Stranger Within the Gates: A collection of short stories by Bertha Thomas, (2008), ed. Kirsty Bohata, Honno Classic

Dancing with Mr Darcy (2009), int. by Sarah Waters, fiction

Struggle or Starve: stories of everyday heroism between the wars, (1998, second edition 2009), Ed. Carol White & Siân Rhiannon Williams, autobiography

Written in Blood (2009), ed. Caroline Oakley & Lindsay Ashford, fiction

Changing Times: women's stories of the 50s & 60s (2003, second edition 2010), ed. Deirdre Beddoe, autobiography

Parachutes and Petticoats: WWII (1992, second edition 2010), ed. Leigh Verrill-Rhys & Deirdre Beddoe, autobiography

*Cut on the Bias (*2010), ed. Stephanie Tillotson, fiction

Wooing Mr Wickham (2011), int. by Michèle Roberts, fiction